A Matter of Life and Death

DAVID COWZER

six**degrees**west

© 2006 - Published by Six Degrees West Limited.

six degrees west

Six Degrees West Limited
9 Herbert Place, Dublin 2, Ireland
t: 00+353 (1) 676 0298
f: 00+353 (1) 676 3865
e: info@sixdegreeswest.com
w: www.sixdegreeswest.com

ISBN 0-9540508-3-5

Design & Illustration: Maxi McDonnell
Typeset: Nicola Edington (e: nicola.edington@tiscali.co.uk)
Printers: J.H. Haynes & Co Ltd

David Cowzer is an award winning copywriter who lives and works in Dublin. After finally taking a year out of the industry to travel and write, "A Matter of Life and Death" is the end product of a life long ambition to produce something that does not include the words "terms and conditions apply" at the end.

For Meike, for everything

Acknowledgements

Special thanks to Gary for the faith, John Giles for the support, Con for the amazing energy, John and Cathy for the expert advice, Maxi, Eavan, Sarah, Nikki and Shane at QMP Publicis and Pembroke for all the help, Donal O'Connell for the challenge, Brendan and Mary for the ironing board, Vera for the tickets and Eddie, Angela and all the family and extended family in Ringsend and beyond for the support and help in writing this book.

Some people believe football is a matter of life and death... I can assure you it is much, much more important than that.

—BILL SHANKLY

—PROLOGUE—

November 2001

The whole pub was tense. You could almost smell the suspense, mixed in with the lingering odour of hops and sweat. Barry ordered three pints and gave the barman too much.

—Have to get used to the euros soon, wha'?

He struggled through the lunchtime crowd back to the others.

—Excuse me... Sorry... Can I get past yeh there (yeh baldy bastard)?

Some eejit turned around too quickly and caught him full on the elbow, nearly knocking the pints out of his hands. He steadied them and slipped through a narrow gap to where the lads were sitting. Not too much spilt. He placed the pints on the table and licked the Guinness from his fingers.

—Good man, Barry.

Conor Twomey drained the last of his pint and took a swig from the fresh one. Nick Dunne-Davis said nothing. His eyes were glued to the big screen. Ireland was attacking down the left. Duff crossed the ball in to Robbie Keane and suddenly he was through, only the keeper to beat. Barry jumped to his feet with the rest of the crowd as Keane was about to score – surely he couldn't miss from there...

—Uhhh!

The pub heaved a collective sigh of frustration.

—Yeh fuckin' stick, Keane!

Barry couldn't believe it.

—How could he miss from there? It would've been easier to score.

—It was a difficult chance.

Conor and Barry looked at each other. What would that gobshite Dunne-Davis know about it? Barry shook his head and did his best to ignore him.

—Me granny's cat would have scored that, said Conor.

—Yeah, right, said Nick. Name me one player on the Irish team who would've scored it.

—Keane, said Barry.

—But he just missed—

—Roy Keane, interjected Barry. When it came to football, he, not Nick, was the boss.

Nick sipped his pint and watched the replay, the ball skidding past the upright. —Where is Roy Keane, anyway? Why isn't he out there?

—He's injured.

—My arse. He'd rather play for Man United than for Ireland.

This time Barry did look at him. Dunne-Davis had never kicked a ball in his life – not a round one, anyway. So what if Roy wasn't in Iran? Hadn't he done more than his fair share to get them there?

He was still glaring at Dunne-Davis when the Iranians scored.

—Fuck! said Nick.

2–1 on aggregate to Ireland now. They couldn't get another one, could they? It was deep into injury time, but the Iranians definitely had the upper hand. Suddenly all the missed chances in Lansdowne started to creep into Barry's thoughts, rushing through his head like someone in RTÉ had linked a satellite up to his skull and was fast-forwarding through squandered golden opportunities. If only they'd got one of them, just one...

—Are you watching Roy Keane? enquired Dunne-Davis sarcastically.

Barry couldn't take it any more. He felt a bitter tide rise up inside him, bursting to be released. All the fury of his frustration was about to be unleashed on the unsuspecting Dunne-Davis. He was going to kill him. Slowly, he put down his glass. The adrenaline pumped through his veins, and he could have sworn he heard his heart hammering against his chest.

Then Nick Dunne-Davis turned to him, eyes wide, mouth open, and grabbed him in a full-on bear hug.

—YESSSS! We're through! We're fucking through!

Barry held on to him and felt his rage return to mere contempt.

—CHAPTER ONE—

May 2002

Nick Dunne-Davis reached over and missed the alarm clock by six inches. His hand fumbled about and found its target after three more lazy attempts. 7.35. He checked the other side of the bed for signs of life. The coast was clear. He compressed his bowels and let go a long burst of wind. —Fucking Guinness... He staggered across to the window and pulled back the curtains, revealing the splendour of a spring morning in Bulloch Harbour. The sun tripped lightly over Dalkey Island and glistened in the deep blue sea. It was a view you couldn't buy, unless you happened to have the bones of a million euro at your disposal.

After power-showering and exfoliating, Nick dragged a razor across the ginger stubble sprouting from his chin. He checked his six-pack in the mirror: getting a bit loose around the middle, nothing a few hundred abdominal crunches couldn't fix. What day was it again? Thursday. He felt like wearing the navy Armani with the powder-blue shirt and the custard-yellow tie – or maybe the burgundy? Yeah, the burgundy was better... A quick cup of coffee, and he was off to meet his sweetheart. This was what got him out of bed in the mornings.

And there she was, waiting for him as always. He actually felt himself becoming aroused at the sight of her curving lines and her perfect body. Was it normal to feel like this about a car? He pulled himself together.

This was no ordinary car. This was a BMW 323 injection coupe in fire-engine red.

Across town, in Ringsend, Barry Kelly was finishing the last of his soggy Weetabix.

—Are yeh comin' in, Da?

Michael Kelly was in the living room, watching Sky News. The weathergirl was coming on next. This was the best bit.

—Your tea's goin' cold! said Jill.

—I'll be in in a minute, love.

Declan looked up from his Cornflakes. —Gobshite.

—Don't speak about your da that way, Jill said. She looked at Sarah to see if she'd heard. Sarah carried on playing with her toast.

—Why not?

—Declan… Barry pointed a milky spoon at his younger brother.

—Well, he is a gobshite.

—That's got nothin' to do with it.

Sarah giggled as she chewed her toast. —Granda is a gobshite, Granda is a gobshite…

—Stop that! Now look what you done, complained Jill.

Declan got up to leave. —Will you sign this for me, Bar?

—What is it? Barry scanned the teacher's note. —No homework again?

Declan looked down at his runners.

—I can't keep signin' these for yeh. Da'll go spare if he finds out. Yeh have to do your work. What's goin' to happen when you finish school?

—Me and Locky are goin' skateboardin' on Baggot Street.

—That's not what I meant. You've got brains to burn. Yeh could do anythin' yeh want. Go to college, even.

—I don't want to be a bleedin' college boy!

—Well, what do you want to be?

—Not a grease monkey like you, anyway.

Jill stopped wiping the jam from Sarah's face. Barry was just about to say something when Michael walked in.

—Where's me tea, so?

Nick smiled at the bird in the Mazda beside him. She was a little younger than him – maybe twenty-three or so – and pretty, in a student kind of way. She pretended she didn't see him, but he knew otherwise. The only thing he wasn't sure of was whether she was checking out him or the Beemer. The lights changed, and he allowed her the luxury of a wink as he roared away, leaving her in his dust. He made it about one hundred metres, to the next set of lights at Foxrock Church, which changed to red as he reached them.

—Fuck!

The bird in the Mazda pulled up beside him again. This time Nick pretended not to see her. He was busy staring at the traffic, which stretched straight ahead of him for the four miles to St Stephen's Green, when his mobile rang.

—N-double-D speaking.

—That you, Dunne-Davis?

Shit. It was Tony Doyle. Nick tried to sound as natural as possible. —Yah.

—Have you anythin' for me?

—I've got something coming in next week, Mr Doyle.

The phone went dead. Nick pushed his hair back and wiped perspiration off his forehead. A driver behind him beeped and pointed to the green light.

—Fuck!

Barry made it to Ballsbridge in five minutes. He jumped

off the Honda 50 and did his best to ignore Nick Dunne-Davis getting out of his car.

—Ah, Barry – just the man I wanted to see. Are you busy today?

—I've a few bits and pieces to do. Some oul' one reversed the test Golf into the front gates, and I think one of the used Nissans's blown a head gasket.

—Cool. I was just wondering if you could give my car a bit of a polish.

No. You can shove your polish up your hole, is what he should have said.

—Well? enquired Nick, absent-mindedly caressing the bonnet with his fingers.

—Certainly, Mr Dunne-Davis.

—Good man.

Nick tossed the keys to Barry and went into his office. Barry pulled on his overalls and felt the first drops of a shower coming down.

—Prick.

After dinner that night, Barry and Jill went for a walk down to the strand. Normally they'd have Sarah with them, but tonight she wanted to stay in because there was a programme on the telly about Westlife. Jaysis, Barry hated Westlife, but he couldn't say a bad word about them in front of her. She was gas. Westlife and David Beckham. She insisted on plastering the walls of her room with the posters. He'd thought it was a bit strange when she'd taken a sudden interest in Man United – a six-year-old girl, into football?

—But I didn't think you liked football, love.

—I do now.

—And wha' about Liverpool? Your daddy could've played for Liverpool if he hadn't hurted his leg.

It was true. Barry had gone to Liverpool as an apprentice at fifteen. One of their scouts had seen him playing for Bolton in Ringsend Park. He'd trained under

Steve Heighway and everything. It was the best summer of his life. And he would have made it, too. He wasn't homesick, like most of the lads. Some of them hated getting up for training every day; not Barry. He even loved cleaning the boots for the pros – legends like Ian Rush and John Aldridge and...

—Does David Beckham play for Liverpool, Daddy?

—Wha'? No; no, he doesn't, love. He plays for the same team as Roy Keane.

—Man United?

—That's righ'.

—Then I want a Man United poster.

—OK, so.

He looked out at a ferry coming in past the candy-striped chimneys of the Pigeon House. Jill took his hand in hers.

—What are you thinking? she asked.

—Nothin'.

—Come on, you can tell me.

—Well, it's just – are yeh happy?

She smiled. —You mean am I happy runnin' around all day after your da and Declan and you and Sarah?

—Well, yeah.

She kissed him on the cheek. —Yes...about you and Sarah, anyway.

Barry knew it must be hard on her, all the same. Ever since his ma died, his da had taken a bit of looking after. When Jill had moved in with them, after Sarah was born, she'd kind of taken over where his ma had left off – cooking the dinners, doing the washing, keeping the place clean. It wasn't in her nature to complain, but he often felt that she wasn't entirely satisfied. And he'd been feeling it more and more lately. They'd been talking about getting married and having another baby – actually, it was Jill who had been doing most of the talking. He hadn't the heart to tell her that they couldn't afford to do either, not unless he got a decent raise at work – and even then, things would be tight.

—You're happy enough, though, aren't yeh, Jill?

Now it was her turn to look out towards the ships.

—Ah, yeah.

She didn't sound one hundred per cent convincing.

—But?

—I would've liked to have gone to college, maybe…but then Sarah came along.

—Yeah. She's a great young one, isn't she?

—I wouldn't swap her for anything. Or you…

This time she kissed him on the lips.

—There must be somethin', but?

Jill thought about it for a bit. Then she turned around and pointed to a 'FOR SALE' sign outside a house on the coast road.

Barry sighed deeply to himself. —Two chances of tha', love.

Michael Kelly was in his customary position in front of the TV when they got home. He looked up briefly from the screen.

—Howya, Da?

Michael didn't answer. He was too engrossed in his programme. The nine o'clock news was on and Anne Doyle was presenting it. She was a fine bit of stuff, and tonight she was wearing a low-cut blouse that revealed just a hint of her ample cleavage. He wasn't particularly interested in what she was talking about – something about the Yanks still trying to find Bin Laden; he was more concerned with the way she said it. That slightly pompous newscaster delivery. Magic.

—Sarah in bed? asked Jill.

—Wha'? Yeah, yeah, she's just gone up.

Jill went up while Barry collapsed onto the old sofa. One of the springs had burst up through the cover and it scratched him on the leg. They really needed a new one, to go with all the other things they really needed.

—Where's Declan? he asked.

No reply.

—Da?

—He's up in bed too.

—At nine o'clock?

Michael wrestled his eyes away from Anne Doyle for a minute.

—I caught him smokin' again.

—Drugs?

He nodded.

Barry looked out the window. —The little...

He jumped up and left Michael alone with Anne Doyle.

—Take it easy on him, son.

Declan was reading his skateboarding magazine when Barry burst in.

—Yeh little bollix.

—Wha'?

—Wha' did I tell yeh about drugs!

—It was only hash, said Declan defiantly.

—I don't care what it was. Wha' would Ma say?

—Ma wouldn't say anythin'. She's dead.

Barry lashed an open hand across Declan's face, catching him full on the cheek with a sharp slapping sound. He didn't know which of them was more surprised.

—Sorry.

He felt his hand begin to sting and watched the red mark surfacing on the pale skin of Declan's jaw.

—I'm sorry, righ'?

Declan stared at him but said nothing.

Declan had only been a kid of ten when their ma had died from the cancer. Barry could still see her in that bed. She had looked like something from another planet, her once-beautiful hair long gone from chemotherapy. And her skin...her skin had been almost yellow near the end. She'd made them both promise.

—D'you swear?

—I swear, Mammy.

—Barry?

He could still taste the tears.

—We swear, Ma. We'll never touch any drugs. Sure we won't?

Declan shook his head solemnly.

—Good boys, good boys.

Barry looked at Declan now – sixteen, and nearly as big as himself. He couldn't really blame him: all the kids were at it, and they said it was less damaging than the drink. Still, though…he'd be into E next, and then God knows what.

—Lookit, Declan, drugs are only for idiots, righ'?

—CHAPTER TWO—

Nick hoovered up the second line of coke from his desk. The familiar burning sensation prickled the delicate membranes of his nose, and in a few short seconds he was feeling invincible – ready to take on the world and kick its fucking arse.

Barry watched him as he cruised out of his office to deal with the young couple looking at the Audi A3. As much as he hated to admit it, he had to hand it to Nick: he was a good salesman. He could bag people who didn't even know whether they wanted a new car or not. He moved with a certain authority, and he told the customers what they needed to hear – even though he knew fuck-all about cars.

—Have a look inside, madam. It's amazing – and that colour really brings out the blue in your eyes.

—D'you think so?

—Absolutely.

And they loved it, all of them. Nick had been top salesman at the showrooms for the past two years. The MD loved him too, because of all the motors he shifted, but that was where it ended. The other salesmen hated him – he was top dog in their dog-eat-dog world – and Barry and Conor steered clear of him as much as was humanly possible. The warm glow of his charm didn't extend to lowly mechanics. They were a necessary evil, like the grease and the oil, and just as expendable.

—We'd be delighted to arrange finance, sir. Nick took out his calculator and punched a few buttons. —Let's see...that's €22,990, plus two and a half for the leather interior and another twelve hundred for the sunroof, plus the CD changer, over three years—

—Er, I'm not sure if I really need the six-CD…

—It's entirely up to you, of course, sir. I know couldn't do without mine for long journeys.

—Well, I suppose you're right.

Barry left him to it. There was a truck full of new Beetles that needed unloading. He and Conor eased them down from the lorry and drove them out to the back of the lot for the pre-delivery inspection. Barry looked at the fake flower beside the steering-wheel and frowned.

—Bleedin' yuppiemobiles. They weren't bad cars, but. He signed the docket and they gave all the Beetles the once-over, just to make sure they were in perfect working order. It was a job Barry took seriously, just like everything else he did in the garage. If it was worth doing, it was worth doing right. That was the only attitude, as far as Barry was concerned. He'd seen fellas come and go in here, lazy so-and-sos who only did the bare minimum and spent their day avoiding work, and he never understood why they were like that. It wasn't just the job; they'd be like that no matter what they did.

He ticked off the 'compression' box on the list and moved on. Conor had Gerry Ryan blaring on one of the car stereos. Some eejit was on, talking shite about Ireland's World Cup chances. He reckoned the team wouldn't make it out of the group. He'd obviously never heard of a certain world-class midfielder who was going to shake up the world when he got to Japan.

Barry was just finishing testing the electrics on a silver Beetle when Conor called him over.

—Lookit. The spare's marked on this one.

Barry had a quick look at the tyre and took it out.

—No hassle. Grab another one off the rack there.

Fucking traffic, thought Nick, as the Beemer crawled towards the gym. Still, he'd had an excellent day at work and he was feeling pretty damn good about life. The fact that the short journey had taken over fifty minutes didn't worry him unduly. How could it, when all these miserable peasants – grinding past in their Toyotas and Nissans, back to their dreary little homes after their dreary little jobs – got to see him in the regal splendour of his 3-series?

He pulled into the car park and waited: not because he was dreading the workout ahead of him – quite the opposite, in fact – but because he wanted to make sure someone would see him getting out of the Beemer. He waited ten minutes before he spotted someone he knew.

—Paul! How's it going, my son?

—Oh, hi, Nick.

Paul Dixon – or Dickie, as Nick liked to call him – didn't appear to share Nick's enthusiasm about their meeting. Probably jealous, Nick thought. After all, he was only driving a Golf – and a '96 model at that.

They walked up the ramp to the plush foyer of the health club.

—Fancy a round this weekend?

—I don't know, Nick.

—Go on; I promise not to beat you too badly this time. We'll play eighteen at Delgany, yah?

—I don't think...

—Come on – it's my treat, including dinner.

—Well, OK, then, Dixon said, feigning a fake smile and nervously eyeing the nearest escape route.

—Good man, Dickie! Shall we say ten a.m. at the club?

But Dickie wasn't saying anything. He was too busy slipping hurriedly into the changing room while Nick got a towel from the bird at reception. —Nice tits, he almost said to her.

—Good evening, Mr Dunne-Davis.

—Nick, please.

She blushed slightly as she handed him the towel. He made sure his fingers accidentally stroked her hand as he took it.

—Cheers.

He reckoned he was in there, if he wanted to. He hung his black Hugo Boss on a hanger and changed slowly into his workout gear. He didn't want to miss anything: the way the navy Adidas singlet hugged his pecs and spread over the taut abdominals that rippled down to his white rugby shorts; the long, lean legs tapering perfectly down to the top-of-the-range Nikes; the caramel tan that was regularly topped up on the sunbeds upstairs.

—Pretty fucking impressive, he said to his own reflection.

Nick was still buzzing from the two cars he'd sold that day – and from the coke. It wound him up like a coiled spring, and here in the gym he could unleash all that pent-up energy. He attacked the bench press first. Most guys did three sets; Nick did eight, rep after rep, until his chest and arms burned. Then he moved on to the most important exercise of them all: abdominal crunches. Ten sets of fifty, five hundred tummy-tightening curls in total, giving him a six-pack that was the envy of all his mates. God, he was ripped up today. The mirrors didn't lie. Six sets of bicep-building arm curls followed; after a forty-five minute run on the treadmill it was time for a quick session in the steam room (great for unblocking the facial pores), and then Nick hopped into the shower. On his way out he tossed the wet towel to the cute bird on reception, landing it expertly on her head and shoulder.

—All yours, Karen.

He had made sure to scan her name-tag on the way in. It never failed to impress the birds.

—Thanks a lot, Mr Dunne-Davis.

She appeared less than impressed with him, but he knew she was only letting on. Either that or she was on the rag. She wasn't a bad bit of stuff at all. He might have considered taking her out, if it hadn't been for the fact that she was hired help. Anyway, she'd probably have a good sniff of his towel before putting in the basket. That was as intimate as she was likely to get with N-double-D.

Just as well I dried my nuts with it, he thought.

Nick made the trip out to Dalkey in less than twenty minutes. The rush-hour traffic was gone, so he put the hammer down, and the Beemer responded to his every command as he glided down the dual carriageway. He was still feeling good. Maybe he'd give Sasha or Alison a call. The old testosterone levels were through the roof after the workout. Better make it Sasha. He found himself wondering if she'd really meant what she said to him last time – the bit about him being a selfish prick.

Michael Kelly was in great form when he came home.

—Howya, Jill?

—Grand, thanks. How are you?

—Marvellous. And how's me favourite grand-daughter?

Sarah ran up to him. —Sweets, Granda!

—Have yeh a kiss for me first?

He picked her up and planted a sloppy wet one on her cheek.

—Ugh! Granda's got stubbly cheeks.

He handed her the bag of Liquorice All Sorts. —He's got your favourites, too. Lookit.

Sarah grabbed the bag and giggled.

—You have her spoilt rotten, Jill said. —What has you in such good humour?

—I won a few quid on the dogs.

Michael went to Shelbourne Park religiously, every Thursday night, with Tommy Burke next door. The two of them spent what was left of their pensions. They'd even talked about buying a greyhound at one stage, but that was years ago, when Michael was still working for CIÉ; before Barry's ma had died.

—How much? asked Barry.

—Never you mind, son. Here.

Michael handed Barry a twenty-euro note.

—What's that for?

—Fish an' chips. I'll have a cod an' large, and whatever yous are havin' yourselves.

—Jaysus, you did win big, wha'? Barry took the money and got up to leave.

—Will I go with you, Bar? said Jill.

—Ah, no, you're all right.

He enjoyed the odd stroll on his own, even just around to the chipper under the bridge. Presto's was right opposite Slattery's, and he might sneak in for a quick pint while he was waiting on the chips. It was a grand evening, so he didn't bother with the jacket. Fish and chips, and his da back to his old self, even for a night; and there was a match on the telly, too… Things were definitely beginning to look up.

The next day, Barry Kelly lost his job.

Nick Dunne-Davis had told him to drop into his office, earlier that morning.

—What are you doing in here? he wanted to know, when Barry came in.

—Er, you told me you wanted to see me.

—Oh, yah, yah. Better sit down.

Nick looked at Barry's greasy overalls and put a hand up. —On second thoughts, this won't take long.

Barry waited for him to speak. This had to be serious; he'd never seen Dunne-Davis at a loss for words before. Barry was just about to ask him was he all right – he looked like shit this morning, must have had a heavy night on the gargle – when Nick finally told him what was on his mind.

—We're letting you go, Barry.

Simple as that. He'd been there since he left school at sixteen. Done his apprenticeship and everything.

—Why, but?

—The current climate...

That old chestnut.

—Since 9/11, business hasn't been so good.

I don't see you starving, thought Barry.

—Orders from the boss, I'm afraid. We're just not selling as many cars as we used to. With the exception of myself, of course.

He couldn't resist that, the arrogant prick.

—So it was either you or Conor. And he's been here longer. That's the only reason.

Fair enough. Barry didn't begrudge Conor. He was a good worker, and he had a family to support as well.

—We'll give you twelve months' redundancy. It should only be ten.

Barry wanted to cry. Why him? Why now? He felt like a little boy sent to the headmaster.

—When do I finish?

—The end of the month.

Barry nodded dumbly and turned to go. He could feel a big salty lump forming in his throat. He didn't want to give that bollix the satisfaction.

—And, Barry...

He didn't bother turning around.

—There'll be a decent piss-up for you.

—CHAPTER THREE—

Barry drained the dregs of his pint and got to his feet, with some assistance from the table and his seat.

—Hold on, Bar, it's my round.

—Stay where you are. I'm gettin' this one.

He waved away Conor's protests, knocking the remains of his pint onto the table in the process. The pub crawl had been Conor's idea, to get Barry's mind off the redundancy. The plan had been to start in the Dawson Lounge and work their way down to Mulligan's on Poolbeg Street, via Kehoe's, McDaid's, Neary's, Sheehan's, the Old Stand, O'Neill's, the Stag's Head, and the Palace – one pint in each bar. They'd started off well enough, with one each in the Dawson straight after work; but moving on from O'Neill's was proving a bit more challenging, now that they'd settled in and the pints were beginning to wrap them in a warm, alcoholic blanket. Conor couldn't remember if this was their seventh or their eighth. He was just beginning to feel better when he saw Barry up at the bar. Poor bastard. It could just as easily have been him.

He looked at his watch. Twenty-five to seven. This could be a long evening.

Jill was just finishing clearing the plates from the table when the phone rang.

—Daddy! screeched Sarah.

—The Kelly residence, announced Declan in his best RTÉ accent. Michael looked at him and grinned. He was definitely feeling better since his win on the dogs.

He might even drag himself around to Fitzharris's for a pint later. Sure, hadn't he earned it?

—Tha' you, Declan?

—Barry?

—Listen...I just wanted to say I'm sorry.

—Wha'?

—About the other night, yeh know?

—Have you been drinkin'?

Declan looked over at Jill and mimed pouring copious amounts of liquid down his throat.

—Is J-J-ill there?

—Yeah. Will I put her on?

—No! Fuck, no – just tell her I'm havin' a quiet pint with Conor and I won't be home for dinner.

Jill made a point of dragging the knife across the plate as she scraped it into the bin. It made a horrible grating sound, like when Miss O'Brien used to scrape her nails on the blackboard to get them to shut up.

—I think she might have worked that out for herself, Declan said. —Are yeh sure yeh don't want to talk to her?

—You're a good man, Declan.

—All righ'.

—A f...fuckin' good man.

Then the phone went dead.

—Well, what did he say?

—Not much. He's havin' a quiet pint with Conor.

Benny Doyle brought the black Mercedes to a silent halt outside the pub in Dolphin's Barn. Tony Doyle waited in the back for his nephew to open the door. He pulled his cashmere coat tighter around his considerable shoulders as he stepped out of the car and walked to the entrance, where the bouncer was waiting with the door open.

—Evening, Mr Doyle.

Benny glared up at him as he followed his uncle inside. The few midweek punters fell silent as the imposing figure of Tony Doyle strode up to the bar. One of them nudged his mate, who had been too busy reading the Evening Herald to notice the two men; his short glass of Jameson rattled off the table as he put it down.

—Mr Doyle. Nice to see you again, croaked the publican.

Tony Doyle glanced around the bar. —Get out, he said.

A moment passed before the patrons of the pub moved quietly and quickly towards the door, leaving half a dozen near-full pints of stout behind.

—I can explain, the publican began.

—You're late, Kavanagh.

—I know, but business has been slow, you know?

—Have you got it?

Kavanagh swallowed hard. —I'll have it for you on Monday, Mr Doyle, I swear on my mother's life, he whispered.

Tony Doyle didn't move a muscle. —What about your own life?

The bouncer's head appeared around the door. —Everything OK, Mr Kavanagh?

Kavanagh took only the shortest of moments to consider his response. —G-Grand, thanks, Alan. Everything's fine.

The large head retreated back outside the door.

—Monday? repeated Doyle.

Kavanagh nodded nervously.

Something rare happened to Tony Doyle. A smile spread across his face – not a very nice smile, it has to be said: the sort of smile that looked like he'd rented it specially for the occasion and it didn't quite fit, like a bad tuxedo rented for a wedding. A tense smile crossed Kavanagh's features, until he saw the glowing anger ignite in Doyle's eyes.

—Monday's too late.

It was Benny's turn to smile. He started by knocking the half-full glasses off the bar with one sweep of his arm. They smashed to the ground with an almighty crash.

Christ, Benny loved this part of the job. The ashtrays were next: he picked up the heavy mounds of glass and hurled them one by one, like a discus thrower, at the neat rows of spirit bottles behind the bar. Glass and whiskey rained down on the sobbing landlord crouching under the bar. Benny hit the Kavanagh family crest painted on the mirror above the till and sent it crashing to the floor. Nice one, he thought. He'd been aiming for that.

He grabbed a stool and smashed it off the bar until he was left with one leg. Using it as a club, he took a few more good-sized lumps out of the bar; then he jumped over it and turned the club on Kavanagh. It made a resounding thump across his back, just like the sound of beating the dust from an old sofa. Benny only hit the fucker three or four times before it broke. He could just about hear his uncle Tony above the screaming voices in his head.

—Enough!

Benny wiped the snot from his nose with his sleeve and gave the oul' fella a hefty boot in the ribs for good measure. Kavanagh groaned and rolled onto his back. Jaysus, Benny thought, I really did a job on him. He grabbed himself a Finch's Orange, one of the few remaining bottles on the bar. He'd earned his money tonight.

—Now, Mr Kavanagh, Tony said. Have we learned our lesson about the importance of punctuality?

Kavanagh managed a weak nod.

—We'll see you Monday.

They crunched out over the shards of broken glass. Benny stopped to plant what was left of his club between the bouncer's legs.

—I found that lyin' around, he said as the doorman dropped to his knees. —Yeh'd want to be careful. Somethin' like that could do someone an injury.

Barry and Connor were nursing a pair of pints in the Stag's Head. The evening sun was easing its way slowly behind the buildings opposite. Barry felt the warm rays wash over his face through the stained-glass window beside him. The booze was beginning to take the edge off things.

—Look at the arse on that! whispered Conor. The owner of the arse in question turned around and glared at him.

—Stuck-up wagon. What are yeh gonna do with yourself, Bar?

—Dunno. Get another job, I suppose.

—Ah, you will, o' course.

—D'yeh think so?

—Not a bother to yeh. The boss'll give yeh a good reference.

They lapsed back into a drunken silence. Barry took a long swig from his pint.

—That's a good pint.

—Lovely, agreed Conor.

Barry got up to go to the jacks. On the way down the narrow stairs, he lost his footing for a second and nearly went on his ear. A young one coming up steadied him as she passed.

—Sorry.

—It's OK.

She smiled at him, flashing a set of perfect teeth. How did they always have such good teeth? Not like the young ones he knew.

His mobile went just as he was in the middle of taking a slash. Jill's name flashed up on the screen. He knew he should really talk to her – but what would he say? Jill, I've been fired, love. We're fucked.

No, he still needed time to work it out in his head. He'd call her from the next bar.

He dropped the phone into the basin when he was washing his hands.

—Bollix!

Sasha Fitzpatrick sat alone in the Club in Dalkey. She'd been furiously avoiding eye contact with a guy in a red polo shirt up at the bar. It wasn't even a genuine Ralph Lauren he was wearing; in fact, there didn't seem to be any label on it at all. He'd probably got it in Dunne's Stores. Sasha knocked back the last of her Smirnoff Ice and caught the barman's attention. She was a regular here, and she enjoyed the service that went with it. A subtle raise of the empty bottle let him know what she required. God, she hoped Nick wouldn't be too much longer. She'd always hated being alone, even in a crowded bar like this one. It made her feel so vulnerable.

The guy in the fake polo looked over again. He was quite cute, actually. His short hair was neatly gelled forward, with a small fringe sticking up, and his eyes were a pleasant shade of blue. Still…she might have been able to forgive him the label-less polo, but not the 501s. Only knackers wore Levi's these days. They were so last-century.

She was busy applying her lipstick for the fourth time when Nick finally arrived.

—All right, babe?

She gave him the daggers. —What time do you call this? she asked, trying to conceal her relief.

—Sorry. Traffic was awful. Just awful.

—Well, you're here now. Where are you taking me?

—Let's get a drink first, yah? Same again?

She nodded curtly as Nick went up to the bar. Sasha was just lighting up a Marlboro Light when she saw her.

—Oh, my God!

It was that bitch Nick used to go out with, Kelly-Anne Moran. Sasha and Kelly-Anne used to be best friends at school, but that all changed once Kelly-Anne stole Nick from Sasha at his twenty-first. It had been a fancy dress in Jester's nightclub; Sasha had gone as Cinderella, but ended up feeling like one of the ugly sisters when Nick went home with Kelly-Anne. True, Sasha had barely spoken to Nick at that stage, but that wasn't the point.

Anyway, who was sleeping with him now? She decided it was best not to linger over that one for too long. But look at the little trollop, laughing and touching his arm as if nothing had ever happened. Who did she think she was?

—Hi, Sasha! beamed Kelly-Anne.

—Kelly-Anne! What a wonderful surprise! Sasha lied. She stood up and kissed the air on either side of Kelly-Anne's face. —I was just thinking we must get together for a drink.

—I'd love to, chirped Kelly-Anne, with an enthusiasm approaching mania.

—Brilliant! I'll call soon.

After that the conversation petered out somewhat. They stood grinning and nodding at each other until Sasha's face started to hurt. Finally Kelly-Anne left, with an embarrassed gurgle, as Nick arrived with the drinks. God, Sasha thought, she hated Kelly-Anne Moran. She was just so fucking pretentious.

Barry's mobile went again as they were settling into their first drink in the Palace. He had it set on Vibrate.

—Fuck!

When it went off in his pocket like that, it always felt like he was pissing himself. He let it ring out. He knew exactly who it was. He was just settling back into the seat when it vibrated again, to let him know he had a message.

—You have four new messages (and one very pissed-off mot).

He took a delicate sip from the amber-coloured mixture. —Jaysus! What the fuck is tha'?

—Vodka an' Red Bull.

—Tastes like bleedin' Benylin, said Barry.

—You're the one who can't drink any more beer.

He took another sip. It wasn't that bad once you got used to it.

—So, how much redundancy yeh gettin'? Conor asked.

—Twelve months.

—Not bad.

Barry stared blankly at the TV screen above the door and said nothing. He'd been doing his best to forget all about it. He was at that awkward stage where oblivion was still three or four drinks away; he was definitely pissed, but not quite langered enough not to care.

—Any idea what you'll do with it?

What kind of a stupid bleedin' question was that? He'd only been told he was being let go a few hours ago. Conor could be a right gobshite when he wanted to.

—You should take a little holiday, yourself and Jill.

Barry looked at his future ex-colleague. Conor was beginning to get on his nerves.

—Now that yeh have the chance to, you know? There's loads of places to go on the cheap these days.

Barry was just about to tell him where to stick his bleedin' holiday when the telly caught his eye again. It was that Heineken ad with Jason McAteer – or was it Carlsberg? Anyway, it was fuckin' magic, whatever it was. He didn't know how they'd done it, but Ireland were playing all these brilliant countries and beating them. He especially liked the bit where Ian Harte scored the penalty to send England home (even though England were shite and Ireland would probably beat them anyway).

And then it dawned on him. It was like a message from heaven, rather than a message from a Scandinavian brewing company, and it spoke to him loud and clear. And it said the only three little words that could help a man in his predicament.

—GO TO JAPAN.

He would take Jill and Sarah to the World Cup – and they'd forgive him for losing his job. After nine pints, it all made perfect sense.

Michael didn't hear the phone ringing. He was far too busy listening to Sharon Ní Bheoláin on N2 news – or, more accurately, studying the way her long blonde hair was draped seductively over her well-toned shoulders. She was a bit like the young one off that Friends programme Jill watched. Where had Network 2 got her from? She didn't sound very Dublin, but it was hard to tell with young ones these days. Must be a culchie; pity they never had country girls like that in his day...

He was contemplating whether or not she was a natural blonde (were the dark roots a bit of a giveaway?) when Jill's voice interrupted him.

—We're going where? Have you lost the fuckin' plot?

She hung up the phone and marched up the stairs to bed. Barry must've said something to upset her like that. It wasn't like her to use bad language in the house.

—Nick! Are you coming to bed or not?

Sasha lay with her hair strategically tossed over the silk pillowcase. Her trim legs and torso were almost lost in the king-sized futon. Nick was onto his third makeup-removal pad, cleansing that difficult bit around his nose – total nightmare for blackheads.

—Be in in a second!

She raised her eyes to heaven and caught a glimpse of herself in the ceiling mirror. Not bad. She liked the way the black stockings accentuated the length of her legs.

—Ni-ick!

It was no use. He still had to tone and moisturise. She pulled one of his rugby shirts from the drawer and wrapped the duvet around her.

Nick was surprised, but not disappointed, when he found her asleep twenty minutes later. It was strange: he always felt pressure to please Sasha, whereas he simply felt all the other girls to please himself. —Ah, well; guess I've got time for a face pack after all, he said, and headed off to chop two fresh slices off the cucumber he kept handy in the bathroom.

Barry staggered sideways down Pearse Street. There seemed to be some kind of magnetic pull emanating from his house, targeting his right hip; the rest of his limbs followed obediently towards Ringsend and home. Fuck, he was starving.

A Garda had stopped him earlier and asked him what he was doing.

—Goin' home, Guard.

—And where would that be?

—Where I fuckin' live, of course!

It had taken him a second to realise that this wasn't the right answer. He'd rubbed his head. —Sorry, I mean down there.

His brain had instructed his hand to point straight down the street, but somewhere along the line his arm had taken on a life of its own and made a detour towards the quays.

—Ringsend Road.

—Right. Make sure you go straight home, now.

—Yes, Guard.

It seemed to take him an age to reach the chipper on the corner. A gang of young fellas were hanging around outside. They were always there at night. He reckoned they were about the same age as Declan, but their faces looked older. They had that bitter edge to their features from scowling and trying to look tough. He didn't like the look of them. They were just waiting for him to make eye contact. He managed to sway uneasily around them and into the hot air of the chipper.

—A battered sausage and a shingle.

He waited while the Italian oul' fella lowered the basket into the oil. It spat and hissed as the oil bubbled over the cold white chips. Barry tried to focus on the clock, but it wasn't easy; the hands kept swaying back and forth. One of them seemed to be near the 1, but then it would melt back a couple of inches towards the 11. The more he tried to focus, the more he thought he was going to puke.

—Salt an' vinegar?

He nodded like his neck was made of rubber. The oul'
fella drenched everything in vinegar – chips, sausage, the
whole lot. He did the same with the salt, dousing the
contents like he was giving the carpet a good Shake 'n'
Vac. Barry hated the way they always did that. He headed
out of the chipper and pressed a handful of chips at his
mouth. One or two might have gone in, but most of them
just clung to his chin for a second before nose-diving to
the pavement.

—Fuck!

He'd be wearing the bleedin' sausage by the time he
got home.

—Got a problem?

One of the young fellas accidentally on purpose
knocked the bag from his hand – the bollix. Barry looked
down at the tangled mess of chips strewn around his feet.
The young fella just stood there, staring straight at him.
Barry wanted to burst him.

—You bleedin' deaf? the young fella asked.

—No, no problem.

Barry turned and walked away towards home.

—Wanker!

They were having a good laugh at him. For a second
he felt like going back and kicking their heads in, but
there were too many of them – and those bastards always
carried knives. He'd better get home to bed.

The smell of the canal made him gag, going over the
bridge, but he managed to keep it down. The lights in
the Ocean bar were swaying away; maybe he'd feel better
after one more... Then he remembered the last time he'd
been in there. It was full of pricks like Dunne-Davis.

He got the key into the door on the third attempt.
The tap made that terrible groaning sound in the kitchen
when he turned it on. He couldn't find the Alka-Seltzer
anywhere, so he popped a couple of Disprin in his
mouth.

—Urghh!

Then he realised they were the soluble ones. The ones he'd spilt all over the floor could stay there – he was afraid he'd fall over if he bent down to pick them up.

He put his finger up to his mouth to shush one of the creaking stairs. And then came the acid test. He opened the bedroom door as quietly as he could.

—Where have you been?

Jill was sitting up in bed waiting for him.

—Howya, love?

—Are you drunk?

—No, no.

Then it happened. There was no warning, not even dizziness or the usual watery taste in his mouth – just a hot projectile stream of steaming brown liquid, all over the carpet.

—Eh, yes.

The chunder sobered him up slightly. Jill shook her head and turned over in the bed. Barry went downstairs to get the Domestos. It took him a good twenty minutes to get it all out of the carpet; those feckin' bits of carrot kept sticking to the fibres – how was there always carrot in it? Even if you hadn't eaten them in a month, they'd still be staring back up at you. He opened the window to let the smell out and climbed into bed.

She still had her back to him, and he still didn't know how to tell her. He'd wait till the morning. It'd be easier with a clear head.

—CHAPTER FOUR—

It wasn't.

Barry's head felt like his brain was rebelling, pounding against the skull that was holding it prisoner.

—Oh, Jaysus...

His stomach heaved as if he were on board a ship in stormy waters, and his tongue felt like it was covered with the remains of a small furry animal. But the smell was the worst: that horrible vomit stench that filled the air, clinging to every breath. He could still feel the acidic burning sensation in his nostrils, too.

When he eventually crawled out of the bed, the floor seemed to be swaying back and forth. He went into the jacks and took a piss. It was nearly brown. The shower made him feel a bit better, though, and he felt he could make an attempt at getting dressed. He pulled on his favourite Adidas tracksuit bottoms and his Ireland T-shirt, the one with 'Keane' on the back that Jill had got him in Marathon Sports.

—Look, love, it's your favourite – Keano.

He hadn't had the heart to tell her it was actually a Robbie Keane shirt. The fact that it had a number 10 on it would have given it away to anyone who knew the first thing about football, but that didn't include Jill.

—Oh, yeah. Magic.

In work they wouldn't be too happy about him dressing like that, even with the overalls on. They had a thing about football jerseys. Well, they could shove it. What could they do – fire him again?

He trudged downstairs and took a deep breath before

opening the kitchen door.

—Yeh can't go to work dressed like that! said his da.

Barry sat down without answering. He wanted to say something, but he didn't.

—Here; that'll make you feel better, son.

Michael plonked a large plate in front of him. Great, a dirty big fry-up, thought Barry. Just what I need.

—Get it into yeh.

—Thanks, Da.

Jill didn't even look at him. She just kept reading her magazine and sipping her tea.

—Is Daddy sick, Mammy? Sarah wanted to know.

—No. He's just silly.

—How come?

—Well, remember at your party when I told you to stop eating sweets?

—Yeah.

—And remember you didn't, and then you got sick?

—Yeah, said Sarah, scrunching up her nose at the memory.

—Well, Daddy had too many pints and now he feels sick.

Sarah giggled at Declan. Barry was still waiting for an appropriate moment to tell them his news. Fuck it, he decided: would there ever be an appropriate time?

—I lost my job, he said, as casually as he could.

Sarah was still giggling, but Jill heard him and put her magazine down.

—What?

—They told me yesterday.

Even Sarah was quiet now.

—But why, Barry? asked Michael.

—Cutbacks – September eleventh — not sellin' as many cars as before. I dunno. That's what Dunne-Davis said, anyway.

—Prick, muttered Declan.

—But you've been there for years, love. Jill's tone had softened. —Breakin' your back for them.

—They're only a corporate shower anyway, Bar. Yeh'd be better off on the dole than contributing to globalisation, sure.

Michael slapped the back of Declan's head. —Shut up, you, yeh tulip!

—Don't worry, Jill said. —Something will turn up.

She took his hand in hers. And that was it over and done with. It wasn't nearly as bad as he'd thought it would be.

Nick didn't bother waking up Sasha. She was fast asleep next to him. Besides, she didn't start work at the restaurant till this evening, and she could let herself out later. He looked out over Dalkey Island: a glorious morning. He checked his skin in the mirror and used the almond facial scrub to scrape off the last of the face pack. He turned around to make sure Sasha wasn't watching before blowing his reflection a kiss.

After his grooming routine, he selected the cream Gucci, the pastel-pink shirt and the black tie. He was going to make a killing today.

Barry was polishing a Volkswagen Passat trade-in when they came in. He thought he recognised them from somewhere, but he couldn't place them exactly. One of them was short and stocky, kind of thick-looking. He was dressed a bit like one of those lads off The Sopranos – black leather jacket, black shirt and tight blue jeans that clung to his arse. Can't be good for the balls, Barry thought. Jill had read it in one of her magazines. That was why she always bought him boxer shorts instead of the jockeys. They took a bit of getting used to, but he had to admit they were more comfortable – except when you were getting on the bike, the odd time, and they caught your meat and two veg in a kind of sling. He shuddered at the thought. The other fella was taller and wore a baggy black suit without a tie. His hair was a bit longer, too, which wasn't hard, since Hot Pants's head was practically skinned.

—Can I help you? Barry asked, in the tone he reserved for dealing with the public: polite and businesslike, without being fawning like Dunne-Davis sometimes was.

They didn't look like the usual customers that came in. Mostly they were middle-aged management types, or rich young yuppies in with Daddy to get their first GTIs.

—We're looking for Mr Dunne-Davis, said the taller fella.

They weren't friends of Dunne-Davis's, anyway. Barry was certain of that. Maybe the prick was in trouble. Deadly, Barry thought. He almost smiled for a second.

—I'll check if he's inside. Can I say who's here to see him?

—Just get him, righ'?

So the skinhead was capable of speech. Barry noticed the other fella nudging him, not too gently, in the ribs.

—Just tell him his cousins are here to see him, he added.

Cousins, me bollix, thought Barry as he went into the showrooms.

Dunne-Davis's mobile went just as Barry walked in.

—N-double-D speaking.

He held up a finger, to indicate that he would deign to speak with Barry just as soon as he'd taken this important call.

—Yes, Sasha? You're still there?

Barry couldn't make out the words on the other end, but whoever it was seemed to be a bit agitated.

—No, there's nothing there... You can search all you like, but I'm telling you, there's nothing in the pad... Look, there's a bottle of champagne in the fridge, right?

He clicked the mobile shut with a deft flick of his wrist.

—What can I do for you?

You can start by givin' me my job back. Then you can do us all a favour by killing yourself, would have been the honest answer.

—There's two men outside to see yeh.

Nick didn't bother hiding his irritation. Sometimes he just wasn't in the mood for dealing with the general public. He got up and went to the door, where he stopped abruptly. He recognised the two men straight away. You didn't forget the likes of Benny Doyle and John O'Neill in a hurry. Nick closed the door hurriedly before they saw him.

—You all righ'? Barry asked.

He clearly wasn't. Barry was beginning to enjoy this.

Dunne-Davis swept his hair back with his hand. He could feel his forehead flaring up like someone had hit a switch on his back. —Er, just tell them to take the yellow Beetle.

Barry noticed the tiny beads of sweat sprouting on Nick's face. —Is everything OK?

—What? Yes, of course it is. Just do it, will you? Please, Barry...

Jesus, Barry thought, he really was rattled. —So they're not really your cousins, then?

—Cousins? Nick almost spat —Er, yeah. They're from the north side.

North side of my arse, thought Barry as he walked across the lot. He handed the keys to the one who looked like he had half a brain.

—He said to take the yellow one. He's with another customer at the moment.

Benny grabbed the keys from his partner and jumped behind the wheel. Barry watched them pulling out of the gates in the canary-yellow Beetle. They looked like they'd just stolen the feckin' thing, especially the way that skinhead was driving it.

Sasha was frantically pulling designer cushions off the sofa. She knew Nick had some sort of drugs somewhere in the apartment. She ripped open the cushion-covers and tore out the fillings. Nothing. She flopped back against the wall. The initial panic of finding Nick gone was slowly subsiding.

She looked around at the mess. A few feathers floated through the air, landing on the piles of clothes and books that were scattered liberally about the place.

—Oh, my God!

Nick's apartment looked like it had been ransacked by burglars. She'd clean it up later. Right now she needed a drink. She remembered Nick's promise of champagne in the fridge and opened the chrome door.

—Fuck. Only one bottle?

Nick Dunne-Davis paced up and down his office. Four strides, turn around, four strides back, turn... He reckoned he'd covered at least two miles in the past hour. He looked at the clock. 4.48 – two minutes later than the last time he'd checked. When the phone rang he rushed to answer it, knocking his knee off the desk in the process.

—Fuck! I mean, hello?

There was no reply. He rubbed his kneecap gingerly.

—Hello?

— Mr Doyle's not impressed.

The phone went dead.

Out in the lot, Barry pulled on his helmet. The two toe-rags still hadn't brought back the Beetle, and he didn't care. It was Dunne-Davis's problem. He fired the old Honda into life, revved the engine and gave Dunne-Davis a big wave as he shot past his window. He wove in and out of the long line of traffic that had Shelbourne Road in a chokehold. He'd be home in exactly three minutes.

Inside his office, Nick was massaging his temples with short circular motions of his index fingers, but the pain was getting worse, like a heavy fog inside his head.

What did the bastards want? He'd been agonising over the possibilities for over an hour. They still had the Beetle – must be holding it as collateral. But what about the gear? Had they taken the wrong one?

There was only one way to find out.

The smell of mince was wafting in from the kitchen. It was Barry's favourite tonight – spaghetti bolognese. He and the da were watching the 6.1 news, although he couldn't concentrate on it properly with Sarah bouncing around on his knee – she was getting too big for that. Michael seemed very interested in whatever the young one reporting from the Dáil was on about.

—Dinner's on the table! called Jill.

Sarah stopped fidgeting and jumped up from the sofa.

—Last one in's a rotten egg, said Barry. He grabbed her arm as she was running away and held on to it. —Hey, no head starts!

She squirmed and tried to free herself from his grasp, but he managed to duck ahead of her through the door. Jill was heaping the spaghetti onto the plates. Why did she always do that? He couldn't understand why she insisted on telling them the dinner was actually on the table when she was still serving it up on the counter. It wasn't as if they were slow in coming in.

—You cheated, Da!

—No, I didn't – you were too slow. Now go and help your mammy, yeh rotten egg, yeh.

—While it's hot, please, Michael! said Jill to the living-room door. He was still watching that feckin' news report. Still, hasn't he a great interest in current affairs? she thought.

Sarah placed the steaming plate in front of her daddy.

—Lovely!

Barry waited for Jill and Sarah to sit down before attacking his meal. He dug the fork in and twirled the long strands around it, making sure he got a good dollop of sauce on it in the process.

—Mmm – lovely. My compliments to the chef.

—I see you haven't lost your appetite, anyway, Jill said, smiling.

Declan came down the stairs and started devouring his dinner without a word.

Barry's mobile rang just as Michael was sitting down. Jill gave him her 'Leave it till after dinner' look. The name flashing on the screen made him stop chewing for a second.

—What does that prick want now?

—What? Jill glared at him for the language and motioned towards Sarah with her eyes.

—Er, nothing... Sorry, love.

He didn't bother swallowing the mound of pasta before mumbling into the phone. —Hello?

—N-double-D here.

Barry hated the way he always said that.

—Who?

—You know who it is. Get your arse down here, now!

Barry hit End on the mobile. Dunne-Davis sounded agitated. He shovelled a couple more mouthfuls in and got up from the table.

—Barry... Jill wasn't impressed.

—Sorry, love. I just have to drop in to the showroom for a sec. Leave it in the microwave for me.

—Who was that?

—Nick Dunne-Davis.

Declan stopped chewing for a split second but didn't look up.

—But, Jill said, —you don't even work for that... prick...any more.

There, she'd said it. She never used bad language in front of Sarah, but she didn't care. He was a prick.

—Can it not wait till after your dinner, Bar? said Michael.

—I won't be a minute.

He looked at Jill to let her know he didn't want to go, but she was ignoring him. She'd made a special effort with the dinner, and now he was walking out in the middle of it. He felt like a right bollix.

He didn't bother with the jacket. It was a nice, mild evening, and he loved feeling the wind rushing through his T-shirt. It made you feel like you were flying – not that he knew what that was like. He'd never even seen the inside of a plane. Imagine, at his age! In fact, the only times he'd been out of the country had been those trips on the ferry to Holyhead for the trials. His stomach churned at the memory of it – the salt air blasting his face as he threw up, again and again, over the side of the boat. The crossing only took a few hours, but it had seemed like weeks at the time. Now he couldn't go near a boat. He practically got seasick in the bath.

The drunken events of the previous evening came back to him. Maybe that was what Dunne-Davis was so uptight about. Barry must have left an abusive message on his mobile, and the prick had only just checked it now. So what? thought Barry. He deserved everything he got, the bollix.

Nick Dunne-Davis stared, misty-eyed, at his car. It hadn't taken him long to figure out what kind of animal would deface a work of art like that. At first he'd thought it might have been Benny Doyle; but Doyle was hardly capable of writing his own name, let alone something like that. Besides, it wasn't his style. No: if you pissed Tony Doyle off that badly, you'd be worrying about replacing your kneecaps, not your paint job. But that thug, Kelly...he had all the motivation in the world.

Nick had it all – and what did Kelly have? An illegitimate brat and a menial job as a mechanic – for the rest of the month, at least. And that was why he'd done it: to get back at his superior.

Nick's sight was becoming blurred. It was almost too painful to bear, looking at his poor 323i... A tear dropped onto his face – followed quickly by a large fist. In his grief, Nick hadn't seen the big black Mercedes parking across the street.

Benny Doyle sank his other fist into Nick's stomach, then dragged his head back up by the neatly gelled coiffure.

—Where's the gear? said John O'Neill, in a voice that made Nick wish he were sitting on a toilet.

Barry could see what was troubling Nick Dunne-Davis even before he turned the Honda into the lot. It was spelled out, in two-foot-high letters, all down the side of his precious BMW. The spray paint was black, and it stood out boldly against the bright-red paintwork. The letters spelled a name that Barry and some of the other lads had for Nick Dunne-Davis, and he recognised the writing instantly.

It was a bit of a shock seeing it screaming out at him, but at the same time, Barry couldn't contain a little smirk. He even felt proud of his younger brother, in a strange kind of way. The little bastard had heard him referring to 'Lick My Anus' many a time at home. Still, he'd a neck like a jockey's bollix to do it.

He'd deal with Declan later, though. Right now he'd better find Dunne-Davis.

It didn't take long. Benny Doyle had Dunne-Davis's neck in a vice-like grip, like he was a huge beer bottle and his head was the top that Benny couldn't quite prise off. Through the chink in the open door, Barry could see the back of the other fella from earlier on. He was sitting in one of the office chairs, and he was holding a gun. Fuck it, Barry thought: he really is in trouble.

Without thinking, he slipped back out to the repair garage and searched for something solid. He grabbed a monkey wrench from the bench and patted it gently against his palm. Funny: they always seemed to do that in the movies, and now he was doing it himself. He tiptoed back to the office door. He could hear his own heart pumping and the dull thudding sound of Benny Doyle thumping Dunne-Davis's kidneys.

—Where is it, yeh little prick?

Dunne-Davis wasn't saying anything intelligible. No change there, thought Barry. In fairness to him, it must be difficult enough to speak with someone trying to slowly remove your head from your shoulders. And the face on the skinhead...Barry couldn't get over it. He looked like he was really enjoying choking Dunne-Davis. That was fair enough – Barry had to admit he'd often thought about it himself – but it was more than that. Your man was getting a real buzz out of it – the way he bit his tongue, and that manic grin on his face... He was totally absorbed in choking the life out of his victim.

Good, Barry thought. That would make what he had to do next that bit easier. He picked his way silently into the office. The wrench in his hand started to shake a bit as he approached the leather-clad back of the fella with the gun.

Oh, shite... He could feel his legs going weak and his head starting to spin. He was going to pass out like a fuckin' oul' one! He'd always felt like this before getting into fights as a kid.

He was shaking all over, but they hadn't seen him yet. He knew he'd better do it quick. Another step took him within striking distance. He drew back the wrench unsteadily, like it weighed a bleedin' ton, and took aim.

Dunne-Davis made a strange croaking sound when he saw Barry. Benny whipped around, following the direction of Dunne-Davis's eyes. —Johnno! he roared, as N-double-D collapsed to the ground like a concertina.

John O'Neill managed to turn halfway around in his chair before being met by a monkey wrench to the forehead. The heavy steel made a dull clank on the bone of his skull and opened a scarlet streak above his right eye. He dropped the gun – it rolled under the desk – and followed it to the floor in a heap.

Benny and Barry stared at each other for what seemed like an eternity before diving simultaneously to the ground. They grovelled around on the floor like two drunks after closing time. Barry felt the gun with his fingertips but couldn't get a firm grip on it. Benny had his forearm pinned to the ground, but he couldn't seem to reach the pistol either; the front panel of the desk was keeping them apart. Barry had it in his hand for a split second, but it was much heavier than it looked. It fell and bounced over to Benny's side.

But Benny was having problems of his own. Dunne-Davis had got the hang of breathing again and was busy trying to pull one of Benny's arms from its socket. It was like trying to find a bar of soap in the bath: neither of them could see the gun, so they had to grope blindly on the floor. Barry caught a glimpse of Benny's other hand, fumbling around under his side of the desk. He drew back the wrench and smashed it down on Benny's hand.

There was a short pause. Then:

—YEEAARRGGHHHH!

Barry had the gun, and he managed to get back on his feet. He lined up Benny's head like he was taking a penno and kicked it, aiming for the top corner. Benny fell to the floor, but he wouldn't stay there for long. Barry got his arms under Dunne-Davis and dragged him to his feet. He was recovering his strength remarkably quickly; he even managed a parting kick to his tormentor's shins. The two of them half-ran out to the lot. Even before they got out of the office, they could hear the others getting up.

Barry ran for the Honda and jumped on from a metre

away. He saw Dunne-Davis trying to open the door of his car, but it was locked.

—Fuck!

Nick had left the keys in his office, and he didn't fancy going back for them. Barry kicked the Honda into life and spun over to him just as the Johnno and Benny staggered outside.

—Get on.

Dunne-Davis looked like he'd been asked the million-euro question by Gay Byrne.

—Get on, yeh fuckin' gobshite!

He was like an oul' one climbing onto a horse. He was only half on when Barry hit the throttle and screamed out of the gates, leaving Benny and Johnno in a plume of smoke behind them. Nick looked around and saw them heading for the black Merc as Barry tore up Shelbourne Road and around onto Ball's Bridge. The lights went red as they went through them, but that didn't stop their pursuers: the Merc burst into Barry's rear-view mirrors. Nice model, he thought. It was an '89 or '90 500 SEL with silver trim. No, it was definitely an '89; he could see the reg now. He'd have his work cut out for him losing these guys.

—Hang on, he suggested.

Dunne-Davis was already squeezing the life out of him when he opened the throttle. The little bike accelerated from fifty miles per hour to eighty in little more than a heartbeat.

—FUUUCK!

They shot down Merrion Road like a bullet.

Even Benny Doyle was impressed. —What in the name of Jaysus…?

He slammed the pedal to the floor and overtook three cars in one go, on the wrong side. The chase was on.

—Me throat! squawked Barry, but Nick couldn't hear him. The wind was roaring past his ears at a hundred miles an hour as they went down Sandymount Avenue. What was this lunatic doing? wondered Nick. He was suicidal. That was the only explanation. The shock of losing his job and the excitement of the scuffle with Tony Doyle's goons had made him flip – and he was going to take Nick with him, the bitter little toe-rag.

—You're fuckin' chokin' me! Barry gasped.

After the third elbow to his ribs, Nick loosened his grip on Barry's neck. He hadn't even realised he was clutching it. He was only concerned with hanging on to the nearest stationary object, which happened to be Barry's throat.

Nick couldn't bring himself to turn around. It was far too dangerous. He could hear the roar of the heavy car behind, though, bearing down on them like a huge eagle swooping over a prairie dog. They were going to be devoured. And, to make matters worse, he could see the flashing red lights of the level crossing looming dead ahead. That meant only one thing: train. This was it. They were going to be run over by the Merc once they stopped at the gates. They had to stop. The barrier was down on one side. Why weren't they slowing down? Kelly was going to stop, wasn't he? Only a madman wouldn't…

—STOP! roared Nick, as Barry accelerated towards the level crossing. Nick wasn't aware of his hair brushing against the lowering barrier as they raced under it. He was much too busy trying to stay on the back of the Honda, after Barry had slammed on the back brake and sent the bike into a ninety-degree spin, heading north down the tracks. Nick's life flashed before his eyes – or so he would mistakenly recall when he got the chance to reflect on it; in actual fact, the only thing flashing in front of his eyes was the large green DART train about to rearrange their body parts.

Barry wrenched the handlebars just before they collided, sending the bike onto the opposite side of the tracks. It was hard going, with that waste of space on the back weighing the bike down. For a minute he thought they'd lost the Merc, until the DART passed the gates, the barriers went up and the car came screeching onto the tracks behind them. Nick could feel his internal organs bobbing up and down over every sleeper as they bumped their way up the track.

A lorry almost took them out as they ducked off the rail line and past Allied Irish Banks. They sped round the corner, past the RDS again, this time going in the opposite direction. And suddenly there was a Garda car in the chase. The lorry had held up the Merc for a few seconds, and the Gardaí were behind the Merc, like a dog chasing a cat chasing a mouse. Ball's Bridge came and went again in a blur, and the red and white Honda streaked past Roly's Bistro and up towards Herbert Park.

The park ranger was in the process of kicking some young fellas with a football off the grass.

—D'yous see tha'?

—Yeah.

—What does it say?

—No football on the grass.

—Exactly. Now get lost before I report yous to the Gar—

He didn't get a chance to finish: two yobbos on a Honda 50 roared past him. He was just about to shout something about watching the flowerbeds when a large Mercedes smashed through the park gates, sending them flying twenty feet into the air in opposite directions. One of them crash-landed in the grass, only metres from where the park ranger was standing. Its edge burrowed deep into the ground, leaving it stuck on its axis like an enormous set-square. The other gate was more fortunate: its landing had been broken by a large rosebush, which was now scattered about the park like confetti. By the time the police car had barrelled over the matching rosebush, the park ranger was in a state of shock. He even handed the young fellas back their ball.

Barry was really enjoying this. It was mad. The adrenaline was pumping through his veins, and he felt like he and the bike were one entity, two parts of the same machine. He was barely even aware of Dunne-Davis on the back any more. It was just him against the Merc. He ploughed down the middle of the tree-lined grass and screamed onto the football pitches, where two junior teams were in the middle of a South Dublin league match. The players dived for cover. In a split second of madness, Barry considered running over the referee, just for old times' sake; but at the last minute he steered around the fat bastard, lying on the ground like a beached whale, and headed straight for the goalposts. The Merc drew alongside him; the Guards were still a bit behind, struggling to keep up with the pace.

The keeper just stood there, staring straight at them, like a rabbit caught in the headlights of a juggernaut. Barry recognised him from his schoolboy days with Cambridge. It was Butter Boyle, short for Butterfingers.

—Get the fuck out of it, Butter! roared Barry.

The keeper seemed to snap to. He dived spectacularly to his right and to safety. —Pity he never did that during a game, Barry muttered to himself as they shot past the upright. The Merc crashed straight through the netting, pulling the posts out of the ground.

Barry aimed the bike for the pond. The weight of Dunne-Davis almost sent him over the handlebars as they thumped down the steps onto the tarmac. The Merc was still right behind them, goalposts, net and all dragging in its wake. Some oul' one's poodle had been snared by the net and was yapping away in terror as it tumbled along the grass. The young fellas skateboarding by the pond dived into the bushes.

And then Barry saw it. He didn't really think about it properly; he just reckoned they might make it, with a little bit more speed.

—Hang on, he said calmly, as he reefed back the throttle as far as it would go. The Honda was doing over ninety when it hit the crude skateboard ramp.

—FUCK! shrieked Nick, as the bike sailed thirty feet through the air over the water.

They slammed down a good ten feet beyond the pond. The Merc wasn't so lucky. Benny slammed on the brakes, but it was too late. The big car wasn't built for flying. It collided with the ramp and flipped onto its side. The Merc made it halfway across the water before belly-flopping heavily into the pond, sending ducks quacking indignantly and launching Benny Doyle through the windscreen. The coroner would conclude later that it wasn't the high-speed flight through the air that had killed him; the crash-landing head-first into the large oak tree had done the real damage.

Barry stopped the bike and turned to look. He felt like Arnie in that scene from Terminator 2, when he looks back at the other terminator after blowing up the truck.

And, sure enough, John O'Neill was clambering his way out of the wreckage. He hauled himself up, dripping, onto the passenger side of the car. Blood was cascading down his forehead, but apart from that he looked all right. This time he didn't follow them, though. The sound of the Garda car sent him hobbling away through the bushes. Barry hoped it was the last they'd see of him.

—CHAPTER FIVE—

After he'd thrown up for the second time, Nick Dunne-Davis calmed down a bit. He insisted that they go back to the showrooms.

—Why, but?

—Because. I need to check something. Just trust me, right?

Barry went back, under protest. The lot was just as they'd left it. There was nobody home. Barry eased the Honda to a stop and waited for Dunne-Davis to clamber off it.

Nick stood and stared at the little bike that had outrun a three-hundred-horsepower car, not to mention the Gardaí. He was still in shock. Surely they couldn't have been going as fast as he had thought? He must have imagined it...

—It's not exactly a Honda 50, explained Barry. 'The nifty' was to speed what Doctor Who's Tardis was to interiors. —I put a Yamaha 150 engine and gearbox into it.

—So how fast is it, exactly?

—Well, there's also the alloy wheels and the racing tyres to take into—

—How fast?

—A hundred and forty. Easy.

—Fuck me!

—Yeah, she's well nippy.

Barry was patting the bike in admiration when Dunne-Davis remembered why they were there.

—That Beetle they took...

—Wha' about it?

—Did you give it the once-over when it came in?

—Yeah, I did a full PDI on it. Why?

—And you didn't notice anything about it?

—No. It was the yellow one, wasn't it?

—Yah.

—Conor did that one. The spare tyre…

—Yes?

—It was marked. I replaced it.

Dunne-Davis covered his eyes with his hand.

—Do you know where you put it? he asked, as calmly as he could.

—Yeah.

Hallelujah, thought Nick.

—I dumped it yesterday.

—What? Fuck it…I don't believe this! He lashed a foot out at nothing in particular.

—No, wait a minute.

—Yes? Dunne-Davis sprang to attention, like a man on Death Row who had just been offered the possibility of a pardon.

—I put it on the rack over there.

Barry pointed. Nick sprinted over to the rack full of tyres.

—Do you know which one it is?

—Yeah, there was a slight abrasion on it.

—Like this?

—That's it.

Nick pressed his nail to the valve and deflated the tyre. The air hissed away, and he got Barry to remove the tyre.

Barry couldn't believe his eyes.

—Wha' the fuck?

So that was what all this was about. Barry didn't know much about drugs, but he knew what that white powder was. It was stuffed into the tyre, wrapped in plastic packs, loads of it; there must have been ten kilos of the stuff. Now that he thought about it, the spare had seemed heavy when he took it out of the Beetle.

—How much is it worth?

Dunne-Davis smiled. —A million euro.

—Holy Jaysus!

—Yah.

—I want nothin' to do with it.

—Ye-ah, said Nick, sounding unconvinced.

—Wha' does tha' mean?

—Well, it's just that it's a little bit late for that now.

—How is it?

—Well, Tony Doyle doesn't forget about this kind of thing in a hurry.

Barry didn't know Tony Doyle personally, but, like everyone else in Dublin, he was familiar with that name. It was synonymous with crime – and not just petty stuff, either. Drugs, armed robbery, murder...they were all part of Doyle's portfolio.

—Well, can't yeh just give it back to him?

—You mean before he kills us? asked Nick.

—Us?

—Look, that was his nephew, Benny Doyle, who hit the tree.

—Fuck...

—And O'Neill walked away from it. Doyle will have traced the Honda back to you already. So we're both screwed. Sorry.

Nick didn't expect instant forgiveness. But he didn't expect the right hook to his nose, either.

—My fucking nose!

Blood poured down into his mouth. He just hoped his nose wasn't broken. That could ruin his profile entirely.

—Prick, Barry said.

He would deal with Dunne-Davis later. He had to get home and make sure Jill and Sarah were all right. What if Doyle went after them too?

Dunne-Davis must have read his mind. —Don't even think about it, Barry. That's the first place they'll look.

—So I just leave my girlfriend and my daughter at their mercy, do I?

—Doyle won't touch them.

—How do you know he won't?

—The Guards saw everything. They'll be keeping an eye out at your place. If Doyle went after them now, it would only implicate him – and he doesn't like leaving trails. Besides, family's not really his style. He's old school and all that. If he goes down, it'll be for someone who's really pissed him off.

—What if I tell him I'd nothin' to do with it?

—Doesn't work like that. Someone has to pay for Benny. It's you and me they'll come after.

Barry couldn't believe it. In the space of two days, he'd lost his job, he'd almost lost his life and he was about to lose his family.

—And the Guards? What if I talk to them?

—You could risk it, but Doyle has half of them on his payroll, said Nick, weighing a bag of cocaine in his palm.

—And the other half?

—That's the problem: you never know which ones are which. It'll be impossible to tell, particularly with the ones that watch the house. He'll make sure he gets some of them in his pocket, even if they aren't in it already.

Barry slouched forward. He was sick of this already.

—So what do we do now? he sighed.

—The only thing we can do. We run.

Barry still had to be restrained from going home. Nick assured him he could call Jill in a few days, when the dust had settled. For now, he had to make him realise how serious this was.

—It's for their own good, Barry. Honestly, the less they know about it the better.

Barry didn't trust that bollix at all. He never had. Right from the first time he'd seen him, he'd known Dunne-Davis was full of it. He looked at the plastic-wrapped white dust.

—And wha' are we goin' to do with tha'?

—We're going to take it with us.

—Wha'?

—Just for insurance. Doyle won't touch your family if he thinks we still have it.

As much as it galled him, Barry had to admit it made sense. He was just beginning to feel a grudging respect for Dunne-Davis when Nick informed him, —Of course, we've got to get out of the country ASAP.

—Out of the bleedin' country? Fuck off!

—Yah, out of the country. Listen, Doyle has people all over the place – even in England. We've got to get far away from here, as quickly as possible.

As if to illustrate the point, the sound of a police car pulling up outside interrupted them. Dunne-Davis peeked around the corner.

—Fuck!

Barry straddled the Honda. —Righ'. Let's go.

—We'll take the Beemer, suggested Nick, before remembering where his keys were.

He waited while Barry reluctantly lifted the saddle and stuffed the packets of coke into the hollow compartment underneath. They pushed the bike silently out the back way. Barry didn't fire it up till they were nearly back up at Ball's Bridge. Dunne-Davis was moaning about not having a helmet.

—I'm telling you, we'll get done by the cops.

He looked conspicuous enough already, in his poncy white suit. Barry only had the one helmet, though, with the LFC emblem on the back of it, and he was fucked if he was giving it to Dunne-Davis. They decided to take the back roads out of Dublin to Enniskerry. From there they'd be safe enough on the N11; they figured the Guards would only be checking Dublin for the bike at this stage. Barry pointed the Honda towards the mountains, and they headed up past the Dodder river and out through Rathfarnham.

It was starting to get dark, and the lights were coming

on all over the city. Barry stopped the bike outside the Blue Light. Fuck, Dublin looked beautiful, illuminated by a million orange specks under the blood-red sunset. Even Dunne-Davis seemed humbled by it.

—D'yeh really want a helmet, now? asked Barry.

—Yah.

—You're sure?

—Of course I'm sure!

—Righ'.

Barry leaned over to one of the big Harley Davidsons parked outside the pub and pulled the helmet from its perch behind the saddle. He handed it to Dunne-Davis.

—Ah, fuck off!

Nick put it on, though. He knew what would happen if he didn't.

And then they were off. Barry knew they must look like a right pair of gobshites – him in nothing but his Ireland T-shirt, at this hour of the evening, and Nick Dunne-Davis…well, the white suit and pink shirt were bad enough (he'd decided the tie might be bad luck after Benny had tried to garrotte him with it), and the brown loafers weren't exactly ideal biking shoes, but the helmet really topped it all off. It was the icing on the cake for Barry. Dunne-Davis looked like a right fuckin' tulip with that Nazi helmet on.

It was completely dark when they got to Enniskerry. Once they hit the motorway, Dunne-Davis offered Barry his jacket.

—You'll freeze without it. I've got sleeves on my shirt, and you're getting the brunt of the wind at the front.

Barry was shocked. He figured Dunne-Davis must be feeling guilty for getting him mixed up in all of this. But he wasn't about to turn the offer down.

—Eh, thanks.

It was true: he was feeling the cold already. Even though it was summer, it was fairly nippy at night, especially shooting down a motorway. He made sure he kept within the speed limits, though. The last thing they needed was to be hauled in for speeding.

It still only took them an hour and a half to get to Rosslare. The plan was to stay the night in a B&B and stow away on the ferry to France the next day. It had been Barry's idea. They had no passports with them, so flying was out of the question. The ferry to Holyhead was no use, either, because Doyle's associates would most probably be waiting for them at the other end. Barry wasn't jumping up and down at the prospect of sailing again, but they hadn't a whole lot of options. France was the logical choice.

—How will we get on the ferry? asked Dunne-Davis.

On the way down he had taken out two hundred euro, which was the limit for one day, from an ATM, and he'd do the same again tomorrow, but that wouldn't get them far.

—Leave that to me, said Barry.

They found a grand little bed-and-breakfast near the port. The oul' one gave them a room for thirty euro a head. She even made them a cup of tea and some ham sandwiches, which they gulped down in no time. Barry checked his watch: a quarter to eleven. Jill'd be going spare looking for him. He wanted to call her, just to let her know where he was. Dunne-Davis wouldn't hear of it.

—You can call her from the Continent. What she doesn't know can't harm her, he insisted.

They were both knackered. It had been a long day. After they went upstairs, Barry lay awake, agonising over whether or not to ring her, while Dunne-Davis snored away. If he'd had his mobile with him, he would have. The worst bit was that she wouldn't know what had happened to him.

Jill was on to her third cup of tea in the kitchen. The

bastard must have gone on the piss again, she thought.

In the living room, Michael was watching the late news on TV3. If he was really pushed, he'd have had to say it was his favourite broadcast of the day. The content was OK, but the delivery was beautiful. It was that young one who used to be on T na G, with the Irish name – Gráinne Something-or-other. She'd a lovely voice on her, kind of husky and sexy. She was going on about some car chase when he saw it.

—Jill! Get in here quick, love!

Jill came tearing into the room just as the reporter was coming on. He was standing beside the pond in Herbert Park, where a large black Mercedes was half-submerged on its side in the water.

—The dead man has been identified as Bernard Doyle, believed to be part of the notorious Doyle criminal family. Gardaí would like the other men involved in the chase to come forward for questioning.

That was when they showed the tape again. It was just like any other home video of a football game at first. Then, out of nowhere, a Honda 50 with two fellas on it burst into the frame, followed quickly by the Merc and then the Guards.

—Mother of Divine, said Michael.

He'd thought he was seeing things the first time, but there was no doubt about it now. It was Barry, with that prick Nick Dunne-Davis on the back. He had his helmet on, but it was definitely him.

Jill was speechless. She hoped to God he was all right.

CHAPTER SIX

Barry banged on the door of the en-suite bathroom. What was Dunne-Davis doing in there? He'd been in there for nearly forty-five minutes, and Barry was bursting for a slash.

—Did yeh fall in, or wha'?

—I'll be out in a minute.

Nick was having major problems with his hair. He'd washed it with the complimentary shampoo and then put shower gel into it, in the mistaken belief that it was conditioner. What kind of place didn't have conditioner? It was all fluffy and wavy now, and where was the hair mousse? He got it looking just about presentable, after another ten minutes, and got back into his silk boxers that he'd worn the day before. He felt like an animal. He pulled on his suit while Barry showered. There were black stains all down the legs of it.

They went down to breakfast together. Barry shovelled the fry into him like it was his last meal. while Nick prodded the greasy pudding with his knife.

—Is it all right for you, dear? asked the landlady.

—Lovely, mumbled Barry.

—Oh, yah, sure... Eh, you don't have any muesli, do you?

—Is that a fruit, dear?

After breakfast they gathered up their meagre possessions and went to pay the oul' one. Nick gave her his credit card, to save the small sum of cash they had. They'd need that later. She was running it through the machine when it stopped, halfway through. Nick smiled reassuringly at Barry.

—Just checking my limit. It always does that.

A couple of beeps followed, and the landlady took out the slip. Nick picked up the pen to sign it.

—I'm afraid I can't accept this, Mr Dunne-Davis.

—Excuse me?

—It's out of date.

—What? It can't be! protested Nick, but he knew it was. The sickening realisation crept up on him: today was the first of the month. They'd sent the new card out to him a couple of weeks ago. It was lying on the worktop in his kitchen. He'd wanted to leave it somewhere he wouldn't forget it.

—Nice one, said Barry, a little too sarcastically for Nick's liking.

If only he'd paid for the room last night... But that was the least of their worries. They weren't going to get very far on two hundred euro between them. Nick paid the sixty euro in cash and decided not to panic. He'd withdraw money from his bank on the way to the ferry. Surely there'd be a branch on the way.

There wasn't. The nearest one that anyone knew of was in Cork, and the ferry was leaving in an hour.

Barry went over to the line of trucks waiting to board the big Normandy.

—Deadly, he said when he spotted Mick Healy's lorry.

Mick was one of the truckies who did the long trek back and forth to Europe picking up the cars for the showroom. Barry had done a nixer on his car a couple of weeks back and was still waiting to be paid. Mick was surprised to see him.

—How's it goin', head?

—Good. Howya? enquired Barry.

—Not too bad. Off on your holliers?

—Eh, not exactly.

Mick took a bit of persuading, but eventually he agreed

to let them take their chances in the bunk behind the cabin of the truck. He had to leave his place in the queue and drive a mile or so from the ferry terminal before they got in, to make sure they wouldn't be seen. It was a tiny compartment, barely big enough for one, but they both squeezed in eventually. The bike was the hard part. They had to wedge it into the back of a 4x4 that Mick was bringing back to the factory in Germany. Jaysus, Barry thought, if only the poor bastard knew the risk he was taking in exchange for a few hundred quid's worth of mechanical work... Still, they were on their way, as long as no one wanted to check the cargo. Mick had driven the 4x4 up onto the top deck of the trailer, to keep it out of sight. He'd done this trip a thousand times and knew all the ferry heads well – but it'd be just Barry's luck if they decided to inspect the truck this one time.

He needn't have worried. They breezed onto the ferry without a problem. The only bad bit was having to lie beside Dunne-Davis in the dark for a couple of hours.

—Barry?

—Yeah.

What did he want now?

—I just wanted to say thanks. For back in the showrooms.

Barry had almost forgotten why he was there. If he hadn't saved Dunne-Davis's arse yesterday – fuck, he couldn't believe it was only yesterday – he'd be on his way home now. He didn't reply. He didn't want Dunne-Davis to think he'd forgiven him. He hadn't. So the two of them lapsed back into an awkward silence until the noise of the cars and trucks stopped.

They waited for half an hour after the last of the passengers had left their cars before venturing out. There didn't seem to be anybody on their level, so they made their way up the stairs to the entrance to the passenger decks. They had to climb a few levels before they reached the door. Barry caught his breath for a second before trying the handle. It eased down gently – nice one.

The doorbell went just as Michael was settling into a half-hour special about the World Cup on Sky News. Jill was out shopping and Declan and Sarah were at school. He'd have to answer it himself. Or maybe he'd just ignore it and they'd go away.

Ding-dong.

—Feck it, anyway...

He rested his mug on the arm of the chair and dragged himself up. He saw two broad silhouettes through the frosted glass. —Shite, he said under his breath as the door squeaked open.

—Michael, long time no see.

Michael was taken aback. He had been dreading the two Special Branch lads who had been camped across the street in the navy Mondeo for the past twenty-four hours. Now he almost wished it had been them. Typical, he thought wryly: just when you might need them, they disappeared.

—You better come in, he said, trying to sound natural.

Tony Doyle wiped his feet on the mat and stepped in. —Wait in the car, he said to the gorilla accompanying him.

Johnno said nothing. That suited him fine.

Michael led Doyle into the living room. —Sit down there. D'yeh want a cup o' tea?

Doyle shook his head. —No, thanks. This isn't wha' you might call a social call.

Michael nodded dumbly.

—So I take it you know what the story is?

Michael shrugged noncommittally. He had a feeling he was about to find out.

Tony Doyle took out a half-Corona and offered one to Michael.

—No, thanks.

—Mind if I do?

—Fire away, said Michael. What else could he say? Passive smoking took years to kill you; Tony Doyle had been known to do it in a matter of seconds.

Michael had known Doyle since they were kids. They'd played football against each other all the way up through the schoolboy grades. Michael had been a handy centre forward for Bolton, while Tony Doyle had been Fatima Rangers' hard man in central defence. They'd had many a good tussle over the years. They'd never actually been friends, but there had been a definite mutual respect between them. Doyle used to kick lumps out of most of the lads he marked, but not Michael; he knew he'd get it straight back from the little so-and-so if he did. Even back then, Doyle had been dodgy. Like the time they'd played in Ringsend Park. They must have been about sixteen. Ray Holmes had just got a brand new suit, his first real one. It was a beaut: a black single-breast, just like the ones Dean Martin used to wear. He'd worn it to the match to impress the lads, and afterwards he was going into town to a dance with his mot. Doyle must have seen him coming into the changing rooms. Just after half-time, he was going for a fifty-fifty ball with Michael when he pulled up with a hamstring – or so he said. When they got back to the dressing rooms after the match, he was gone, along with Ray Holmes's new suit.

Doyle blew out a long puff of smoke that settled in a blue-grey fog across the room.

—Where is he, Michael?

—I don't know.

Doyle did nothing, just rolled his cigar with his teeth a few times.

—I'm tellin' yeh. He hasn't been back here – no phone calls, nothin'.

—Just disappeared into thin air, did he? Like the fuckin' Ascension?

He didn't sound angry. Michael could have sworn he was actually smiling.

—You don't scare me, Tony Doyle, he lied.

Doyle looked at him. His eyes suddenly turned cold; then, just as quickly, they were back to warm again.

—I never did scare yeh, yeh oul' bollix.

Good. That sounded like a compliment, thought Michael.

—But he must have told you somethin'? This isn't schoolboy football, Michael. This is serious.

—I know it is.

Michael knew it was something to do with drugs. Everyone knew Doyle ran that racket all over the south side of the city. But Barry? It just didn't make sense. He'd never have anything to do with drugs. Hadn't he nearly burst Declan for smoking the hash?

—But I know Barry. He's not into…that scene.

Doyle tapped his fingers on the armrest. He was staring at Michael, trying to work out if he was lying or not.

—I don't know how he got mixed up in all this, an' I don't really need to know. I'm just tellin' yeh it's not like him. I know yeh don't believe me, but…

Doyle sat forward in his chair. —He's your son and you want to do righ' by him. I can understand that. Any father would do the same thing. But he's got somethin' belongin' to me, Michael. Somethin' worth a lot of money. Not to mention wha' happened my nephew. I can't just let that go.

Michael shook his head gravely.

—Now, I know he's hidin' out somewhere with that other bollix. I'm still not sure exactly how mixed up in this thing he is. But if you hear anythin' from him – anythin' at all – I want to know about it. Righ'?

Michael nodded.

—Righ'. Doyle got up from his chair. —I'll see meself out.

Michael let out a deep sigh that came from the pit of his stomach. He wished Barry would just let him know that he was all right.

Johnno was reading The Star when Doyle came out. There were a couple of inches about the chase inside, and a few still shots from the home video. Doyle's name had been mentioned in relation to Benny's, but there was nothing linking Johnno to it. There were references to a drugs scam, but neither Dunne-Davis's name nor Barry Kelly's appeared. Johnno rubbed his forehead gingerly. It was still smarting from the double blow – he'd needed seventeen stitches in all. He put the paper down and turned the key in the ignition.

—Any joy?

—Nah, said Doyle.

—D'yeh want me to have a word with him?

Doyle shook his head. —He doesn't know anythin'.

That was fair enough. Johnno was well capable of dishing it out when he had to – and taking it as well, if they were really tough. Countless years in the ring had hardened his mind and body. He wasn't like that psycho Benny. Benny had done it for fun, but only when he knew they wouldn't fight back. There'd been a few times when Johnno would have sorted Benny out himself, if he hadn't been his uncle's nephew. And Johnno wasn't the only one. Benny Doyle had led a charmed life because of who he was. He had got away with murder, literally, on more than one occasion. But he'd got what he deserved in the end. They always did.

—Where to, boss?

—I think we might take a little trip out to Dalkey.

It was just starting to clear up outside, and Tony fancied a drive along the coast. As long as they beat the feckin' traffic...

The big Jaguar purred down the coast road and out beyond Blackrock. Dun Laoghaire harbour was full of yachts; they looked great, with the big sails bathed in brilliant sunlight. Johnno flicked a switch above the mirror and the sunroof glided back. Even Doyle seemed to be enjoying the ride.

He'd never admit it publicly, but Tony Doyle wasn't

exactly heartbroken at the loss of his nephew. Benny had been more trouble than he was worth. He'd cost Tony a couple of small fortunes by not using his head – at least, not using it to think with. No, Johnno was a much better man to have at your side. At least he'd half a brain as well as his other, less cerebral talents. If they could just get hold of that merchandise that Dunne-Davis had stolen, things would be all right. He'd enjoy watching the little prick suffer.

But not Michael Kelly's young fella. Tony decided he would show him some mercy because of who he was. He'd make it nice and quick for him.

They were just leaving the harbour when it started. Barry felt like he was a teenager again, on the ferry over to Holyhead. That gentle spinning feeling that made him dizzy, and the nausea that made him feel...well, sick. Every time the boat moved up and down – which was about every five seconds, as far as he could tell – he could feel it: that fry he'd eaten. It was rolling around the top of his stomach, waiting for its chance to escape. His legs felt weak, and he was hot and cold at the same time.

—I love boats, don't you? chirped Dunne-Davis.

—How long is the trip?

—Oh, it's a good long one...

—How long? groaned Barry.

Nick did a few mental calculations.

—I'd say about twenty hours.

Twenty hours — that was nearly a full fuckin' day! Barry knew he'd never make it that long. He'd have to break it down into smaller parts if he was going to survive it. Right, it's half four now, he said to himself. If I can make it to six without puking, I'll be OK. That was all he had to do: concentrate on not getting sick.

—Are you all right, Barry? You look a bit pale. You're not going to puke, are you?

He shoved Dunne-Davis out of the way and burst

through the door onto the deck. He just reached the rail before launching his breakfast into the water below him. He felt a bit better after that.

Tony Doyle felt quite at home in Dalkey. He reckoned he could get used to life out here. It was nice being so close to the sea. And the young ones...fuck, they were gorgeous. Johnno had noticed them too. You'd have to be blind not to.

—Look at the set on tha'!

Doyle nodded appreciatively. Maybe when he retired he'd make the move. For the moment, he needed to be closer to the city centre, closer to his ever-increasing market.

They checked the address again. This was it, all right. Dunne-Davis had style, Tony would give him that – and so he should have, with all the cash he'd made from their little bit of import trading. They'd both being doing very nicely out of it until now. But Dunne-Davis had to get greedy. Just like all the rest. Silly man. Should've taken his ten per cent and saved his neck, Tony thought.

Johnno checked the buzzers outside the building and pointed to the one with 'NDD' written on it. He pressed it, just for the hell of it, gave it a good long buzz and waited to make sure there was no one home. Nothing. He was just about to press another one and pretend he'd forgotten his key (he'd heard these yuppie types never even said hello to each other in these luxury apartment places; no sense of community) when a voice struggled through the intercom.

—Yes?

Johnno looked at Doyle, who nodded back at him.

—Yes, we're just here about the gas. Mr Dunne-Davis called us.

—He doesn't have gas, came the tart reply.

Doyle frowned.

—That's why we're here, ma'am. We need to do an

estimate before installation.

There was no reply, but after a few seconds the intercom buzzed. They were in. Dunne-Davis's apartment was the penthouse, so they took the lift to the sixth floor.

Their knock on the door was answered by a very hungover-looking young lady.

Not bad, thought Johnno.

—You don't look like you're from the gas company, said Sasha.

—Can we come in, love? asked Doyle genially.

Sasha had spent the past two nights, or maybe three, at Nick's – she couldn't remember. All she could recall with any certainty was taking his spare key and his credit card the other day. There had been something hazy involving champagne, and something clearer but no less nauseating about Leeson Street. The rest was a complete blur – except the taxi driver. Oh, my God, Sasha thought. She hadn't, had she? She hadn't had the fare for the ride home, so she had invited him upstairs and… She had! He had been horrible, from what she could remember, and old – like the older one standing in front of her… This must be him, back for more with one of his mates. What kind of a slapper did he take her for?

—You filthy bastard! she screamed, as she drove a well-aimed kick into Tony Doyle's groin.

Doyle went down like a sack of spuds. Nobody had dared do that to him since he was eleven. It took Johnno a second to react – he was as shocked as Doyle was. He finally dragged her off Doyle and manhandled her inside. Doyle kicked the door shut behind him and waddled over to the sofa. Johnno threw Sasha down on the other sofa – not hard, though. He hated getting rough with women. It wasn't his style. She was screeching and clawing at him with her nails, though – she'd tear his fuckin' stitches out in a minute!

And then he did it. He slapped her. It was just a reflex, over before he knew he'd done it. He felt that horrible guilty feeling wash over him. Sasha sat up on the sofa, sobbing quietly. At least she wasn't hurt too badly. He'd used an open hand, but it had still made a terrible clatter.

Doyle cleared his throat noisily, like he was about to start hawking up blood. He didn't. Instead he fumbled in his inside pocket for his pills and popped two of them down, dry. His heart was at him again.

Barry reckoned he was over the worst of it. He hadn't eaten anything at all since the unfortunate incident involving his breakfast. Maybe he'd just fast until they got off the boat. In the meantime he decided to go to the cinema. It really was a fuckin' great boat. It had everything – bars, restaurants, shops, even game zones where kids could play computer games. You could spend your whole holiday on it and never get bored.

He waited till the usher had her back turned – she was busy trying to control some kids at the door – and then slipped in behind her. This was grand. He hadn't been to the pictures in ages. He used to go all the time with Jill, but they never seemed to get around to it any more. He wondered what she was doing. He'd call her as soon as they got to France, just to let her know he was safe and when he was coming home.

When was he going home, though? Dunne-Davis hadn't said anything about that yet. Barry had given him the slip in Molly Malone's Bar, when Dunne-Davis had gone to the jacks. He was beginning to get on Barry's nerves, even more than usual. Barry had asked him whether it was a good idea to be spending the little money they had on booze.

—It's medicinal, he'd said in that stupid Dalkey accent of his.

Barry wasn't even particularly interested in the movie – it was Ali, with Will Smith in it – but anything was better than watching that other gobshite getting drunk and talking shite. It turned out to be all right, nothing special, but he enjoyed being on his own in the dark for a couple of hours. The film relaxed him – apart from those tossers talking every few minutes – and he felt better coming out than he had going in. He even felt like he could handle Dunne-Davis for a while. Then it would be time to get a bit of kip. They hadn't decided where they were going to sleep yet – probably in one of the lounges.

When he got to the bar, Dunne-Davis was where he'd left him. He wasn't alone.

Sasha Fitzpatrick was trying desperately to express her opinion of Nick Dunne-Davis. It wouldn't have made for very polite conversation, if anyone had been able to hear a word she was saying. But the gag that had been attached firmly around her mouth made self-expression all but impossible. She screeched indignantly at the ceiling, but it made no reply.

John O'Neill had tied her to the chair and taken her blindfold off once they got her to the old warehouse. He'd removed the gag as well and let her scream her head off for a while – no one could hear her, after all – but he'd had to reattach it. He'd been genuinely afraid his eardrums would burst. And the language out of her...where did she learn words like that? He hadn't even heard of some of them himself.

Mr Doyle had insisted on holding her here. He was convinced she was in on the scam, and therefore fair game as a hostage. Johnno wasn't so sure. He couldn't see even a tulip like Dunne-Davis involving a headcase like her in all of this. He concluded – correctly, as it happened – that she had just been in the wrong place at the wrong time. Still, there was only one way to find out. He hoped she'd tell them quickly, so he wouldn't have to hurt her – not seriously, anyway.

Nick Dunne-Davis introduced the woman to Barry.

—Madame Galliano, may I present Barry Kelly?

Barry shook hands and was surprised when she kissed him on both cheeks.

—Hello, Barry. She looked at Nick and smiled. —And please, call me Claudette.

Barry sat down while Nick went up to get more drinks. She must have been fifty if she was a day – a fuckin' oul' one! All the same, though, she wasn't like most oul' ones Barry knew. You could tell she looked after herself. She had a bit too much make-up on, but you could still make out the high cheekbones and delicate features. Her shoulder-length blonde hair was straight out of a bottle, but there was definitely something sexy about her. Maybe it was the accent. He'd never met a French woman before. She must have been a fine thing in her day, he reckoned.

—So, eh, what do yeh think of Ireland?

—I love it. My husband and I, we have a cottage in Killarney. I go to it when I need a small break.

—Very nice, said Barry.

And that was about all he managed to say to her. Dunne-Davis came back with the drinks and they were like a pair of teenagers. It was embarrassing. Barry didn't know where to look as they canoodled in full view of the other passengers, not a bother on them.

She eventually got up to go to the ladies'.

—Well? enquired Nick.

—Well what? said Barry.

—Are you keen?

—Keen for what?

—Keen for the old threesome.

—Wha'?!

—Come on, she's mad for it.

—You're the one who's fuckin' mad.

—Honestly, come on. It'll be great fun – the old spit-roast, yah?

—The wha'?

—You know, one at either end. I'm telling you, she's gagging for it.

—Fuck off!

Barry couldn't believe what Dunne-Davis was proposing. It was low, even for him.

—She's married, an' anyway. (And so will I be, if I ever get out of this, he thought.)

—That means nothing. They're always the game ones.

—Yeh mean you've done this type of thing before?

—Dozens of times!

—I said no. Now fuck off.

Dunne-Davis was beaten. —All right. It's your loss, though. At least I've got us a place to sleep. It's cabin 732. Deck 7. Give me an hour or so.

He winked at Barry as Claudette sat down. She was peculiarly attractive for an oul' one...but no. Barry knew he wouldn't be able to live with himself. And the thought of Dunne-Davis as well was enough to make him puke.

They finally excused themselves and left him to contemplate the inky sky outside on his own.

Sasha had screamed herself out and was exhausted.

—Now, if I take this off, Johnno said, —you're not going to scream, are yeh?

She shook her head. She was still confused. It was obvious now that these guys weren't taxi drivers. She also knew that Nick was somehow involved. He had to be. There was no way he could afford a million-euro apartment on his salary, even if Daddy had helped him out with the deposit. No, he was definitely into something – and she had a feeling she was about to find out what it was. These guys had ransacked his pad looking for something, and she had a fair idea what. She could play dumb, but why should she? It would only make her predicament worse. And what had she got to gain by protecting Nick? He certainly wouldn't protect her, would he? She would tell them everything she knew. The only problem was, that didn't amount to very much.

Johnno removed the gag.

—Now, young lady. Where is it? Doyle's tone was polite but menacing.

—Where's what?

He slapped her hard across the face. She'd been expecting it, but the force of it still shocked her.

Doyle was taking a personal interest in this one, after her earlier assault on the family jewels. Johnno wedged himself in between them. He couldn't stand seeing Doyle at his most vicious, particularly with a woman. He grabbed her by the throat and hoped it looked convincing.

—The drugs. Don't play the innocent with us, love. We know you're in on this.

—Fuck off. Fucking north-side knackers!

Doyle kicked the chair she was sitting on, and Johnno had to hold on tight to keep her from falling off.

—We're not north-siders, yeh little wagon. Crumlin's south-side, said Doyle, insulted at the accusation.

—It's all the same to me! she sobbed.

Doyle hit her again. This time she did fall off the chair, only she was still tied to it, so it landed in a heap on top of her. Johnno picked the two of them up. This was getting out of hand. He put a hand on Doyle's shoulder to calm him.

—Leave this one to me.

Doyle's eyes, still blazing like a madman's, locked onto his for a moment. Then he turned and stormed out the door.

She was trembling all over. Johnno offered his handkerchief, but she couldn't move her arms, so he held it to her nose. She blew hesitantly. He wiped away the large tears running down her cheeks.

—Fucking bastards, she said, expecting another slap.

Instead, Johnno knelt down to meet her at eye-level.

—Tell me what you know. Make it easy on yourself. Don't bother trying to protect Dunne-Davis. He's not worth it.

—I don't know anything, honestly.

He believed her. Maybe he was a fool, but he did.

She was tough, but she wasn't as tough as she thought she was. Johnno had seen women take much worse beatings from Doyle before, but those women were different. Harder, somehow. They'd been taking it all their lives, first from their das and brothers, then from their husbands. She wasn't like that. He knew this was the first time she'd really been hit. He had to admire her. Maybe she did know something and was protecting Dunne-Davis – though it was hard to believe she'd risk losing her good looks for a slimeball like that... He didn't buy it. He wouldn't admit it, but it was easier for Johnno to believe her.

—Tell me about Dunne-Davis.

She hesitated, but only for a second.

—He's a prick.

Outside cabin 732, Barry could hear what sounded suspiciously like something firm slapping against bare flesh. Then he heard the chant: —Who's your daddy? Who's your daddy? Which was ironic, really, given that Madame What's-her-name was old enough to be Dunne-Davis's mother.

He didn't wait for the answer. After another couple of laps of the Normandy, he ventured up on deck. The night sky was beautiful. It was calm and clear, but he was still freezing in his T-shirt as the ship powered through the gentle foam. He wasn't feeling sick like before, just a touch of dizziness that hadn't been helped by the two pints of Guinness. He might brave breakfast in the morning, though.

By the time he got back to the cabin, the shouting, slapping and moaning had stopped. The only sound was the gentle snoring of Nick Dunne-Davis. Barry eased the door open and went inside. It was tiny. After taking a slash in the bathroom (even tinier) he cleared a hollow in the clothes and shoes that lined the floor and lay down. There was a spare blanket at the end of the bed. Deadly.

He managed to get to sleep surprisingly quickly.

He only woke once during the night. It was what Nick referred to as an N-double-D special. It started off deep in his intestines, with a low rumble like distant thunder; by the time the large pocket of wind had reached its point of exit, it resembled a small hand grenade in terms of volume and force. For a second Barry thought they'd been hit by a torpedo, before he realised what it was. Nick also stirred briefly in his slumber. —False alarm, he mumbled, and went back to sleep, to dream of the many conquests of his past and the many more of his future. Barry only dreamed of one thing that night: Japan.

—CHAPTER SEVEN—

Barry didn't wake again till morning. He heard Claudette closing the door gently behind her. Good. He waited while Dunne-Davis stirred in the bed and swung his legs over the edge. Barry didn't open his eyes; it was too early to speak to that prick. Nick went into the bathroom and closed the door. By the sound of things, he was finishing what he'd started last night.

Barry waited another few minutes, until he heard the shower raining down on Dunne-Davis. Then he let himself into the bathroom – it still stank, even with the fan on – and flushed the toilet.

—Fuck! roared Dunne-Davis, as the water in the shower turned scalding.

Barry waited another few seconds for the cistern to fill and flushed it again.

—JESUS CHRIST! Stop doing that, will you?

He flushed it once more for luck. That would hurry the fucker up. It did, too: Nick only spent fifteen minutes in the shower, even though he'd found Claudette's designer body wash with lavender. After Barry had showered, they made the short trip up to the Burren Buffet for breakfast. It was help-yourself, and they did. Muesli, fresh fruit salad and scrambled eggs with smoked salmon did Nick. Barry was feeling adventurous and went for the full Irish. He was definitely feeling better. The rashers and sausages were A-1, and he washed it all down with freshly squeezed orange juice and four cups of tea.

Back on dry land, Sasha wasn't faring so well. She'd spent the night in the dank room, on a few old cushions thrown on the cold, hard floor. Johnno had untied her and given her an old blanket, which was better than nothing, she supposed. The windows were way up by the roof, so there was no way out there. She tried the door after he left, in the vain hope that he might have forgotten to lock it. He hadn't. She had spent most of the night staring at the corrugated roof thirty feet above her.

She had come to the conclusion that they'd let her go once they found Nick. She didn't want to dwell too much on the fact that she could identify them now. Surely they'd exchange her for whatever drugs Nick had stolen from them? But that was assuming the bastard ever came back. She reckoned, correctly, that he had probably left the country with the drugs. She actually found herself praying, which she hadn't done in years, that he'd come back. She was onto her fifth Our Father of the Rosary (was it ten Hail Marys or ten Our Fathers? She decided to say both, just to be on the safe side) when she was interrupted by the door creaking open. The heavy steel frame dragged across the concrete floor. Her heart raced.

She was expecting Doyle, but it was the other one – Johnno. She'd heard them speaking to each other the day before:

—Johnno?

—Yes, Mr Doyle?

—Go down and put two hundred on Limestone Lad in the 2.30.

She didn't know whether knowing their names was good or bad. It would be good, if she ever got out of here alive.

—I brought you some breakfast, he said, holding out a banana.

—Great, she said sarcastically —I don't suppose it comes with coffee?

He shook his head.

—I need to use the bathroom.

That was an understatement. She'd been contemplating whether or not to go in the corner for the last couple of hours, but had decided against it. The smell would be terrible if she was here for any length of time.

Johnno nodded for her to follow him to a small outdoor toilet. It was hideous. He stood outside the little portaloo while she squatted over the chemical toilet. Christ, she hated these things! They'd had them at that U2 concert in Slane; you had to spend twenty minutes queuing up, only to be greeted by all that mess staring back up at you from three feet below. She did feel better now, though.

Outside, she scanned the horizon, desperately searching for a landmark. It was no use. There was nothing familiar. They must have taken her to the north side – or to Crumlin, wherever that was. It was like something you'd see on the news – a war zone. Bits of rubble lay where an old shed had once been; a battered car, rusted beyond recognition, was up on bricks. Apart from that, there was nothing but a couple of fields surrounding the decrepit warehouse. They were tucked away behind decaying grey walls, which informed her that Baz wuz ere on 16/9/98 and that Micko was a wanker. She didn't doubt it.

Johnno led her back through the little maze of corridors and shut the door behind her. Sasha felt a hot tear run down her cheek and brushed it away. She'd have to toughen up if she was going to survive this. It was funny, but for the first time in her life, being alone didn't terrify her. Tony Doyle was another matter.

Barry spent the rest of the day up on deck. He didn't feel as sick up there. The sun was out, and he'd found a nice sheltered bench at the back of the boat. He was reading the sport section – there was a pullout bit on the World Cup – but he couldn't concentrate. The only thing he wanted to do was call Jill. It wasn't that he wasn't looking forward to his first trip to continental Europe; he just wished that Jill and Sarah were there to share the experience with him. When he thought about it, this was the first time he'd been away from them since Jill had moved into his da's house. And this wasn't exactly a fuckin' summer holiday he was going on. He'd be lucky to come out of it with his life.

He thought about that. Dunne-Davis had told him not to worry about anything; he had a plan that would get them out of this mess. —Everyone's a winner, he'd said. Barry was looking forward to hearing it. If it didn't work, he'd fuckin' kill Dunne-Davis himself, long before Doyle ever got near him.

Back in cabin 732, Nick was too busy saying goodbye to worry about the mess they were in. He was beginning to enjoy this little trip. Claudette had given him two hundred euro, to add to the hundred and twenty-eight they had left.

—There is something else you would like?

Nick bowed his head sheepishly. —There is one thing.

—Tell me, Nicky.

He flashed his perfect smile. —Any chance I could have your walnut face-scrub?

They piled back into the bunk of Mick Healy's truck. Nick had wanted to inspect the Honda, to make sure the merchandise was still there, but Mick wouldn't hear of it.

—Forget about it. I'm taking a chance as it is. Who'd nick that piece of shite, anyway?

Barry couldn't have cared less about the drugs. He was more concerned with his little Honda 50, and he had to admit that it was unlikely someone would be interested in stealing it. Even if anyone were, they'd have had a job getting onto the top ramp of the trailer, breaking into the 4x4 and getting the fucker out without someone noticing. He felt like a bit of a bollix, but he couldn't tell Mick about the drugs stashed under the seat.

—You're right, o' course, Mick, agreed Barry, nodding at Nick to stay quiet.

—You lads'd be better off walking off and meeting me down the road, suggested Mick. —They don't check tickets getting off. Sure, yous are home and dried now.

Dunne-Davis was having none of it. —Ah, no; sure, we may as well get off the way we came on. Y'know?

—Fair enough, said Mick.

He closed the door behind them. It was just the two of them and the darkness again. Dunne-Davis started that stupid whistle that he always did, the one where he pushed the air out through a tiny gap he made with his tongue behind his teeth. It was always the same tune, too. Barry didn't know what it was, but he knew it was driving him mad. He'd even caught himself humming it today.

—Fuck up, will yeh?

—What?

He didn't even know he was doing it. That made it worse.

—Whistlin' out of yeh. It's wreckin' me head.

Dunne-Davis said nothing. He could be snotty enough when he wanted to be. They waited in silence for the sound of the car engines igniting.

—So, are yeh going to tell me what the story is?

Nick waited until Barry was just about to ask again before answering.

The plan was this. They would travel to Amsterdam on the Honda. Nick had checked the distances and times on the internet while they were on the ship. (He was quite proud of himself. His only previous experience of the Web had been searching for porn at work and checking out the BMW accessories website.) It was roughly eight hundred kilometres to Amsterdam, and it would take them at least eight hours if they did it in one go. But they wouldn't do it one go. For a start, it was much too far for Barry to go without a break.

—I'd be fuckin' knackered, he pointed out.

Secondly, it was already past dinnertime by the time they got organised. It'd be getting dark soon, and Barry wasn't that keen on travelling at night – particularly since he'd never been in a foreign country, apart from those couple of trips to England. Aside from that, he didn't trust Dunne-Davis to navigate at the best of times, even if he had got a C in French in his Leaving.

And, finally, there were the borders. That was the clincher. Did you still need passports to get through them? Barry hadn't even got his driving licence with him. And if they were searched, the game would be up. Better to find a way around them than to risk it. The Belgian one would be first.

In the meantime, they had a more immediate problem to contend with. Barry didn't realise he was on the wrong side of the road. He just never thought about it. And Dunne-Davis didn't bother to tell him, either. He'd been so delighted when his drugs were still intact that he'd done a sneaky line of Charlie, behind Barry's back. Barry didn't know what had got into him. He had to warn him a couple of times to sit down on the back of the bike. It was bad enough he was wearing that Nazi helmet and his white suit – like the fuckin' man from Del Monte crossed with Adolf Hitler; now he was attracting far too much attention for Barry's liking. After the second near-collision, Barry realised his mistake and steered them onto the correct side of the road. Dunne-Davis didn't notice; he was too busy giving the fingers to the van that had almost mashed them into the asphalt.

Dunne-Davis had a contact in Amsterdam who might be able to sort something out while Doyle cooled off.

—How long will that be? said Barry.

—Don't know. Maybe a couple of weeks. Maybe more.

That all sounded OK to Barry. It was the next bit he didn't like. It basically involved cutting the coke with something else and selling it to Nick's contact for twice the price.

—Like waterin' it down, d'yeh mean?

—Exactly.

—With wha'?

—Can be anything. Flour. Talcum powder. Doesn't matter.

Barry wasn't sure.

—It's simple, Dunne-Davis explained. —Dealers do it all the time before they sell it. Not to the same extent, maybe, but still.

—Yeah, but that's before they sell it to gobshites like you, with more money than sense. We're goin' to be selling it back to a real dealer, aren't we?

—Not really. This guy I know isn't what you might call a dealer…more of a recreational user with ties to the bigger fish. He's really only a middleman, but he's always at me to cut him in on something. Reckons he can access a lot of cash in a hurry.

—That's handy, agreed Barry.

—Right. Anyway, we do all the bags except one. We leave one as it is – not the one we offer him to test, though.

—Why not?

—Because they never check that one. It's too obvious. We'll leave one at the top of the bag that looks like it's been tampered with.

—The real one.

—Right. We don't put anything at all in that one. It's one hundred per cent Colombian as it is.

—Wha'?

—Pure. It's one hundred per cent pure.

—And what if he does check the one we offer him? Or any of the others?

—We'll cross that bridge when we come to it.

Barry looked sceptical.

—They won't kill us for it, anyway. Probably.

Nick tried to look cooler than he felt.

Barry didn't like it one bit. Posing as fuckin' drug dealers, after he'd promised his ma on her deathbed that he'd never have anything to do with the stuff. And even if they did get away with it, who was to say Doyle would accept the deal? Granted, he'd double his money, but that wouldn't bring his nephew back.

Still, what other choice did they have? They couldn't stay on the run forever. It was just one of those things: fucked if you do and fucked if you don't.

Johnno strode into the bookie's with fifty thousand euro under his arm. He hoisted the old Celtic bag onto the counter.

—Mr Doyle wants to place a bet.

The young fella behind the counter looked nervous.
—Hold on.

He disappeared into a back office, leaving Johnno and the other punters watching the multiple TV screens dotted around the walls. There was horse-racing on every one of them. Johnno could have happily sat there all day if there was boxing on, or even football, but not horse-racing. He didn't see what people saw in it – except Doyle. He knew exactly what Doyle saw in it: money, and lots of it. Doyle loved nothing more than throwing a few grand on the horses, but he wasn't too keen on losing. Usually he'd phone in his bet without giving a credit-card number, and only send Johnno around if he actually won. The rest of the time, he told the unfortunate bookie to put it on his account. And there wasn't a bookie in the city brave enough to request that the Doyle account be settled up.

This time was different, though. This wasn't some dumb animal running at Leopardstown. These were eleven thoroughbreds who were going to run riot in Japan. And with most bookies offering fives on Ireland getting five points from their opening group – well, Doyle figured he just couldn't lose. Johnno wasn't so sure. Fair enough, there was a good chance of a win against Saudi Arabia. And a draw against the Cameroons – that was definitely achievable. But a draw against the Germans?

—Three-time winners, he'd told Doyle.

—They're shite now. Even England hockeyed them over there.

—I know that, boss. But they always come good at the finals. Why don't yeh just phone it in?

Doyle glared at him. He liked people to believe he was a man of his word. Any insinuation to the contrary wasn't tolerated. In his mind, the fact that he'd been ripping off bookies for years was nothing more than a perk of the job; just business. He got to come out ahead of the game, and they got to keep their businesses protected. Still, the less said about it the better, as far as he was concerned.

—Fifty grand on Ireland to get five points.

There was nothing more to be said. Once Doyle made his mind up, there was no going back. Johnno picked up the bag to leave.

—And Johnno…make sure you get decent odds.

He knew what that meant.

The young fella came back out of the office.

—Mr Casey will see you now, Mr O'Neill.

—Cheers.

The kid lifted the hatch in the counter and held it up for him. Robert Casey was sitting behind his desk in the small office. He stood up when Johnno came in.

—Mr O'Neill. How are you today?

—Grand, thanks.

Casey's palm was clammy when he shook Johnno's hand. —Have a seat. Would you like tea or coffee?

—Coffee, please. Black.

He went outside. Johnno fiddled with the handle of the bag until Casey came back and handed him the cup.

—Thanks.

Casey sat down and pretended not to notice the bag.
—Now, what can I do for you?

He waited for Johnno to take a sip from the steaming mug. Johnno placed the mug back on the table. He'd let the fucker squirm a bit longer. He waited until Casey looked as if he would burst. The tension was killing him. Perfect.

—Mr Doyle would like to place a bet.

Casey's whole face dropped. His features didn't actually budge from the fake smile he'd bullied them into; they just slid south from his forehead, in an avalanche of skin and sinew.

—That's great, he heard himself say through clenched teeth.

—Fifty thousand. Johnno lifted the bag onto the desk and patted it. —You can count it if you like.

—That won't be necessary. And what are we placing it on?

Johnno took another mouthful. Fuck, it was good coffee.

—We are placing it on Ireland. To get five points from the opening group in Japan.

—Right. I think we're offering five to one on that particular—

—Think again, said Johnno.

Casey said nothing. He looked at the bag. At least O'Neill had actually brought some money in this time. But that meant nothing. He'd offer ten to one on that Doyle would take it straight back if Ireland failed to get the five points. And what if they did get them? How much did he stand to lose?

—Mr Doyle feels that ten to one is a more reasonable price.

—Really?

Ten to one. Half a million euro. He might just cover that. He didn't have much choice.

Barry was making good time. He felt completely energised flying along the French motorways. It was totally different from Ireland. The roads were great. It was a piece of piss, once you got used to going on the right-hand side. And there weren't any potholes or anything else to slow you down. They were only a country apart on the map, but they were worlds apart in his head. The evening sun was warm on their backs, and he hardly noticed that there was nothing but a T-shirt between him and the elements. He was just beginning to think he could get used to this when his passenger reminded him of his existence.

—Pull over up there, Dunne-Davis said.

Who the fuck does he think he is, ordering me around? thought Barry.

Dunne-Davis pointed at the service station off the motorway up ahead. Barry had been meaning to fill the tank anyway. He said nothing, but steered the bike off at the exit. Dunne-Davis went inside and paid for the petrol.

—Lookit, said Barry, pointing to the big McDonald's beside the station, when he came out.

—Are you hungry?

They were both starving. It had been a long day and they hadn't eaten since breakfast.

—May as well fill up while we're here, suggested Barry.

Ordering was easy enough. They had pictures of everything behind the counter, just like at home. Barry hadn't a word of French, though, so he pointed to the picture with what he hoped was a Big Mac meal on it.

—Grand, monsieur?

—Er, yeah. Grand, thanks.

Maybe it wasn't such a difficult language after all. He remembered Jill used to love it in school. But, then again, she used to love nearly everything at school. He couldn't get out of there quick enough: Dunne-Davis was making a fool out of himself, trying to order in French. All he could say, as far as Barry could tell, was 'Oui'. He must have ordered half the bleedin' menu at this stage.

After the feed, they rode another hour or so towards Paris. They'd decided to bypass it, even though Barry secretly wanted to see what all the fuss was about. He'd promised Jill they'd go there for their honeymoon if they ever got married.

—Don't worry, you're not missing anything, Dunne-Davis assured him. —Nothing but boring art galleries and ignorant fuckers.

Barry didn't necessarily agree, but he knew he'd have to leave it for another day. Instead, they found a campsite on the outskirts and decided to chance their luck.

—Leave it to me, man, said Nick.

Barry wasn't going to argue. He left Dunne-Davis at the campsite's TV room. He had an urgent call to make.

Michael was reading the paper in the living room. Jill was around at her mother's and Sarah was up in bed; he had the place to himself, except for Declan. He was out in the kitchen, doing his homework – at least, that's what he'd said he was doing.

Michael still hadn't told them about Tony Doyle or any of that drug business. It would only break Jill's heart to think Barry was mixed up in that kind of carry-on. Besides, he didn't believe it himself. No, he needed to talk to Barry and find out what the story was. The undercover lads were still hanging around the place, but they seemed to be losing interest.

He looked up for a second at the sound of the doorbell. He didn't bother stirring; it'd be one of Declan's mates. He heard him answer the door. Off on his feckin' skateboard again, instead of studying for his exams.

Michael was just settling back into Johnny Giles's article about why Ireland was going to do well in the

World Cup when the door opened. It was Tony Doyle. Again. What did he want this time?

—Someone to see yeh, Da, said Declan.

Michael put the paper down and sat up properly.
—Thanks, son.

Declan closed the door behind him.

—Nice young fella, said Doyle, almost like he meant it.
—I hope he doesn't turn out like his brother.

He eased his large frame into an armchair and smiled at Michael. He glanced at the newspaper.

—Any news?

Barry couldn't work out how to use the phone. He needed a card for it. The feckin' thing wouldn't take coins. He called the free number for the international operator and asked to make a reverse-charge call to Ireland. The stupid wagon on the other end put him through to the Dutch operator the first time, so he spelled it out for her the second time.

—Ire-land! I-R-E-L-A-N-D. Not Holland!

—Ah, yes! One moment, please.

The Irish bloke on the other end was even worse. A complete spanner altogether.

—And where are you calling from, sir?

—France.

—What's the weather like there?

—Lovely.

—It's a beautiful country, isn't it?

—Yes. Could you—

—And the language! D'you speak French at all, sir?

—No! Listen, I want to talk to me bleedin' girlfriend, not to you, righ'?

—Certainly, sir. And what's her name?

Barry told him the name and number and waited to be connected. It was ringing, anyway.

—Hello? said Declan.

—Yes, I have a collect call from France for Jill McKenna.

Will you accept the charges?

—Eh, she's not here, sorry.

He was just about to hang up, the fuckin' eejit, when Barry roared down the line. —Declan! It's me, yeh gobshite!

—Howya, Barry? I seen you on the telly—

—Just say yes!

—Wha'?

—Say yes, you'll accept the charges.

—Yes, you'll accept the charges, said Declan in his most formal tone.

The operator hung up.

Michael was getting sick and tired of this. It was bad enough not knowing what had happened to Barry, without this psychopath dropping in every other day.

—Lookit, I told yeh I don't know where he is.

Doyle just sat there, staring at him.

—We haven't heard a word from him, and that's the God's honest truth of it.

—So you're tryin' to tell me yeh haven't a clue where he is?

Michael rubbed the bridge of his nose. —No. He could be in Timbuk-fuckin'-tu for all I know.

Doyle looked like he was seriously considering teaching Michael a lesson when the door burst open.

—Da! That was Barry! He's on his way to Amsterdam!

Barry had to hand it to Dunne-Davis: he certainly had a way with women. By the time Barry got back to the TV lounge, he was chatting away to two young ones, not a bother on him. And, naturally, when they were off to bed they invited the men back to their tent. The two of them. Barry wasn't mad keen on the idea, but it was better than sleeping rough.

He hadn't bothered listening to their names when Dunne-Davis had introduced them. They were Dutch, or was it Danish? One of them had short dark hair and a grand pair of tits on her. The other had pure blonde hair, all the way down to her arse, nearly. She was a bit on the heavy side for Barry's liking. Not that he'd any interest in either of them. Dunne-Davis could do what he liked, but that didn't mean Barry had to.

The girls had shown Barry where the tent was, and he wheeled the bike around. Dunne-Davis had stroked a couple of pillowcases from a washing line and was busy cramming the bags of coke into them.

—You sleep on that one and I'll take the other one, right? he said to Barry.

—I presume you're talkin' about the pillows?

Dunne-Davis didn't get it. Barry took the CD player, covered in powder, out from the bottom of the bike's storage compartment. Deadly; he'd thought he'd lost that. He hadn't seen it since he'd listened to that U2 album a couple of weeks ago.

Dunne-Davis grabbed it from him and arranged the powder into one neat line with his fingers. He placed his nose over it and hoovered it up in a couple of noisy gasps. He blinked a few times and smiled.

—Waste not, want not.

Barry grabbed the Discman back and waited for Dunne-Davis to unzip the tent. He didn't like what he saw inside. It was fuckin' tiny. It was officially a two-man, but they would have been squashed on their own, never mind with the two young ones in there as well. When they did finally squeeze in, it was almost unbearable. The heat was stifling; Barry could feel the sweat forming on his back. They were all wedged together like sardines, with a couple of sleeping-bags thrown over them.

And then it started. Dunne-Davis and the blonde. At first it was just kissing, the odd slobbering sound here and there. Then they got more into it. The breathing was getting heavier and they were writhing up and down against each other. Surely, Barry thought, he wasn't going to nail her in front of himself and the other one? Even Dunne-Davis wasn't that bad, was he? A long moan from the blonde answered his question. Barry couldn't believe what was happening to him – or, more accurately, what was happening to the blonde. Not that she was complaining. The whole tent was shuffling back and forth from the motion of their humping.

He was beginning to think it couldn't get any worse when the other one turned around and stuck her face in his. She pressed her tits against his chest. Jaysus, what was she doing? Before he knew what was going on, she had her tongue in his mouth. It was wriggling around his gums like a demented goldfish. He tried to squirm his way out of her grip, but she must have got the wrong impression, because she clamped her hand over his manhood and started to force it up and down like it was a fuckin' bicycle pump. He tried to pry her hand free, but she gripped it even harder and began panting in rhythm with the other two. Barry was convinced she was trying to remove the feckin' thing from his body. In the end he had to shove her away with both hands and struggle to his knees.

—Er, just goin' to the jacks, he croaked.

—Don't be long! she panted.

He nearly pulled the tent down in his eagerness to escape. Dunne-Davis hadn't seemed to notice the commotion. Fuck him. Barry wasn't going to spend the night with those perverts.

There was still a light on in the TV lounge, so he went to check it out. Maybe he could crash there. He grabbed the Discman and made his way over the pine needles and gravel in his bare feet. They stung a bit, but it wasn't nearly as bad as being castrated by a Danish slapper.

The lounge door was open and there was no one inside. Deadly. He turned the light off and stretched out on a couch. This wasn't too bad at all. He put on the headphones and got comfortable; nothing like a bit of the oul' U2 for relaxation. He pressed the Play button and the CD spun into action. Barry shot up when the music came on.

Oh, oh, oh, oh, oh, oh-oh
Oh, oh, oh, oh, oh, oh-oh
Uptown girl!

What the fuck was this? It wasn't U2, that was for fuckin' sure. He frantically hit the Next button a few times, but it only got worse: 'We've Got a Little World of Our Own' was next up.

Barry couldn't believe this was happening to him. Westlife! It was fuckin' Westlife! How the fuck did that happen?

This was all he needed. Sarah must have borrowed the Discman without bothering her arse to put his disc back in. He ripped the headphones off and flung the CD player across the room. It was enough to make a grown man cry.

Barry did what he always did when he couldn't sleep. He started to imagine himself on the open road, just him and his bike, with the wind at his back and the sun on his face. As he slowly relaxed, he formed a crystal-clear image of himself in his Ireland shirt, on the Honda, riding through the countries of Europe, over the great steppes of Russia and out beyond Asia, until he reached the ultimate destination – Japan and the World Cup. With this image in his mind, he drifted into the most peaceful of sleeps.

—CHAPTER EIGHT—

The Kellys were debating the news over breakfast.

—I think it's great, said Declan, slurping down his cornflakes.

—Why would you think that?

Jill just couldn't understand him sometimes.

—Well, y'know…he's seein' a bit of the world and all.

—What did he say to you, exactly? asked Michael.

Declan raised his eyes to heaven as if this was the dumbest thing he'd ever heard. —How many times do I have to tell yeh? He…is…going…to…Am-ster-dam.

Michael slammed his mug down on the table, shocking himself even more than the others. —Listen, you, yeh little… Have you any idea of the trouble he's in?

Even Declan was momentarily speechless.

Michael had had to tell Jill what was going on, but he was fairly sure that Declan couldn't be trusted with that kind of information. The less he knew, the better – particularly after he had practically given Doyle a forwarding address for Barry. —That man who was here yesterday is a nasty piece of work, he continued. —A very nasty piece of work.

—But I didn't mean to tell him! protested Declan.

—I know yeh didn't. But that doesn't change the fact that Doyle knows where he's headed. Now, I'll ask yeh again: did he say anythin' about callin' back?

Declan shook his head and tried to remember the conversation. He was finally beginning to appreciate the serious nature of the situation.

—No. All he said was he was in a tricky situation and

he was trying to sort it out. He said he'd be back as soon as he could, and not to worry about him.

Declan turned to Sarah, who was busy trying to unstick her jam and toast from her hair. —And he said you're to do what your mammy tells yeh.

Barry and Nick got on the road early, after Barry had been woken at six by the cleaners. Nick slipped out of the tent while the two girls were still sleeping. He was sporting a large grin, which Barry did his best to ignore.

—You missed out there, son.

Barry tried not to look at him as he wheeled the bike towards the exit.

—Your one was even better than mine, Nick informed him.

They breakfasted on some croissants, stolen from the kitchen of the campsite. Dunne-Davis was complaining about smelling like a whore's arse, but Barry insisted they get going without showering – not because they were under any real time pressure, but because he enjoyed seeing Dunne-Davis like this. He'd never seen him with his hair standing on end and a couple of days' growth sprouting unevenly from his jaw. His once-pristine white suit was crumpled and stained, but he'd lost none of that cocky swagger that Barry hated. He still persisted in walking five feet in front of Barry, even though there were only two of them. Maybe it made him feel superior or something. It made Barry feel like giving him a good boot up the hole.

Barry's own clothes were holding up OK. His T-shirt was beginning to smell a bit, but the tracksuit bottoms were fine. He didn't want to inspect his boxers too closely. Anyway, they could always get some new stuff in Amsterdam if the worst came to the worst. For now, the wind blowing through his T-shirt freshened him up a bit. Nothing like a bit of natural deodorant.

They made the Belgian border pretty quickly. At least the sign said it was the Belgian border. There weren't any checkpoints in sight, but Barry decided to double back and find an alternative route, just to be on the safe side. This involved riding through fields of varying terrain for a few miles until it was safe to get back on the main road. Dunne-Davis was particularly unhappy about the bumpy ride across a ploughed field.

—Slow down, he shouted into Barry's ear.

Barry pretended not to hear him.

—Did you hear me? I said slow down!

Barry continued straight ahead. He opened the throttle up a bit to drown out Dunne-Davis's protests. His arms were burning, all down the backs of them, from fighting the steering. The last thing he needed was that prick on the back giving him grief. Dunne-Davis wrapped his arms hard around Barry's waist as they went over a large bump. The bike shot into the air for a few feet and landed hard.

—Slow down, you fucking lunatic! He was beginning to panic. Good.

They hit another bump and Barry's head jerked backwards, breaking Dunne-Davis's nose for sure. He could hear the sharp snap of cartilage, even through his helmet. He felt like a right bollix, especially when Dunne-Davis fell off the back of the bike.

Barry killed the engine and dismounted. Dunne-Davis didn't make for pleasant viewing. There was blood pouring from his nose, all down his suit. The landing hadn't been a smooth one, either; his arse had taken the brunt of it. He sat in the middle of the field, holding his nose to stem the blood. There were tears running down his face.

Barry didn't know what to say.

—Yeh all righ'?

Stupid question.

—At least it was a clean break, he offered.

Dunne-Davis glared at him. The nose was swelling up all right, but it wasn't crooked. He wouldn't be snorting any of that rubbish through it for a while, anyway.

Barry extended his hand. Dunne-Davis took hold of it and dragged himself up.

—Sorry, right?

Dunne-Davis made no reply. He just pulled his hand away and walked over to the bike. He wouldn't even look at Barry.

They passed through Belgium without a word. Dunne-Davis was holding his nose for most of it, until Barry helpfully offered him a clothespeg from the campsite – it had been stuck in one of the pillowcases – to stem the flow. He clamped it over his nostrils and pointed to a petrol station off the motorway. He went in to pay while Barry filled up.

Barry was pleasantly surprised when Dunne-Davis came back out with two ice-creams: a peace offering, perhaps? He was just about to thank him when he saw what Dunne-Davis was doing. He didn't even bother opening them. He just pressed them onto his face, so that they formed a makeshift ice-pack around his nose.

Fair enough, Barry thought. He couldn't expect instant forgiveness. The first time he'd hit him, back in the showrooms, he'd been justified. It was only fair, after what Dunne-Davis had got him involved in. This time he had been wrong. Even if Dunne-Davis was a prick, he'd been offside. Out of order. The accident had definitely been in the 'accidentally on purpose' category, and they both knew it.

Still, the bleeding stopped eventually. Fortunately most of it had been soaked up by Dunne-Davis's suit. Barry couldn't have handled it messing up the paintwork on the Honda. They rode on in silence.

Sasha felt terrible. She hadn't washed in days and, quite frankly, she was beginning to smell. It was a new experience for her. It was like standing on the DART beside some grubby little man with bad B.O., only this time it was her own odour offending her nostrils. It still wasn't overpowering – in fact, she really had to inhale deeply under her armpits to smell it – but it was definitely there. She hoped that Johnno guy wouldn't smell it off her.

Then again, why should she care what he thought? He was just a criminal – not as bad as that bastard Doyle, but a criminal just the same. There was something different about him, though. He didn't scare her like Doyle did; she couldn't explain it, but she felt kind of safe when Johnno was there. Maybe it was his eyes. They weren't hard and cold like Doyle's. Doyle's looked like he wasn't even alive, most of the time. They were dull and lifeless – until he got angry; then they flared up into embers of pure evil. Johnno's were brighter. They were blue, brilliant blue, and somehow warm at the same time.

Sasha could hear his footsteps outside; she knew it was him by the weight of them. The door creaked open. She wasn't disappointed.

—I brought you a present, said Johnno.

He placed the plastic bag on the ground. The warm aroma filled her senses and made her tummy sing. She was ravenous.

—D'yeh want chicken and cashew nuts or beef in black bean sauce?

—Chicken.

She nearly tore it out of his hands.

—Easy there.

She fumbled with the foil until the lid flew off. It bounced off her leg and drenched her trousers in sticky sauce. She didn't care.

Johnno handed her the chopsticks and sat down on the milk crate opposite her. She wasn't a bad-looking sort at all, even without the make-up on and with the hair in a mess. Her eyes were huge and brown, like two enormous ripe chestnuts.

—I've never been to dinner with a north-sider, she told him.

He grinned. —Enjoyin' that?

She didn't answer for a second. Her mouth was crammed full, so she just nodded.

—How long are you going to keep me here? she asked between swallows.

—Just till we find your boyfriend.

—He's not my boyfriend.

It was true. In her heart of hearts, Sasha had long since given up on Nick. She had held a candle for him for years, but she had always known that eventually she would have to let it burn out. And eventually had just become now.

Back in Belgium, the strain was beginning to tell on Barry. He was kicking gravel with his foot, making a little hollow in it, for no reason. The two of them were sitting on a bench in silence. Dunne-Davis had said nothing to him for hours. Barry wondered, not for the first time, why he'd bothered to save him from Doyle's gorillas at all. He should have left him there. He couldn't help feeling a little bit guilty about switching the tyres, though – after all, that was what had landed them in this mess in the first place, wasn't it? He copped himself on: Dunne-Davis importing millions of euros' worth of cocaine was what had landed them in this mess. Besides, he had only been doing his job switching those tyres.

That made him feel worse. Even if they did manage to pull this thing off, what about his job? He hadn't got one to go home to. He knew he shouldn't blame Dunne-Davis for that, if he thought about it – he'd only been the messenger. Still, it did make things easier. He wondered what Dunne-Davis was thinking. The way he was staring over at him… Probably wishing me dead, Barry thought.

Nick was wishing that all this had never happened. He was in major trouble. He could handle losing his job, which he surely would if any of this ever got out. That meant losing the apartment in Dalkey – a rough break – and the Beemer. That would be like losing a limb. Worse, for fuck's sake! At least they could give you a prosthetic arm or leg, but what substitute was there for the ultimate driving machine? No, all of that was pretty bad – bad, but bearable – but it was the thought of his looks that was really getting to him. Where would he be without his chiselled profile? It was almost too much to contemplate. His nose throbbed and burned every time he tried to breathe through it. He hadn't dared to look in the mirror yet.

He knew it had been an accident. There was no way Barry would ever do something like that on purpose. Fine, he might have been just a knacker with next to no education, but he was also a decent knacker, when you thought about it. And, now that Nick did think about it, he couldn't remember speaking to Barry since the tragedy had happened. He couldn't remember much about anything, in fact. He'd been in shock. He guessed that they must be in Holland by now.

He decided to check his nose in the mirror. Maybe it wouldn't be too bad. Maybe he could visit a plastic surgeon in Amsterdam – get a little liposuction around his chin and a bit of Botox around the eyes, while he was at it... Things weren't really that bad. A nip here and a tuck there and he'd come out, like Priscilla Presley, better than he went in!

He went over to check his nose in the rear-view mirror. It was a big mistake.

—FUCK!

By the time they got back on the road, Barry was genuinely worried about Dunne-Davis. He was taking the whole nose thing very badly. Barry had tried to convince him that it wasn't that bad – and it wasn't. Yes, it was a bit swollen, but that wouldn't last forever. Dunne-Davis had it all out of proportion. He was like one of those anorexic women who see themselves as huge in the mirror, even though they're actually tiny: he was convinced his nose was of Barry Manilow proportions, when in fact it was really only Barbara Streisandesque. Barry did his best to talk him round, but Dunne-Davis was adamant.

—I'm ruined, he sobbed. Over and over, until Barry felt like he was going to hit him again. He'd have to control himself if he didn't want to add murder to the growing list of crimes he'd committed. Eventually he gave Dunne-Davis his CD player, just to shut the fucker up.

It only made things worse. If Barry had been totally honest, he'd have had to admit to ulterior motives: he'd been quietly confident that Westlife would push Dunne-Davis over the edge, given his fragile mental state. It didn't happen. Not only did it seem to lift his spirits, but the bollix kept singing along into Barry's ear – like he was actually enjoying it! Maybe 'singing' was the wrong word; 'bellowing' was a better description. Even above the buzz of the engine, Barry could hear every torturous out-of-tune word he screeched.

Oh, oh, oh, oh, oh, oh-oh,
Uptown girl!

He was just doing it to get back at Barry. There was no other explanation. Fuck, he was a malicious bastard. And Barry couldn't say anything, either. He wouldn't give Dunne-Davis the satisfaction. Better to just grin and bear it.

The gloves were definitely off now, though. This was total war. By the time he saw the signs for Amsterdam, Barry wished he'd hit him harder.

Nick Dunne-Davis had a reputation to think of. That was why there was no way he was going to roll into Amsterdam on the back of a Honda 50 sporting a filthy white suit stained with oil and blood and God knew what else. Barry wasn't keen on the idea, but eventually he agreed to stop near a farmhouse on the outskirts of Amsterdam. The plan was to wash their clothes in a stream at the end of the field and dry them off in the sun. Even Barry had to agree with that part: there was no way they could show up to meet Dunne-Davis's contact looking like they did.

So they stripped down to their underwear. Barry took off his Robbie Keane T-shirt and dunked it under the icy water. There were big salt-stains spreading out from under the arms, but they were definitely coming out as he scrubbed. Dunne-Davis wasn't faring so well. His suit was ruined. Even an industrial-strength dry-clean wouldn't have saved it. He was rubbing away at the blood and grease like a lunatic, but it was no use: the suit was way beyond redemption. He flung it against a tree.

—Fuck it!

—It's only a suit, said Barry, in a sympathetic tone that he knew would drive Dunne-Davis mad.

—Only a suit! squealed Dunne-Davis. He was apoplectic. —Only a suit, is it? And what the fuck would you know about suits?

Barry remained calm, which incensed Dunne-Davis even further.

—I know enough to know that that one's fucked, anyway.

—Fuck! repeated Dunne-Davis unnecessarily, as he stumbled awkwardly out of the water, accidentally drenching Barry on purpose.

—Jaysus! Watch where you're goin', will yeh?

Dunne-Davis stomped off into the fields without another word. Barry decided to whip off his boxers and give them a rub. —May as well do me socks while I'm at it, he said to himself. The water was nice and refreshing now. The icy shock had given way to invigoration, and he ducked his whole body, head and all, underneath.

—Yeeoow!

It felt good. After a couple of minutes he paddled out

into the blazing sun. He'd be dry in no time. He laid out the clothes on the bank to catch the full rays and stretched out beside them. Lovely.

The clouds were drifting lazily past. One of them looked exactly like Britain. He could have fuckin' sworn it. It was grand lying here in the sun, not like at home. He was actually comfortable – warm, even. There wasn't any breeze to freeze the bollix off you. He never bothered lying out in the sun at home. They'd taken Sarah out to Dollymount a few times, but he couldn't get into it. One minute the sun would be shining down and you'd be grand, nice and warm; then it'd slip behind a cloud, like someone had turned the lights off. And then the wind would decide to blow you out of it. And just as the sun was threatening to make an appearance, you'd feel the first drops coming down. It was miserable. Sometimes you could just lie there for a few minutes and get soaked until the shower went and the sun came back; most of the time, though, it didn't bother its arse coming back. Four seasons in one day, me bollix, Barry thought. There were only two seasons in Ireland: a wet and miserable winter, and a slightly milder but just as wet winter. Then there were those gobshites who drove their cars onto the beach. What was all that about? He never understood those fuckin' eejits who drove all the way to the beach and then sat in their cars listening to the fuckin' GAA or some other shite on the radio. What was the point? They'd bring flasks of tea and sandwiches and all, and then they wouldn't even bother their holes getting out of the car!

He looked down at his legs stretching out below him. A few drops still glistened in the light, but he was almost dry. The clothes would take a while. Let them take their time. There was no rush. He was almost beginning to feel good about things. It was amazing what a bit of sun could do for you. They'd go to Amsterdam and meet Dunne-Davis's mate, or contact, or whatever the fuck he was – Dunne-Davis was fairly sketchy about that part. Then they'd do the deal and go home. Simple as that. Doyle would get his money, with interest, and they'd be free men again. Back to reality.

Reality was good. There was nothing wrong with it. Some blokes found it boring and had to escape, through drugs or birds or whatever, but not Barry. Barry liked reality. At least, he liked his own reality, with Jill and Sarah and even his da and Declan. He liked living in Ringsend and having people he'd grown up with all around him. There was a sense of belonging that yuppie fucks like Dunne-Davis, the ones buying the new apartments that were sprouting up like concrete boils all over the face of Ringsend, knew nothing about. They brought rising house prices with them, and fuck-all else. The Dunne-Davises of this world wouldn't have been seen dead in Ringsend ten years ago, but the Celtic Tiger had changed all that. Every fuckin' eejit had to have a new car, and the city couldn't cope. The traffic that choked the streets meant people were spending more time in their cars than they were at work. It was only a matter of time before a neat little village on the doorstep of the city drew the attention of the property developers. Ringsend had changed beyond recognition. The irony was that people like Barry, whose family had lived there for generations, couldn't afford to live there any more. There was no point in moaning about it, either; it was just a fact of life. Buying a place was out of the question for him and thousands like him, and it always would be. When he got home, he'd just have to get another job and soldier on. That was the reality.

And then reality did something very strange.

It started with what sounded like a gunshot. And there was a very good reason for that: it was a gunshot. It was followed rapidly by another gunshot. And that was followed by Nick Dunne-Davis charging through the fields, screaming like a butcher's boniff and headed straight towards Barry. That would probably have been enough to shock Barry's brain into disbelief; the fact that Dunne-Davis was wearing a red and white floral-patterned summer dress with splits down the sides almost pushed him over the edge.

—Start the fucking bike! Dunne-Davis roared.

For the first time in his life, Barry wished he were hallucinating.

The sight of an angry farmer aiming a shotgun out the window of a Land Rover finally kick-started his brain into action. Dunne-Davis was very athletic, there was no doubt about it, but the farmer was definitely gaining on him. Even Carl Lewis would have had his style impaired by a knee-length dress that couldn't have been more than a size 10; Barry wouldn't have sworn to it, but he reckoned Dunne-Davis was at least a 16, if not an 18. The farmer screamed something in Dutch that Barry guessed – correctly, as it happened – translated as 'Pervert!' He slowed down briefly to reload and fired another volley in Dunne-Davis's direction. With a bit of luck, Barry thought, he'd kill Dunne-Davis and let him go. Unfortunately, neither scenario appeared likely, so he fired up the Honda and grabbed his clothes. Dunne-Davis hurdled straight onto the saddle and shuffled backwards to make room for Barry to jump on.

—Holy fuckin' Jaysus! screamed Barry, in an octave he had previously believed to be the exclusive preserve of pre-pubescent girls.

Thinking back on it, Barry would remember it as the most painful experience of his life. He still woke up at night screaming when he dreamed about the tackle that had broken the two bones in his right leg and ended his career before it had started – but that was a stroll in the park compared to this. The black leather saddle must have been edging towards the two-hundred-degree mark. He could have fried eggs on it. He certainly felt like his nuts had been sautéed in burning oil.

He vaulted up off the saddle, which proved to be his second big mistake. The delicate skin between his legs had bonded with the near-boiling leather, and it didn't respond well to the sudden attempt at extrication.

—Nnnnggrrrhh! he screamed through his nose.

When his penis eventually did come unstuck, the worst of the pain was over. Then there was just the stinging pins-and-needles sensation of first-degree burns that would last for two or three days. He somehow managed to turn the bike over and get them moving, but their hasty departure had resulted in the loss of everything but his T-shirt, which he held on to for dear life. He was totally naked, straddling the bike like a jockey. The worst bit was Dunne-Davis holding his hips for balance and tearing the skin off him with his nails. It was funny: even in all the commotion of being chased through a field by a homicidal Dutchman, he still had time to imagine the situation from Dunne-Davis's point of view. It couldn't have been a pretty sight. With a deft flick of the wrist, Barry whipped the T-shirt onto the saddle and lowered himself onto it. It was like dipping into a scalding hot bath at forty miles an hour. The motorway was only a hundred metres away, and Barry was praying that the farmer would give up once they reached it.

He did – but even then, they felt like their problems had only just begun. Cars and trucks honked their horns wildly from all directions. A naked man riding a souped-up Honda 50 down the motorway, with a man in a summer dress on the back, was a fairly unusual sight even for Amsterdam. It was all too much for one oul' one travelling in the opposite direction: Barry saw the shock frozen on her face, and then heard the crunch of metal and glass against the concrete barrier that separated the lanes. He checked his rear-view mirror and saw her car right itself. Thank fuck. He struggled to get the helmet off the handlebars. Once his head was safely inside, he wished the rest of him could follow. It was easily the most humiliating experience of his life.

They turned off at the next exit, a couple of kilometres further on, and took shelter behind a bus stop at the side of a tulip field. Barry pulled on his T-shirt and looked around vacantly. He was in shock. Normally he would have felt obliged to burst Dunne-Davis, but he felt strangely numb – light-headed, even. The adrenaline that had been coursing through his veins had burnt itself out. He sat down gingerly on the grass and stared at Dunne-Davis. The state of him…it would have been funny if it hadn't been so serious. For the first time that Barry could remember, he was actually interested in hearing what Dunne-Davis had to say for himself.

—Suppose you're wondering why I'm wearing this? said Nick Dunne-Davis sheepishly.

Barry nodded dumbly.

Jill was going out of her mind. She had been sitting by the phone for the past two days, waiting for him to call. Just one simple phone call. If only he'd call, she could warn him about Doyle, tell him to keep away from Amsterdam. She couldn't stand not knowing whether he was all right or whether… It was better not to think about that. She'd heard stories about what happened to people mixed up in drug wars – horrible, stomach-churning accounts of painful deaths, of torture and mutilation and…

This was terrible. She was driving herself mad. She had to do something to take her mind off things. She got up from the stair where she'd been camped since Tuesday. Declan had slagged her about it, and she'd nearly bitten the head off him.

—Like your new office, Jill.

—Feck off, you! It's your fault I'm sittin' here prayin' for the phone to ring…

She didn't mean it, though. He was just a bit thick. Not even thick – just young and naïve. She knew he hadn't meant to let Doyle know about Barry. But Doyle did know, and she felt like she'd burst because she couldn't warn Barry that he might be walking straight into a trap. They'd always looked out for each other, and now, when he really needed her to, she couldn't. She wanted to scream. Instead, she trudged wearily into the living room, to Michael.

—I'm just goin' out for a walk, she said. —Will you

answer the phone?

He looked up from his paper. —I will, o' course. Go ahead. It'll do yeh good to get a breath of air.

He was right, too. By the time she reached the strand she was feeling better – not optimistic, just realistic. Even if Doyle did have contacts in Amsterdam, that didn't mean they'd ever find Barry. It was a big city, after all. Maybe he could do whatever he had to do and come home. And the next time she went for a walk he'd be with her, holding her hand and walking too fast, the way he always did. Then he'd point to one of the boats coming in, and she'd have to pretend to be interested. He'd go on about why Liverpool were going to win the league – or why they weren't, depending on his mood – and all the other stuff he went on about. She hoped he'd come home soon.

Barry wasn't surprised. He was shocked, but he wasn't surprised. It was exactly the type of thing he'd come to expect from a slimeball like Nick Dunne-Davis. And the way he'd explained it – not a bother on him, as if it was the most natural thing in the world...

He'd stormed off into the fields, in a huff because of his suit. After a while he'd calmed down a bit and noticed a farmhouse across one of the fields. Closer inspection had revealed that there was a particularly attractive young lady contained within the farmhouse. (Barry was dubious over this point. Dunne-Davis would have got up on himself if he could turn around quick enough.) He'd made sure there was nobody else in the house before knocking on the back door in nothing but a pair of boxer shorts.

—I mean, in fairness, what woman could resist?

Nick spread his arms open to emphasise the vision that had greeted the young lady. According to him, they had exchanged a few pleasantries before going on to exchange bodily fluids.

—Yeh did in yer hole! said Barry, but he knew they had.

Nick had asked his latest conquest if she had any clothes she could spare, on account of the embarrassing predicament in which he had found himself. She had responded in the affirmative – and in surprisingly good English – and left him alone for a bit. When she'd returned with the red dress, they both had a good laugh and Nick agreed to try it on.

—Purely out of curiosity, of course.

He was adamant over this point. He didn't want Barry to think any less of him. He needn't have bothered: Barry couldn't have thought any less of him if Nick had said he'd mated with a Jack Russell terrier. Anyway, the young lady in question had found his attire irresistible, in a slightly twisted way (and Nick had found the experience to be rather stimulating too – not that he'd ever admit it; he had his pride, after all). One thing had led to another, and before he knew it they were enjoying wild, passionate sex again.

—And then the farmer came home. We didn't hear him, what with the shagging and all. Caught me with my trousers down.

—Trousers?

—Well, whatever.

—So he wasn't too impressed when he caught yeh in bed with his wife?

—It wasn't his wife, Nick corrected him.

—Wha'?

—It was his daughter – but it was his wife's dress.

Barry took a second to process this information.

—Yeh dirty bastard.

And that was how Nick Dunne-Davis had come to be charging across a field dressed like Mr Pussy. Barry repeated his earlier assessment.

—Yeh dirty, dirty bastard.

Eventually they found another farmhouse with a full washing line. Barry got a pair of faded blue jeans that were almost a perfect fit – just a little long in the leg. Nick traded his frock for a pair of cords and a check shirt.

—Check it ou'. It's Garth fuckin' Brooks.

—Fuck off, replied Nick.

He felt like an idiot. Even worse than he had in the dress. The cords weren't even Diesel, for God's sake. He just hoped he wouldn't meet anyone he knew in Amsterdam – not until they got sorted out with some decent kit, anyway. Fuck food; he was going to spend the money on clobber. Eating was overrated, but you could never be too well dressed. And they had the problem of Barry's feet. Nick had managed to keep his shoes on, but Barry's were back at the stream; in fact, they were probably halfway out to sea at this stage.

They helmeted up and rejoined the motorway for Amsterdam. Barry steered the bike off at a large retail outlet adjoining the highway. Nick gave him fifty euro to buy a pair of runners and waited with the bike and its valuable cargo. Barry managed to get a half-decent pair for forty and spent the rest on cotton sports socks (three pairs) and boxer shorts (two pairs). He felt like a new man.

—Lookit, he said, presenting his booty to Dunne-Davis. —Not bad for fifty euro, wha'?

Dunne-Davis didn't reply. He just got off the bike and left Barry to examine his new wardrobe. He must have been gone about twenty minutes before Barry caught sight of him strolling casually out of the shop and past the security guard, with a large bag under his arm. He climbed onto the bike.

—Hit it, he suggested.

Barry obliged.

—CHAPTER NINE—

Amsterdam was Nick's second home, he explained to Barry. They found a fairly reasonable hostel around Leidseplein and booked a twin room. They left the Honda in the little courtyard and carried the pillowcases full of coke up the flights of stairs to their room. Barry threw his new clothes on the bed and flopped down onto it.

—Show us what yeh got, he said to Dunne-Davis.

Nick emptied out the contents of the bag one by one. First he took out two red toothbrushes and threw one to Barry.

—Nice one.

Barry's teeth were beginning to hurt. He hadn't brushed them in days, and he could feel the sticky film hardening around them. He watched as Dunne-Davis produced a long-sleeved navy T-shirt, which he also threw onto Barry's bed.

—You'll need that when it's cold at night.

—Er, thanks very much.

It was stupid, really, but he felt like a kid on Christmas morning. It was amazing how essentials like new underwear seemed like luxuries when you were on the run. That was it for Barry, though. The rest was for Dunne-Davis, which was fair enough. And the rest turned out to be a new pair of khaki combats, a Nike T-shirt, a couple of pairs of boxers and socks and another long sleeved T-shirt with a large '69' printed on the front. Barry didn't want to think about that.

—How much? he asked.

—Ten euro.

—Not bad.

He didn't want to know how Dunne-Davis had done it, either. It was ironic that a rich kid like him could be such a good thief. Or maybe it wasn't. Barry's da had always said that the more money they had, the less morals they had, or something like that. For the moment, Barry wasn't complaining.

He went into the bathroom at the end of the hall and spent a good five minutes brushing the crud off his teeth. When he got back, Nick Dunne-Davis was strategically placing the 'pillows' under the bed.

—Not the most original spot, is it? said Barry.

—Have you got a better idea?

—Just leave 'em on the bed. They look like pillows anyway.

Dunne-Davis shrugged and placed them delicately under the other pillows, taking care not to spill any white powder anywhere. His nose tingled at the thought of all that candy. The swelling was definitely going down, and his nostrils were beginning to perk up in anticipation. Not now, though. They had work to do. Once they'd set up the deal and cut the merchandise, he could relax and enjoy himself. Naturally, he'd keep a few grams for recreational purposes after the deal went down – providing everything went OK, of course, and he wasn't sleeping with whatever lurked under the waters of Amsterdam's canals. Still, he reckoned it couldn't be as bad as sleeping with whatever passed for fish in the Liffey these days.

—What d'yeh want to do now? asked Barry.

Nick smiled to himself.

—Why don't we go for a coffee?

Barry had never seen anything like it. Amsterdam was beautiful. There were canals everywhere and trams buzzing alongside them as they walked. They crisscrossed the entire city, vying with the cyclists who seemed to be everywhere. There was hardly a fuckin' car to be seen.

It was brilliant – the total opposite of Dublin. And everything was within walking distance. It was like a big village, with flower markets and the type of stuff Jill would love.

—Isn't it fantastic?

—Disneyland for grown-ups, agreed Dunne-Davis.

He pulled out two pair of expensive-looking sunglasses and handed one to Barry. —Here, I forgot to give you these.

Barry took them and noticed the 'Police' label on them. He hoped Dunne-Davis hadn't stroked them from a cop, but he didn't really care. They were the business. He caught a glimpse of himself reflected in a shop window and barely recognised the character he saw. Stubble covered his jaw, and the shades made him look kind of cool. The only thing that gave him away as being Irish was the T-shirt. He sneaked a quick look at Dunne-Davis and reckoned that, out of a suit, he looked five years younger than his thirty-odd.

They ambled through the sunshine and decided to get a feed at one of the chippers that lined the street corners. Dunne-Davis ordered fish and chips for both of them. —Leave this to me, he told Barry, so Barry expected him to order in Dutch; but the gobshite just spoke English really slowly, like he was talking to a halfwit. Your man just nodded, like he'd seen a million tossers like Dunne-Davis before. The fish and chips weren't exactly of the Borza variety, either. They got something known as matjes hering, which as far as Barry could tell was a herring with the head cut off, marinated in some kind of chilli sauce. The chips were fairly standard, except for the sauce: it was fuckin' peanut! It wasn't too bad, though. They finished them up and headed off to one of the coffee houses that were sprinkled liberally around the city.

—They're fond of their coffee, wha'? said Barry.

—They certainly are, agreed Nick, as they stepped down into the Bulldog Palace Coffee Shop. —You can get beer and…stuff in some of the places, too.

Barry went straight up to the bar. It was a bit like one of those American-style bars in Dublin, though it was hard to tell through the smoke and dim lighting.

—Pint o' Guinness, please.

The barman looked at him as if he'd ordered a bucket of steaming piss. —No Guinness.

Barry remembered where he was. —Oh, yeah. Sorry. A pint o' Heineken, so.

This time the barman looked like he was going to say something stronger. —No...alcohol.

Barry turned to Dunne-Davis for support, but he wasn't there. He was over in a booth at the far end of the bar. Barry looked up and down the bar: dozens of varieties of juice and mineral water. There was some sort of milkshake blender and a large coffee machine behind there, as well. He pointed to the apple juice.

—Apple juice, please.

Dunne-Davis came back and picked up some cigarette paper and one of the many Zippo lighters that adorned the bar. Barry took his apple juice and followed him down to a small table near the entrance. It all began to make sense as he watched Dunne-Davis rolling a joint the size of a 99 cone.

He looked around nervously.

—Is tha' legal?

—Perfectly, said Nick, licking the edges of the paper.

—Fuck's sake.

Barry sipped his apple juice in silence until Dunne-Davis had finished rolling. He flicked the lighter and started sucking on the end of the joint.

—Want some? he enquired, blowing a lungful of smoke straight into Barry's face.

—Fuck off!

By the time Barry dragged him out of the place, a couple of hours later, Dunne-Davis was giggling like an idiot. It had been days since he'd had so much as a

Marlboro Light. He was like a fuckin' three-year-old. He hadn't a clue where they were going.

—I thought yeh knew this city?

—I do.

—What's so fuckin' funny?

Dunne-Davis just pointed at Barry and broke his bollix laughing. It reminded Barry why he wasn't into drugs. Where was the fun in a grown man behaving like a baby?

—Where we goin'?

After another fit of hilarity, Dunne-Davis gasped: —Oude...Oude Kerk. The Oude Kerk. Barry half-led, half-dragged him over the little humpback bridges towards the train station. He stopped to ask directions from some English lads in football tops, but they just laughed at him, the bastards.

—Wahey, Paddy!

When they eventually got there, Barry couldn't believe his eyes. He'd known there was some kind of red-light district, but he hadn't expected it to be so in your face. The entire street was full of houses – nothing unusual there; it was what was inside the houses that shocked him. Young ones, wearing nothing but lingerie – and oul' ones wearing even less. And they were sitting in the big bay front windows, bold as brass. Some of them just sat there and looked bored, while others blew kisses and made obscene gestures. Some of the places had signs with prices on them, like you were ordering a fuckin' burger from a menu: I'll have a blowjob and chips, please. It was unreal.

Dunne-Davis pointed an arm that swayed across three or four windows.

—We're going in there.

—We are like fuck!

The next morning Barry woke up late. Dunne-Davis was snoring away, so he made sure he made as much noise as possible getting out of bed. He turned on the little radio alarm – it was one of those little plastic jobs with one speaker that sounded like a long-distance phone call – and clicked the volume up until it vibrated on the locker. He opened the window and let in a flood of noise from the street. He even tried opening and slamming the door a few times, but the bollix wouldn't wake up. After a good shower and shite, Barry came back in to the room: Dunne-Davis was still asleep. There was only one thing for it. Barry picked up the glass of water beside Dunne-Davis's bed and held it over his face. Then he whispered, very quietly, —Wake up.

When Dunne-Davis failed to respond, he let him have it. He poured the full glass over him before Dunne-Davis actually moved.

—Huh? He sat up and shook his head from side to side like a dog drying himself.

—Couldn't wake yeh, explained Barry cheerfully.

Dunne-Davis sat up in the bed as his senses came back to him. The previous evening's proceedings were slowly replaying in his head. He didn't feel too bad, apart from the dryness in his throat.

—Well? said Barry.

—Well what?

—Are we goin' to meet this contact of yours?

Dunne-Davis spent the obligatory half-hour in the shower. After a light breakfast of dry rolls and yoghurt, they bought ten kilos of flour and brought it back to the hostel. There was a small wooden table in their room that they could use for mixing. Barry hoisted the flour onto the table and lay on his bed.

—I'm not touchin' that shite.

Dunne-Davis looked pissed off but didn't say anything. Instead he emptied the coke out of the pillowcases and opened the first packet. It was going to be a messy job. After a couple of hours staring at the ceiling, Barry got bored and left him to it.

There was an internet booth in the hostel, so he put two euro into it and looked up the Irish Independent website for the sports news. He would have sent Jill an e-mail, but what was the point? His da had given away the computer because of the amount of time Declan was spending playing games on it. He was an awful man for the old video games.

There wasn't much sports news, really, just all the hype about the World Cup. It was only a couple of weeks away now. Ireland had beaten Sunderland in Niall Quinn's testimonial match. Big deal. Roy Keane wasn't playing in it because of another injury or something – probably just taking it easy, getting himself right for the real thing. Barry just hoped he'd be home in time to see the World Cup properly. It mightn't be so bad being unemployed for a month or so, after all. He checked the Liverpool site as well, but there was nothing about transfers on it. Everybody was waiting to see what happened in the World Cup, who would do well, who would be the find of the tournament. There were always some African players no one had ever heard of who ended up being superstars. The European clubs would get them on the cheap and turn them into world-beaters. Barry just hoped there weren't too many of them on the Cameroon team. They were in Ireland's group and were quietly fancied by some of the pundits at home.

It took Dunne-Davis hours to cut all the coke and flour. The really hard part was getting it back into the packs. Barry had to go out and buy more of them when he ran out. There was white powder all over the place, so he had to get a dustpan and brush as well. When Dunne-Davis had finished, they had twenty kilos of the stuff, packed into one-kilo bricks. They still had one untouched pack, as well, for cutting the deal. They put it all into a big green rucksack Dunne-Davis had stroked earlier.

—Right. Ready for action, he said, subtly snorting a stray line or two from his forearm.

Barry waited anxiously in the room while Dunne-Davis went to make a phone call. He was back in no time.

—It's all sorted. We're meeting Karl at his club tonight.

—And he's goin' to buy it?

—No. He's only the middleman, like I said. He'll introduce us to a contact who's interested in buying.

—And how d'yeh know this Karl?

—I was in school with him. He's a DJ over here. Remember? The guy I was telling you about.

—So you're sure he's all righ'?

—Positive. His dad and my dad were partners in the same firm. Known him since Irish college. We're to bring the gear with us tonight.

—All of it?

—Yah. Your man wants to buy the twenty kilos. He's willing to pay one and a half million euro for it.

—And you owe Doyle a million?

—Yah. We give him a million and a half and everything's sweet.

—Hmm, said Barry.

—What?

—I don't think we should bring the lot of it. What if it's a set-up?

—It's not a set-up. Me and Karl go way back.

—Yeah, but this is big money. I don't care if you were ridin' each other in boarding school. I say we leave it here and bring the sample. Then, if he's happy with it, we can always meet him tomorrow.

Dunne-Davis looked over at the rucksack stuffed with white gold. He hated to admit it, but Barry was probably right.

—Right.

The club was buzzing when they arrived. Barry wasn't

sure about their attire. Dunne-Davis had insisted they wear the shades, even though it was pitch-dark out.

—We've got to look like drug dealers, he explained. —Image is everything.

That was fair enough, but Barry had to keep lifting them up to see where he was going. At one stage he was only six inches from mashing his nose into a lamppost.

—Are yeh sure we're not too scruffy-lookin'?

—It isn't possible to be too scruffy for these places, Nick assured him.

The bouncers stopped them anyway and said something in Dutch. They were the biggest men Barry had ever seen, nothing like the usual twats in bomber jackets at home: these guys must have been twenty stone each and well over six feet. They both wore suits and were evidently bilingual, which put them two languages ahead of the morons in Dublin. But these guys were actually pleasant and accommodating. They ushered them in as soon as Dunne-Davis had introduced them.

—N-double-D and Barry Kelly to see DJ Karlos.

—Enjoy your evening, gentlemen, said the slightly less gargantuan of the two.

—Er, thanks very much, said Barry, still a little surprised.

It was the first time he'd ever been in a place like this – a real club. Drum and bass pumped out of the gigantic speakers that lined the walls, and people were dancing and writhing in unison everywhere. And the girls...they were fantastic. Most of them were dressed in tiny little bikini tops and skirts that barely covered their arses. One of them, a dark-haired young one who seemed to be in a world of her own, was dancing on top of a speaker, mesmerised by a bottle of water she was dancing with. Her skirt was so short that Barry was sure he was about to see the Promised Land, until he was interrupted by Dunne-Davis.

—Want a drink?

—Wha'? Er, yeah.

He looked around. Practically everyone was drinking bottled water, for reasons that were obvious even to Barry.

—Bottle o' beer.

He followed Dunne-Davis over to the bar that stretched all down one side of the club. It must have been forty metres long. A young one no more than sixteen came up and hugged him, just flung her arms around him and held on to him for a minute. He hadn't said a word to her. She stared at him with eyes as big as saucers and eventually let go.

—Here. Dunne-Davis handed him an ice-cold Grolsch. It tasted good. Barry rubbed the clouded bottle against his forehead, which was beginning to form warm beads of sweat. His eyes had just about adjusted to the dim conditions and the shades.

Dunne-Davis waved at DJ Karlos. He spotted them and waved back with one hand, while his other hand worked the decks. 'Hey Boy, Hey Girl' pulsed out across the club. It was the first song Barry had recognised, and even that was only because it was one of the ones that Declan insisted on blasting in his room. He thought it might be the Chemical Brothers, and he smiled briefly at the irony of the name. The crowd whooped in delight and picked up the pace; a sea of heads bobbed up and down as the lights swooped across them, illuminating manic grins and wild-eyed faces. Some of them even seemed to be...they couldn't be...they were! Some of them were sucking soothers! The fuckin' eejits.

—What in the name of Jaysus? It was like something out of a film to Barry.

He was distracted by DJ Karlos, who'd bounded down from his perch above the crowd.

—How's it going?

—All right, man? Dunne-Davis was delighted to see him.

DJ Karlos offered his hand to Barry. —Karlos.

—Barry.

Karlos didn't actually shake his hand, though. Instead he locked thumbs with Barry and wrapped his fingers around his wrist, the way the homeboys in the movies did it.

He ordered a beer for himself and another round for the lads. —Cheers, he said, raising his bottle.

It was too loud for conversation, so he got straight to the point. —Did you bring it?

Dunne-Davis nodded at the rucksack. DJ Karlos looked well pleased and motioned for them to follow him upstairs.

—Wanker, muttered Barry as they followed him.

When they got to the large lounge, the wanker in question was much chattier. He talked shite with Dunne-Davis about the old days for a bit, and he didn't seem to mind Dunne-Davis's arse-licking. It was pathetic, Barry thought: just because your man had made a few quid playing other people's records...

—That chill-out mix you did was, like, amazing!

Karlos shrugged in fake modesty. He was enjoying the adulation, the little prick.

—It just left me speechless.

Not for fuckin' long enough, said Barry to himself.

—So, Karlos asked, —have you got something for me?

Dunne-Davis nearly tore the bag open. So much for being cool. Barry just hoped DJ Karlos hadn't seen the bed linen and underwear stuffed inside. Dunne-Davis handed him a small packet and waited patiently while he cut it into three neat lines with his credit card. He snorted the first and offered the next one to Dunne-Davis, who did likewise.

—Fuck, that's good shit. Karlos seemed impressed.

Dunne-Davis laughed nervously. Barry declined the third line, so Karlos hoovered it up. Barry was feeling really edgy. For the first time that night, he was glad he was wearing the shades. He didn't want Karlos to see the fear in his eyes.

—Do you mind if I hold on to this for personal use?

—Not at all, said Dunne-Davis.

—I can pay you for it.

—Don't be silly, man. I wouldn't dream of it.

—Cool. I'll just go and see if they're here yet.

DJ Karlos got up and left the two of them alone. Barry ripped off his shades.

—Do yeh think he bought it?

Dunne-Davis paced the room, inspecting the Van Gogh prints that lined the walls.

—Absolutely. He's a good bloke.

Barry raised himself from the leather sofa and looked down at the heaving club below. He caught sight of Karlos, talking to two dodgy-looking characters and pointing up at the lounge.

Something was up. All Barry's instincts said so. They just didn't look right, even for drug dealers. One of them had a scrawny 'tache, the kind only a select set of skangers in Dublin would be proud of.

—Maybe I'm just bein' paranoid...

—You are, interrupted Dunne-Davis.

—...but I don't like the look of our customers.

Dunne-Davis joined him on the mezzanine and confirmed his worst fears.

—Oh, my God!

—Well?

—Doyle's men. Definitely. I recognise the one with the ronnie.

They looked at each other, then at the fire escape at the far end of the corridor. Dunne-Davis grabbed the bag, but Barry snatched it from his grasp and flung it back on the couch.

—It'll give us a couple o' seconds, he said as they burst through the escape door.

He wasn't wrong. The two toe-rags were moderately surprised by the bag of dirty underwear and bed linen that they were compelled to check.

By that stage, Barry and Dunne-Davis had bounded down the concrete steps and were pounding along the cobblestones to the nearest place of refuge, which turned out to be a tiny coffee house a couple of blocks away. They ducked into the cosy bar and held their breath while their pursuers fled past.

Barry exhaled deeply.

—So much for your mates.

—I can't understand it. The fucking prick. How could he do that to me?

Dunne-Davis was genuinely upset. —Fuck him.

—Did yeh happen to mention where we were stayin' to your DJ mate?

—No, I don't think so.

—Yes or no?

—He asked me, but I said I didn't know the name of the hostel.

—But yeh told him where it was?

—I told him it was in Leidseplein.

—Yeh fuckin' eejit.

Barry turned the key in the door and pushed it open slowly. It groaned along its hinges and came to rest against the wall. He held his breath and hit the lights.

—Nothing, he said.

Dunne-Davis appeared from the corridor where he'd been cowering and brushed past him. They gathered up everything into the new rucksack Nick had 'acquired' from the coffee house and left as quickly as possible. As they were passing reception, Barry rang the little bell for service.

—What the fuck are you doing?

—Gimme some money.

Dunne-Davis reluctantly handed him the wad of notes and waited while the lady came out.

—Are you leaving us already?

—Yeah. Could yeh do us a favour? said Barry, handing

her the money. —Could yeh tell our friends we've gone to Brussels? Only, they might call in later, y'know?

—Brussels? Yes, certainly. Thank you.

—Thanks.

—CHAPTER TEN—

They sat in silence in the basement of the little coffee house. It was another one of those non-alcoholic places, so they had to sip water while deciding what to do. Eventually, Dunne-Davis got up to take a whizz. He could stay in there forever, as far as Barry was concerned.

—Are you enjoying your trip?

Barry looked up to see who had asked him such a stupid fuckin' question. He was a skinny young fella, probably Dutch by the look of his red cords and scraggly hair.

—Does it fuckin' look like it?

The young lad sat down beside him.

—Relax, bro. You should try something else.

—Fuck off, suggested Barry. He looked around to see what was keeping Dunne-Davis. He didn't feel like talking to this gobshite all night.

—There's no need to be like that. What's your name, man?

—Me name's none of your fuckin' business, man. Righ'?

Barry didn't mean it to sound as threatening as it did. He just wasn't in the humour for conversation.

The kid got up to leave. —Enjoy the trip, asshole.

—Sorry, offered Barry, but the kid was gone.

Dunne-Davis eventually came back and sat down.

—Well?

—Fuck off.

Barry took another sip of water. He had some serious thinking to do.

Things were bad. Dublin was out of the question. So was anywhere in Ireland, or Britain, for that matter. They obviously had to get out of Amsterdam, but where could they go? The Brussels false trail would buy them some time, but they'd have to find somewhere where the long arm of Tony Doyle couldn't reach them. And, speaking of Doyle, how the fuck had he known they were in Amsterdam? Dunne-Davis had been adamant that Karlos wasn't involved with Doyle's crew, but somebody had tipped him off. Someone from home, Barry thought. It had to be. Dunne-Davis must have opened his big mouth. The prick couldn't resist bragging to his druggie mates. Still, Barry knew he'd better not call home for a while, just in case.

Then there was the question of offloading their goods. Barry didn't like the idea of selling drugs one bit. Lugging them across Western Europe appealed to him even less. But, for the moment, their main priority was finding somewhere to lie low; they could worry about the drugs later. Maybe if they waited long enough Doyle would forget about his nephew and they could just give him back the coke...

Some chance, Barry thought. Fuckers like Doyle never forgot, never mind forgave. They'd have to work out another way. The whole thing was a mess. He should never have become involved. Why couldn't he have just done what every other selfish bastard would have done, and left Dunne-Davis to his fate? If he had the chance again, he told himself, that was exactly what he'd do. But he knew it wasn't true. He looked over at Dunne-Davis.

He couldn't be entirely sure, but he was fairly certain Dunne-Davis had a human head the last time he looked. And he was almost certain that he hadn't had a large trunk on any of their previous encounters. Barry finished the last of his water and fished out the small white square of paper that was stuck to the side of the glass. The smiley face on the paper winked up at him and began laughing out loud, in the manner that is the exclusive preserve of the hallucinogenic chemical.

Barry was no expert, but even through his wooziness he had a fair idea what the friendly young lad had dropped in his drink. Particularly when the smiley face opened its mouth and started singing, —Ac-id! Ac-id!

Nick was confused. Barry was acting very strangely. The stress of their near-death experiences must be taking their toll on him. He seemed very lucid one minute, and then he'd be completely vacant the next – totally out to lunch, and it didn't appear that he'd be returning for dinner. And then he'd say something brilliant.

He had it all worked out – except for the bit about Carlsberg; Nick wasn't sure about that. Barry kept going on about seeing the light and claiming that Carlsberg had shown him the way. And then he'd point to the Carlsberg logo through the window and laugh.

In fairness to him, though, it wasn't the worst plan Nick had ever heard. And anything was better than going back to Dublin. Nick wasn't completely convinced that the little Honda would carry them all the way, particularly considering the sea they'd need to cross. Barry conceded that one and even agreed that they could catch a train, at least part of the way.

The rest seemed to make sense. The World Cup in Japan was the last place Doyle would expect them to go. And after the Amsterdam fiasco, Nick was prepared to go to the moon if he had to. Besides, wouldn't Japan be full of Japanese women?

Back in Dublin, it was pissing down.

Typical bloody Irish summer, thought Sasha as the rain pelted the corrugated steel roof above her head.

She was almost getting used to it now: the isolation. The loneliness, and the pathetic sense of elation when anyone – even Doyle – came to visit her private prison.

Well, maybe elation was the wrong word, but anything that broke the monotony was welcome. She knew by heart the number of grooves in the roof – 328 – and the amount of bricks in each wall: 2,730 in the side walls, 1,342 at the gable ends. She almost yearned for what was about to come.

She knew it the second Johnno walked in. It was in the way his shoulders sagged and his chin pointed towards the concrete floor.

—Mr Doyle's not happy, said Johnno quietly.

—Good. Bastards like him don't deserve to be happy.

—Things haven't worked out the way he planned.

—Maybe he should consider a change of career?

—Maybe I should too.

Sasha looked him up and down. How had he ended up working for that scum? She was sure he wasn't inherently bad; he'd just taken a wrong turn, somewhere along the way.

—He wants to know what yeh know about Dunne-Davis's contacts in Europe.

She didn't bother answering; what was the point? She just laughed and shrugged her shoulders.

—I have to ask yeh. He's headin' for Brussels. Did he ever talk about anyone over there? Any names, or places he might stay? It'll make things easier on you, Johnno added, trying not to sound too threatening.

Sasha shook her head.

—I suppose you better get on with it, she sighed, doing her best to appear braver than she felt.

Johnno looked at his shoes.

—I'm sorry.

—I know you are.

The pain went away after the first couple of slaps. They were the worst. She knew he was pulling his punches – it was no coincidence that her teeth were never touched, or her nose. There was nothing that wouldn't heal in time. Still, an open hand across the face from a hundred-kilo man could certainly ruin a girl's make-up.

After four or five, he stopped and turned away. He couldn't face her. Fuck, he hated this job! And he hated that she hated him because of it.

—Sorry, he said, and walked out.

Sasha slumped back against the wall. She was feeling decidedly upbeat. She'd been expecting him to kill her.

At one hundred and ten miles an hour, something occurred to Nick Dunne-Davis: he was going to die. It wasn't the first time he'd had such thoughts recently, particularly when he was a passenger on the little bike, but this was different. On the previous occasions he'd felt strangely safe in Barry's hands, deep down inside. It felt like Barry knew what he was doing, somehow – like he was some sort of guardian angel on a Honda 50, sent to take care of Nick. But it didn't feel like that now. Barry seemed to be out of his mind.

The tables had turned. Normally Barry was Mr Responsible and Nick had the luxury of having all the fun. But now Barry had flipped from the pressure, and it was Nick's turn to be the designated adult. It was a role he wasn't entirely comfortable with; in fact, it was a role he'd never had any interest in playing before. But he resolved to do the best he could and give adulthood a fair shot, assuming, of course, that they managed to come out of this with their lives – which, it had to be said, was looking increasingly unlikely.

—Barry, I think you better slow down, he suggested, in a high-pitched shriek.

No reply. Surely Barry could see the police checkpoint ahead? They were in Gemany by now. Hadn't Barry seen what they did to people who failed to stop and present their "papers" in all those World War II films? The plan was to get to Berlin and take a train from there to Moscow (Nick's suggestion; he was rather proud of that one), but Barry hadn't mentioned anything about bursting through armed policemen at one hundred miles an hour.

Nick was sure he would have remembered that bit.

—Can you hear me, Barry?

Barry couldn't hear a word Nick was saying. Even if the engine hadn't been screaming in his ears, then the rat-tat-tat of machine-gun fire would surely have drowned out his passenger's protests. In Barry's defence, he hadn't actually seen the checkpoint. He was concentrating on the visual feast of the streetlights whizzing past, and the spaghetti-stretched headlights and taillights of the traffic all around. It was like one of those speeded-up videos, lights and colours streaking into one another. He could feel every tiny glitch in the road; each pebble was like a speed bump to be navigated. In actual fact they were doing around a hundred miles an hour, but to Barry it felt more like four or five hundred. Every so often it would feel like they'd almost stopped; then he'd have the sensation of being shot through the air like a rubber band. It was all happening around him, and he had no choice but to participate. But every now and then a nagging little voice said in his ear:

—You're enjoying this, aren't you?

Nick could hear the police motorbikes behind them. He didn't need to look around. There were three of them in hot pursuit. Here we go again, he thought. He was almost used to it by now. His body seemed to instinctively lean in and out of corners in tandem with Barry's. After the terror of the first couple of chases, he was beginning to see the attraction of biking. It would never match the fulfilment of cruising in a BMW, but as a purely visceral rush it wasn't bad at all. And nothing Barry did with the little bike surprised him any more – until he steered it off the main road into the pine forest.

And even that wasn't exactly surprising. Terrifying, yes, but it was almost what Nick had come to expect. And, if he was brutally honest, it was exactly this type of lunacy that had got them this far. So he just went with it – sat back and held on for dear life as they shot between the trees in the darkness. The police bikes roared behind them, the sound of their powerful engines magnified and echoed by the giant trees. The forest was alive with hundreds of screaming horses powering over the soft carpet of mulch. Barry was flinging the Honda 50 expertly around tree-trunks, using the moist surface to slide in and out among them. For all Nick's trust in his driving ability, he really began to get nervous when Barry killed his headlights. Now it was getting crazy.

But to Barry's mind it was entirely logical. He was simply using the Force. Because now he was Luke Skywalker, flying through the forest on an airbike, with his old Jedi master reassuring him of his power. 'The Force is strong in you. Switch off your headlights,' said the voice of Obi-Wan Kenobi – Barry could hear the splendid Royal Shakespeare Company voice, as clear as day. He didn't need things like headlights. Let the stormtroopers behind him worry about them. The Force would guide him safely through the darkness and out to the other side. It was as if the bike was on a predestined path. It cut a swathe through the undergrowth, dodging trunks and roots, and taking the peaks and troughs in its stride. He felt like he could open it up even more and put greater distance between them and the forces of the Dark Side.

And it worked. The German police bikes gradually gave up the chase, one by one. Without the glowing target of the taillights, it was just too dangerous for anybody retaining a shred of sanity. By the time Barry realised what was going on, they had reached the other side of the forest and freedom.

They were greeted by an empty road that wound its way towards Berlin. Nick suggested that they avoid the autobahns and their inevitable roadblocks. Barry nodded dumbly. He was slowly returning to reality. His mouth felt bitter and coarse, and there was a shooting sensation down his spine every few minutes; it was a bit like pins and needles, except it was sharp and fast and covered his whole body. Every now and then he could feel acidic saliva oozing from the glands in his cheeks. And he could feel his body and mind slowly returning to his control. He felt like shit.

CHAPTER ELEVEN

Nick couldn't get rid of his helmet fast enough. It had been OK when they were travelling through the night and the roads were empty, but as soon as it started getting bright the traffic appeared – the day started very early in Germany – and that Third Reich effort would attract a lot of attention. Nick decided to take his chances and flung it into a field. He could get another one in the little town they were coming into. He knew he'd have to watch the money, though. They had a little over two hundred euro left, which would hopefully cover the train tickets to Moscow and a little food.

The guy in the motorbike shop was helpful enough, and Nick got a battered old racing helmet for ten euro. It would have to do. He bought some croissants and pastries in a little bakery that smelled like heaven. That would keep them going until they reached Berlin.

He handed a warm croissant to Barry, who accepted it without a word. He seemed moody and uncommunicative.

—Are you all right? enquired Nick.

—Fuck off, replied Barry.

That was encouraging. At least he was back to his old self again. The wild look in his eyes had been replaced by a weary stare. It was hardly surprising. Michael Schumacher would have been struggling after a performance like that.

After another couple of croissants, they were ready to move out. Barry seemed a little wobbly getting on the bike, but he'd be grand. Before mounting, Nick checked that the gear was safe and secure under the saddle – all that bumping and jumping around the forest might have burst a packet or two; but a quick root in the rucksack eased his worries. Everything looked OK. Barry pointed the bike east towards the rising sun and kicked it into life. It was going to be a beautiful day in Berlin.

They rode down the magnificent tree-lined avenue that led to the Brandenburg Gate, where conquering armies had returned to victory parades for hundreds of years. The Reichstag to their left was resplendent in the morning sun. The large glass dome perched on top of it reminded Barry of some kind of futuristic transparent beehive. They could just make out people scurrying around inside, like little ants clad in designer clothing.

They followed the main thoroughfare down to Zoo station and came to a halt outside the massive entrance. Nick jumped off the bike.

—I'll check it out.

Barry removed his helmet. The sweat was pouring off him. It cascaded down in mini-waterfalls from his hair; it ran into his eyes and stung them dry. He decided to take off his T-shirt and wring it out. It peeled off him like a second skin. The gentle breeze felt good against his naked torso. Nobody was paying too much attention to him, so he relaxed a bit. That was better. He could feel the wind drying the moisture from his armpits.

He would have killed for a drink – or died for one, for that matter; whichever came first. He dug out a two- and a one-euro coin from his pocket. The trousers were sticking to him, so he had to have a good root to free them up. Whatever that fucker had slipped in his drink, it seemed to have worn off. Surely he'd sweated enough fluids to clean out half a dozen of the bastards by now?

He slotted the coins into the vending machine and hit the chunky Gatorade button. The three seconds it took to dispense seemed like an eternity in purgatory. He was so close to paradise, he could almost taste it. And it was paradise when the ice-cold liquid eventually crashed over his taste buds, like a huge wave smashing onto a bone-dry beach. Barry gulped the entire bottle down in one long, delicious pull. The sun was really beating down, boring a hole right through him. There was traffic humming all around, and there seemed to be dozens of cream-coloured taxicabs in every direction – just like home, he thought wryly. The chimps in the zoo across the street screeched and squawked over the traffic.

It was a mad place, and Barry liked it. He watched a homeless-looking man drop some coins into the same vending machine and crack open the ice-cold can of beer that popped out. Beer! From a fuckin' vending machine! Barry couldn't imagine that lasting long in Dublin. You'd have kids of eight and nine tearing the machines apart to get at the booze. Fuck the coins: a crowbar would be more effective. Sure, you couldn't even leave a Coke machine on the side of the street at home; and here he was watching some poor old bum getting a Berliner Kindl from one. He reckoned he'd seen it all.

The next thing he saw was Nick Dunne-Davis coming down the steps of the station.

—Right, we're sorted, he said.

—What's the story?

—The train leaves tomorrow morning. It's a thirty-two-hour trip to Moscow.

Barry's original plan had involved riding the Honda all the way to the Sea of Japan and then taking a ferry to Tokyo. Nick had no problem with the choice of destination, but he had no intention of travelling halfway round the world on the back of a glorified hairdryer. Barry had eventually agreed to the train, and decided – against all his instincts – to trust Nick to look after the finer details, which basically involved bribing their way to Tokyo.

—And the bike?

—There's a cargo carriage on the train. It costs a bit

extra, but we've got enough.

—So wha' do we do for the next twenty-four hours?

—Check out Berlin, I suppose.

It was a wonderful city. Barry loved the history behind it. He'd always enjoyed history at school; in fact, it was probably the only subject he'd really liked – that and PE, of course. Dunne-Davis wasn't as keen as Barry was, but they took one of the walking tours of the city anyway. They left from right outside Zoo station and they lasted all day. And the best bit was that it didn't cost them a penny. They just hung around on the fringes listening to the guide while he gave the introduction – he was German, but his English was pretty good – and as soon as the group of tourists moved off, Barry and Nick sidled up alongside them and blended in. They passed the old cathedral that had been left as a bombed-out shell in memory of the war. Everything around it had been pummelled into the ground, so it was a bit of a miracle that the spire was standing at all.

—Fascinating, said Dunne-Davis, a little too sarcastically for Barry's liking.

When the tour was over they made their way to the Potsdamer Platz. It was like something from the next century. Steel and glass twisted and spiralled into the sky, making Barry feel like he was in a sci-fi movie. They lay in the sun in the park opposite. Barry decided to give his T-shirt a rub in the fountain when no one was watching. He laid it out on the grass to dry. It was evening now, but there was still a fair bit of heat left in the sun. Berlin was a fantastic place, but it still made him wish he were back in Dublin.

They found a place on a street corner that sold cheap food. In fairness, it wasn't exactly like locating the Lost Ark; there seemed to be one on every second corner in

Berlin. Dunne-Davis asked for two Bratwurst and they stood at the plastic tables, with the suits and commuters on their way home from work. The Bratwurst consisted of a large sausage about six inches long, wedged into a three-inch hotdog roll. Barry lobbed ketchup and mustard on his and regarded it dubiously. It just looked fuckin' stupid, with the two ends of meat sticking out. He took a tentative bite and chewed it delicately.

—Jaysus, not bad.

Dunne-Davis nodded in agreement. It wasn't Patrick Guilbaud's, but it wasn't as bad as it looked either. They had one more each and decided to bunk onto the U-Bahn. That was another thing Barry noticed: everything ran like clockwork. If the timetable said there was a train due at nine minutes past seven, then you could bet your left bollock that a train would be there at nine minutes past seven. And everybody stamped their tickets. There was no one around to make them, but they did it anyway.

They went a few stops, for the craic, and came out beside a large bar. It was like they'd arrived in Turkey: when they went in, they instantly raised the non-Turkish population by two hundred per cent. Barry was a bit nervous, but nobody paid them any attention – literally: it took them half an hour to order a drink. They stayed there till about three and managed one more beer – which was just as well, considering the state of their finances. Maybe people just drank slower in Germany. No one else seemed to be getting served any quicker than they were, and they didn't seem to care, either. Barry thought it was a bit odd to spend five hours in a bar and only have two pints. How did they make any money?

Dunne-Davis suggested taking a stroll, so they did. They came across a backpackers' hostel and decided to try their luck. Everyone seemed to be fast asleep in bed and there was nobody on reception, so they sneaked their way up to the TV lounge. There were a couple of German lads in football tops on their way to bed. They didn't say a word. Barry noticed the slippers they were wearing were just like his da's. He was going to crack a joke but decided against it; they didn't seem like the friendliest blokes in the world. After they left, Barry and Nick stretched out on the couches and hoped they could get a bit of kip before being thrown out.

Barry couldn't help thinking about Jill. He tried hard not to, but it was useless. He pictured her, asleep in bed – their bed – with her hair tied back, wearing the stripy pyjamas she'd got in Dunne's. She had got them for him, but he never wore them; not because he had anything against them, just because he couldn't be bothered with pyjamas in general. A T-shirt and shorts did him grand. So Jill wore them. And she was probably tucked up comfortably in them at that very moment. He hoped she was sleeping better than he was.

He did get a couple of hours' broken sleep before being woken up by two English girls in the kitchen. They weren't clattering around or anything; it was just that he was sleeping so lightly. It couldn't be any worse than listening to Dunne-Davis. Barry didn't know which was more offensive, the snoring or the farting. They didn't even smell that bad; it was the sheer volume of them that was so revolting. What had he been eating? It wasn't as if they had vastly differing diets or anything. As if to emphasise the point, Dunne-Davis let go a long, high-pitched trumpet, like a bugler blowing the wake-up call at dawn. That made up his mind for him. He woke Dunne-Davis with a gentle knee to the thigh – not enough to give him a dead leg, just a little 'thank you' for the pleasant evening they'd spent together. Dunne-Davis stirred and sat up slowly. He picked up the rucksack he'd been sleeping on and rubbed the impression the zipper had left on his cheek. After he did whatever it was he had to do in the jacks (Barry didn't want to think about it), they were on their way. They strode straight past the oul' one at reception and kept their heads down.

They caught the U-Bahn to Zoo station. Barry was pleased to find the Honda where he'd left it. After an attempted conversation with a cashier, they gathered enough information for a brief panic attack: the train wasn't at Zoo Station and never would be. It was leaving from another station across town. But they had an hour to get there, so there was no need to get too uptight.

They made it with half an hour to spare. As they were looking for the platform, Barry noticed something on one of the TV screens in a shop window.

—Hey, look at this.

It was Roy Keane. On German fuckin' television! They must be scared shitless of us, Barry thought happily. Well, it was actually the BBC World Service, but nevertheless, there he was, staring intensely (did he ever stare any other way?) out at the world.

—Keano!

—That's great, said Dunne-Davis, but Barry knew he didn't mean it. —Can we go now?

Roy looked a bit down in the dumps, but then he was always a bit grumpy. That was what gave him his edge. Then they cut to Mick McCarthy. Barry liked McCarthy. He'd done almost as much as Keane to get Ireland to the World Cup. It was strange them being on telly, though. Maybe Keane was injured? Barry put that ridiculous notion out of his head. He knew that nothing short of losing a limb would prevent Roy from playing in Japan – and even then, he'd probably hobble around the pitch on one leg, scaring the bejasus out of anyone who went near the ball, including his own team. It was going to be the pinnacle of a magnificent career. The world's best player on the best stage in the world...and Barry was actually going to see it all, in the flesh. He felt that he, like his hero, was ready to take on the whole world.

Michael Kelly couldn't believe it. He sat dumbfounded in front of the telly. He was speechless. People said that all the time, but it was only a figure of speech: if you were speechless, how could you even say the words 'I'm speechless' when you won a hundred quid on the Lotto, or some other shite like that? But Michael really and truly couldn't speak. He opened his mouth a few times (in fact, it had been open the whole time; he had just been too shocked to notice) and tried to get his tongue to do as God intended, but the fuckin' thing just wobbled about his mouth like a drunk at closing time.

—Uhhh! he cried weakly, to the rest of them in the kitchen.

Maybe he was dreaming. That was it: it was just a nightmare. He'd fallen asleep in his chair with the TV on. He was waking up slowly, and his dreams were being influenced by what was on the telly – like when you dream you're freezing your arse off on an iceberg, only to wake up and find the duvet on the floor. That was all it was. He'd wake up in a minute...any minute...

—And the main headlines again: Republic of Ireland star Roy Keane is going home from the World Cup.

—Aaghhh! Michael whimpered.

It was a nightmare – but it was a real nightmare. He hadn't felt like this since Helen had died. It was almost that bad.

Barry and Nick found their seats on the train. They'd stuffed the merchandise under the saddle of the Honda and locked the storage compartment before leaving it in the cargo carriage. Barry had persuaded Dunne-Davis that that was the safest place for it, in case they were checked crossing the border. That was another problem they'd have to deal with when the time came.

—Leave it to me, Dunne-Davis had said. —I've got it all worked out.

Barry was sceptical, to put it mildly. He'd caught Dunne-Davis sneaking a packet of coke into the rucksack 'for bribery purposes'. He just hoped they wouldn't end up in the arse end of Siberia cracking ice with pickaxes. But Dunne-Davis had assured him of the dodgy nature of Russian officials, so he had let it go.

The seats weren't too bad. They were basically just two benches, in a cabin with a sliding door. There didn't seem to be anyone else in with them, even though it was a four-berth cabin. Barry wasn't sure if that was good or bad. Dunne-Davis was hard work at the best of times, but thirty-two hours stuck in a tiny room with the prick was going to be a real test. He reckoned that, if he tried to do it one hour at a time, he might make it through the journey without throttling him.

—So what makes Roy Keane so good, anyway? I don't see what all the fuss is about.

Barry revised his plan: better make it minute by minute, rather than hour by hour. He bit his tongue and stared out the window onto the platform. He noticed the pigeons nesting in the rafters. He saw that it was two minutes before departure time. He marvelled at the thick black hair on the legs of the railway worker. They would have been hairy for a grizzly bear; they were exceptional on a woman. Maybe it was a man in a skirt? It didn't really matter, as long as he or she took Barry's mind off the gobshite sitting opposite him...

—The Irish media always go on about him being world-class, but why does he never beat anyone with the ball, or score spectacular goals like Beckham?

Barry almost lost it. It was typical of an ignoramus like Dunne-Davis to compare Roy to someone like that. He tried counting the pigeon droppings on the bench outside. He told himself that it wasn't Dunne-Davis's fault; he wouldn't know whether a football was pumped or stuffed.

The train was slowly grinding away from the station. Only another thirty-one hours and fifty-nine minutes to go. Barry was doing well.

—I reckon he's overrated, continued Dunne-Davis.

Barry crushed the can he was holding. Unfortunately,

it was still half-full. —Roy Keane has the legs of a racehorse, the body of a warrior and the heart of a lion, he said through clenched teeth.

—Yeah, and the head of a skanger, added Nick, very, very quietly.

Tony Doyle reached for his angina pills. This was all he needed.

First that snot-nosed little wagon wouldn't squeal on her boyfriend. Then Dunne-Davis had vanished into thin air, presumably along with the million euro of gear, just when they had him in their clutches. And now this. This selfish waster was about to rob him of half a million in winnings. It was typical of the spoilt brats of today. In Doyle's day, you would have paid to play for your country. Now he was listening to Roy Keane moaning on about the pitch being too hard in the luxury complex where they were staying. It would have been laughable if it hadn't been so serious. Then McCarthy came on, and he started moaning about the insults he had been subjected to. They were like fuckin' schoolboys. A swift kick up the arse was what they needed.

There was a knock on the office door and Johnno came in.

—Boss.

—Have you seen this?

—Yeah.

—Isn't it fuckin' shockin'?

—Shockin', agreed Johnno. —What are we gonna do?

Doyle thought about it in silence for a bit.

—D'yeh want me to get the cash back?

—No.

Doyle knew he could always get the money back if things went badly. For now, he had a better idea.

—I think the odds have just lengthened.

Johnno nodded. —I'll go and make sure they have.

—Good lad.

Doyle sat back in his chair and wondered how much longer it would be necessary to hold onto Dunne-Davis's young one. What if she really didn't know anything? Either way, she'd have to be taken care of sooner or later.

—CHAPTER TWELVE—

Back in Germany, the train was quiet. Dunne-Davis had eventually shut the fuck up after Barry had offered to beat him to a fine pulp. It was the bit when he'd started going on about how skilful Robbie Keane was that had finally done it.

—Do you not think that he's the best Keane in Ireland?

Now that Barry thought about it, he reckoned that Dunne-Davis had been winding him up – at least some of the time, anyway. So they sat there in silence. It was grand. Barry watched the fields whiz past. Nick had robbed a Barely Legal magazine from the newsstand in the station and was flicking through it. It had been on a rack outside the place, so it had been a piece of piss to stroke. He turned the magazine on its side and peered at it from a different angle.

—Eh, just going to the jacks, he said, getting up.

—Wanker, said Barry to himself, but loud enough so Nick could hear. It must have been a whole forty-eight hours since he got his hole, he thought. Then he returned his attention to the window. It was a beautiful country, all the same. Barry had hardly been outside Ireland in twenty-six years, and here he was in his fourth European country in a week. He was wondering when they'd be coming into Poland, when Dunne-Davis sauntered back in, looking a little flushed.

—Enjoy it? said Barry dryly.

Dunne-Davis didn't reply. He sat down and took out one of the rolls they'd stocked up with at the train station.

It took him a bit of fiddling with the plastic wrapper; it was hot and sticky in the cabin, and the plastic had almost melted onto the cheese. He got it eventually and started munching away noisily. Barry fished a packet of crisps out of the rucksack. He couldn't get over how dry they were. They didn't seem to taste of much, but they filled a gap. He wolfed them down in no time and opened one of the large bars of chocolate. It didn't matter that it was half melted; it was delicious. The old Germans certainly knew their beer and their chocolate. He wasn't so sure about the crisps, but two out of three wasn't bad. He'd get some chocolate and bring it home for Jill and Sarah, if he ever made it home in one piece. For now, he was just happy to have Doyle and his cronies miles behind them, and the thrill of the World Cup ahead of them.

He wondered if Doyle had found out where he lived yet. Then he decided not to think about things like that. He had to trust Dunne-Davis on this one. Those bastards were vicious, but it was just business. They didn't resort to taking it out on your family. Or so he prayed to God. He couldn't live with himself if something happened to any of them. Anyway, Declan had said they were all grand on the phone. He'd call them again as soon as he had a chance.

He felt the train slowing down and looked at Dunne-Davis.

—So what's this ingenious plan of yours?

Ingenious was definitely too big a word for it. Truth be told, 'plan' was also a little on the ambitious side. It involved Dunne-Davis lifting up his seat, climbing into the hollow beneath it, and then closing it over him.

—You're fuckin' jokin', of course.

—No, honestly, it'll work.

—Ah, for fuck's sake! Barry could see it now: six months in a Polish prison, sharing a small cell with a large man named Oleg.

—Just open yours and get in. I did this Interrailing, years ago. They never check. I'm telling you.

Barry looked at the bench on his side. He shook his head and pulled it up.

—Bollix!

There was a heater in there, bolted to the floor. The train had stopped, and Barry had seen a guard getting on... Maybe he could duck into the cabin next door; there didn't seem to be too many people on the train. He slid the door back gently and popped his head into the corridor.

—Feck!

The guard was outside a cabin a few doors down. Barry didn't think he'd seen him, but there was no way out. He lifted up Dunne-Davis' seat.

—Move over.

—What?

It was tiny, but there was nowhere else to go. Barry dived in and closed the seat just in time. The guard's footsteps clacked around the cabin, but he didn't open the seat. They waited.

—Did you fart?

—No, lied Dunne-Davis.

—Yeh did, yeh dirty bas—

—Shhh!

The footsteps were back. The door groaned shut and they tapped around the cabin. Oh, fuck, thought Barry. What was he doing? The footsteps stopped, and the seat creaked above them. The fucker was sitting on them! Barry felt the tiny cavity shrinking around him, and Dunne-Davis elbowed him in the ribs.

—Shhh!

He must have groaned without realising it. It was horrible in there. He felt like he couldn't breathe. His face was pressed against the underside of the seat and he literally couldn't move a muscle. He had never thought of himself as claustrophobic, but he was seriously reconsidering that. His breath was becoming laboured, and his head felt like it was going to break free from his body and float off into the atmosphere like a helium balloon.

—Ugghh...

This time he heard it. Dunne-Davis shoved him hard, and his head hit off the seat. Whoever was sitting on it shouted something in German and jumped up.

—Scheisse!

The cover opened and sunlight flooded in. They stared up at the large figure towering over them.

—Er, all right? ventured Nick.

Jill couldn't take much more of it. They were worse than children.

—He's dead righ', said Declan.

—What? Michael demanded.

—The FAI are just a shower of old farts, sittin' around in their blazers gettin' fat on taxpayers' money.

—D'yeh hear this?

Michael was looking to her for support, but he was wasting his time. She had more important things to worry about than a silly football row.

—It's true, Declan said. —The Irish team weren't even allowed to fly first class until Keane put his foot down. It was only the oul' lads who went first class up until recently.

—How would you know that? You're not even interested in football.

—I'm interested in this, though. This isn't just about football.

Michael was flabbergasted. How anyone could side with that mé féin-er was beyond him. —And what about Quinn and Staunton and...his whole team turnin' on him? Explain tha', if you're so smart. How come they're all supportin' McCarthy in all of this?

—McCarthy's a muppet, replied Declan.

Michael hated that word. All the kids used it now.

He supposed it was cool. And here was his own son using it to describe the best manager Ireland had had in years. Fuck Charlton – he'd had much better players to work with. McCarthy had taken a team of average pros, journeymen with most of their clubs, and brought them to the World Cup, dismissing the likes of Holland along the way!

—Even I know that Keane was the one that got us to Japan, Declan said. —McCarthy had nothin' to do with it.

—And how do you explain his own teammates? countered Michael.

—They're just yes-men. They're not even good enough to mix Keane's drinks – even though I heard he doesn't even drink, 'cause he's a real professional. Not like the rest o' them wasters – too fond of the gargle, they are—

—They're professional footballers! If you'd ever played a team sport in your life, instead of risking life and limb on that feckin' skateboard, yeh'd know what I'm talkin' about. Any fella who won't room with his own teammates, or – and this really takes the biscuit – won't eat with his own teammates, is a wagon! He can fuck off back to Manchester where he belongs!

—That's righ', he's too good to be wastin' his time with those losers!

Michael got up and stormed out of the room. Jill had never seen him that animated before, nor heard him using that kind of language. Neither had Declan, for that matter – not since his ma had died, anyway. It was strange, seeing him so excited. Strange, but not necessarily bad.

—Give us the salt, will yeh? Declan said to Jill.

—And what did your last maid die of? she replied, leaving him alone and saltless.

When she went in to him in the sitting room, an hour later, Michael was still brooding. The Keane saga was all over the television. Jill couldn't understand it. She'd read that India and Pakistan were about to go to war with each other, and this was all they were reporting? In the papers, even the threat of a nuclear war played second fiddle to this football rubbish that was spread across the front pages. It was pathetic.

—I'm just going out for an hour, she said.

—Yeah, all right, love.

She closed the door behind her. She felt a bit odd; guilty, in a way. But what harm was there in just meeting the guy? She was only curious. Besides, it would take her mind off things for a while. She was beginning to wonder if she'd ever see Barry again.

She put the thought out of her head. She'd have to hurry. She was meeting him at the house in Sandymount in ten minutes.

The big German's name was Jan, but you pronounced it 'Yan'. He was in his fifties, tall and well dressed, with elaborately designed spectacles. Barry liked him, after the initial shock of their meeting. His breathing was back to normal now, and Jan seemed to see the funny side of the incident. His English was excellent, and he told them that he was travelling to Moscow on business.

—So are we, said Nick.

—Really? What kind of business are you in?

—The motor trade.

Jan couldn't help casting a doubtful eye over them. They certainly didn't look like businessmen – in fact, they looked like a pair of dirty backpackers down on their luck – but he let it go.

—You are Irish? he said to Barry, nodding at his T-shirt.

—Yeah.

—I think you will do very well against Germany in Japan.

—Really?

—Yes. We are not so good now.

—I don't know about tha', now, said Barry sceptically.

Jan turned to Dunne-Davis. —And what part of England do you come from?

—Ireland.

—Excuse me?

—Er, I'm Irish.

—He just sounds like a Brit, added Barry helpfully. —We call them West Brits at home.

—I see. West Brits.

Dunne-Davis wasn't impressed. He stared out the window and reddened slightly. Looking at Barry reminded him of how they must appear. He pretended to bend down and tie his shoelace, discreetly inhaling under his armpit on the way. It was foul. He needed a shower like he had never needed one before. He sat back and took out his packet of Marlboro, offering one to Jan, who politely refused. He had bought a few packs back at the station in Berlin. They didn't seem to have any Marlboro Lights, but he was sure the Russian guards wouldn't care. He exhaled the smoke out the window. It made him feel a little better.

The train dragged its way through Poland all day. They rolled past run-down farms with lonely, tin-roofed houses; some of them were painted in beautifully bright colours, blues and reds and yellows that lent a splash of hope to their surroundings. Occasionally a ruddy-faced farmer would stop and wave at them as they ploughed on through the heart of the countryside.

Nick wondered what they did for amusement around here. There couldn't be too many nice restaurants or bars, that was for sure. He supposed they didn't know what they were missing; that was why they were so content. Barry and the Kraut were busy talking about football – Barry was telling the guy about their great odyssey to Japan... Jesus, would they ever get tired of it? Nick was beginning to feel pretty tired himself. It wasn't that late, but the travelling could certainly knock it out of you.

Something about the gentle swaying motion of the

train and the constant click-clack of the tracks made him drowsy. He pulled the bed down from over his head and climbed up onto it. The other pair could talk all night for all he cared, but he was going to get some sleep. They were probably in Belarus by now. He hoped they wouldn't have any more passport checks for a few hours at least. He could do with a good night's rest.

Barry found himself apologising for the sphincter symphony being conducted by Nick Dunne-Davis. Jan laughed and shrugged it off at first, but after an hour or so of constant bombardment the joke was definitely wearing thin. They had to leave the window wide open, and the two of them sat there furiously ignoring the frequent eruptions that punctuated the evening air. Barry polished off a rubber ham roll that served as dinner, since there didn't appear to be a dining car on the train.

He decided to do the decent thing and let Jan have one side of the cabin to himself. He slid in under Dunne-Davis's bunk and lay down.

—You are very brave, said Jan.

—Wha'?

Jan pointed up at the sleeping windbag above him.

—Oh, yeah. Good night.

—Good night.

After the obligatory twenty minutes spent wishing he were in bed with Jill, Barry fell asleep. He didn't wake again until the severe-looking fellow in the black trench coat was standing over his bunk.

He looked like something from a Russian spy movie. Jan handed him his German identity card and the guard scanned it scrupulously, running his finger across the photo over and over again. It was as if he was expecting it to come off in his hand, almost hoping that it would, so he could personally be the one to condemn Jan to hard labour for the rest of his natural. What were those places called again? Gulags, or something like that. Barry had read about them somewhere, back in his real life. He had visions of himself and Dunne-Davis in one of them, skinny as supermodels in the biting cold.

The guard muttered something to him in Russian. At least, he supposed it was Russian; it could have been fuckin' Klingon, for all he knew.

—Russki? he barked again.

—Er, no.

—Deutsch?

Barry shook his head blankly. The guard didn't seem to be impressed with his dumb-Paddy routine.

—Here. He shook Dunne-Davis until he almost fell out of the bunk. —Wake up, yeh bollix.

Dunne-Davis looked, bleary-eyed, at the impatient guard. Then he seemed to realise where he was, and Barry could see his senses snap back to him.

—Oh, yah. Right.

He flung his legs over the edge of the bunk, pulled a couple of packs of Marlboro from somewhere and held them out. The guard just stood there, staring at them. Dunne-Davis's hand shook.

Fuckin' brilliant, thought Barry.

After what seemed like an age, the guard finally accepted the smokes without a word. Dunne-Davis lowered himself carefully down to the floor – the man did have a gun, after all, and he looked like he wouldn't need much of an excuse to use it – and motioned discreetly towards the corridor with his head. The big Russian held the door open and let him out. Barry lay back on his bench and exhaled deeply.

They were out there for nearly ten minutes. Barry could hear voices, but couldn't make out a word. Your man seemed to have some English; he must have, if they were talking for that long. Finally, Dunne-Davis came back in and rummaged through the rucksack. Jan appeared to be sleeping; at least, he was lying on his bunk with his back turned to them. Dunne-Davis gingerly removed a small plastic packet of white powder from the rucksack and disappeared again. There was more talking, and what sounded like a laugh from the guard; then Dunne-Davis came back in and climbed up to his bunk.

Barry waited patiently for the news. He waited some more, his patience dwindling. Surely Dunne-Davis wasn't snoring again? Jaysus, he was some can of piss, there was no doubt about it. Barry jumped up and shook him from his slumber. Dunne-Davis stared at him like he had just done the rudest thing in the world.

—Well? demanded Barry.

—It's all sorted, replied Nick, before slipping back into peaceful oblivion.

CHAPTER THIRTEEN

Barry had to wait till Jan went out to the jacks in the morning.

—So what's the story?

Dunne-Davis poked his head over the edge of the bunk to look down at him. He leaned over and made sure the door was closed securely.

—Right. We're sorted until we get to Moscow.

—I guessed tha' much.

—Then, once we're there, we'll be met at the station...

—Wha'? Met by who?

Nick flirted briefly with the idea of pointing out that it was 'by whom', but Barry didn't take kindly to correction by Nick – in fact, Barry didn't take kindly to Nick in general – so he decided, wisely, to let Barry wallow in his own ignorance.

—Don't ask. Friends of Sergei's.

—Who the fuck is Sergei?

—The guard, of course.

—Righ'.

That made sense to Barry.

—He reckons his friends might be interested in our... merchandise.

—Fuck off! But he's a soldier.

—Yah, but they're nearly all involved.

—Wha' d'yeh mean, 'involved'?

—Y'know, they're in the Mafia...the Russian Mafia.

—Righ', said Barry, pretending to understand fully.

He didn't like the sound of it. The place must be really corrupt if even the soldiers were in the Mafia. And what chance would he and Dunne-Davis have, dealing with the likes of them? They were amateurs taking on professional criminals, real bad-ass so-and-sos – not like that DJ tosser back in Amsterdam, or even Doyle's gorillas. They wouldn't get away from these punters as easily.

Dunne-Davis must have read his mind. —But don't worry...

Barry always worried when people said that to him. Especially when they were people like Nick Dunne-Davis.

—...I told them we were IRA.

—You did fuckin' wha'?

Dunne-Davis could be fairly reckless sometimes, but as far as Barry knew, he wasn't completely suicidal.

—I had to. They wouldn't deal with us otherwise.

Barry revised his opinion. Dunne-Davis was suicidal. There was no other explanation.

—You didn't have to say we were in the fuckin' 'RA!

It was going from bad to worse. Barry lay back and covered his eyes with his arm. Why had he listened to Dunne-Davis? True, it would have been tough going on the bike, but at least they'd only have had one psychopathic gangster to deal with. Now they could have a whole army of them to worry about.

Any of the blokes he knew in the IRA would kneecap you for even thinking about dealing drugs. That's if you were lucky. He'd made a point of steering well clear of them at home. They were dangerous, in the same way that swimming with sharks if you were covered in fish guts was dangerous. There were a couple of them in that Concerned Parents Against Drugs crowd. Most of them really were concerned parents, but Barry knew one bloke in particular who took his concern that little bit further – like to the point of cutting a dealer's thumbs off with garden clippers.

Not that Barry had any sympathy for dealers. They were scum. These guys dealt in heroin and human misery. Dunne-Davis was just a spoiled rich kid doing it for the thrill. Barry didn't know much about cocaine. As far as he knew, it was mainly yuppies used it, but it did seem to be getting more popular among ordinary people too. It didn't turn people into zombies, like heroin, but it was still drugs.

Back in a warehouse in Dublin, Johnno was applying a blindfold to Sasha's face. The bruises were yellow and black now. They were healing nicely. She wouldn't have any permanent scarring, but that didn't make him feel much better. Doyle hadn't taken any interest in her recently; it was like he was satisfied that she didn't know anything. She seemed nervous, even though she was doing her damnedest to appear cool. Johnno tied the blindfold firmly, but not too tightly, behind her head. He thought about smoothing her hair down with his hands, but it felt wrong. It would be hypocritical.

—Don't worry, he said as softly as he could.

Her shoulders loosened, but she was still scared. He led her by the arm – the skin was incredibly soft against his rough palm – out to the Jag. He opened the back door and eased her head under the roof.

—Where are we going? she asked, when he turned the engine over.

—Don't worry, he said again.

Sasha stopped talking then. Whatever her fate was to be, she accepted it – for the moment, anyhow. She knew that, when that final moment came and they held the gun to her head, she'd struggle. It was human nature. Something deep inside her still wanted to live, and that instinct would burn until something or someone finally extinguished it. For now, she tried to relax her taut muscles and did her best not to think about what was to come.

If only he'd tell her, it wouldn't be so bad. Even if he said: —Look, this is it. At least she'd know. She could use whatever short time she had left to prepare, if that was possible, for what was to come. It was the uncertainty that was torturing her. She couldn't stand it much longer.

Barry had hardly said a word all day. What was the point? Jan was reading a trade magazine about lawnmowers or something. That must be his business, or maybe he was just in the market for a new one. Barry didn't bother asking. Dunne-Davis was reading his Barely Legal behind an old newspaper he'd found. Then he got up and started fidgeting around the cabin.

—What are yeh doin'? (Barry resisted adding 'yeh gobshite', purely out of respect for Jan.)

—Looking for my razor, replied Nick.

He found it and ducked out to the toilets at the end of the carriage. One of them was free. He removed his T-shirt and ran the hot tap. Nothing happened. He tried the cold. At least that was working. He drenched his torso and scrubbed furiously. Then he did his face. He sprayed a good dollop of shaving foam (borrowed from Jan) onto his hand and lathered it around his three-day growth. Jesus, his eyes looked like shit! There were black bags underneath them, and the skin was in dire need of a couple of slices of cucumber, at the very least. A full facial would be ideal, but it would have to wait. The blunt razor struggled through the tangled stubble, pulling it out more than anything else. Nick almost had to gouge it out of his cheeks, and the bit around his mouth was agony.

—Fuck!

Another red patch sprouted blood on his neck. This was impossible. He finished as best he could and splashed water over his blood-pocked cheeks. It stung like mad. At least he didn't smell quite as bad any more.

He made his way back to the carriage and sat down. It was only a couple of hours to Moscow.

The car was definitely stopping. Sasha reckoned they'd

been travelling for about fifteen minutes, but it was very difficult to say. The blindfold disorientated her. They could be anywhere by now. She felt Johnno climb out of the car – it actually lifted slightly, with his weight gone; then he opened her door and helped her out. She could feel what seemed to be a concrete path beneath her feet, so she reckoned that he hadn't taken her up the mountains. That was a positive, hopefully.

There was a jangle of keys, and one of them went into a door. He led her into a building and over to a sofa.

—Stay here.

She could hear him drawing the curtains. Then he went out to another room and did the same. She heard his steps on stairs, and the same sound from upstairs. What was he doing? There was nothing to stop her from tearing off the blindfold and running outside – nothing but fear.

His steps coming back down the stairs put the thought out of her mind. It was replaced by a more disturbing one. What if he had brought her here to rape her? She'd caught him watching her before, when he thought she wasn't looking. Well, he could forget about that. She'd rather he killed her. She didn't care how attractive he was; that had nothing to do with it. And no matter what people had thought of her or called her in the past, she wasn't going to lie there and be violated by anyone. But if that was what he wanted, why hadn't he just done it in the warehouse, where no one could hear? Anyone in the same postal area would hear her if he tried it now. She'd make sure of that.

—OK, yeh can take the blindfold off.

She removed it and squinted in the half-light. It looked like a suburban house, the terraced kind she'd seen on Coronation Street.

—This your place?

He didn't say anything. He just walked to the door and motioned for her to follow. When she got to the top of the stairs, he was waiting. She heard the sound of running water. He wasn't going to drown her, was he?

Johnno held the bathroom door open. The bath was filling up with hot water. Sasha went in, expecting to be grabbed by the hair and plunged in head-first. Instead, the door closed behind her.

—You've got fifteen minutes, said a voice behind the door.

Then he went downstairs and she heard the television come on.

She looked around, half-expecting some kind of trap. But there was nothing. She let her dirty clothes fall to the floor and turned off the taps. He'd even put bubble bath in! It was the best soak she'd ever had. The water caressed her skin and eased her aching limbs. She lay there until he came up and knocked on the door.

—I'll be out in a minute!

—There's some clean...clothes and that for you out here.

She waited till she heard him retreating to the living room again before she got out out. The fluffy towel enveloped her whole body. She tentatively turned the door handle and peeked out. There was a Dunne's Stores bag on the floor. She dragged it in and inspected the contents. One black bra and one pair of knickers, also black. She checked the labels: the bra was a size too big and the pants were a size too small.

—Typical, she muttered.

They weren't exactly sexy lacy numbers, but they weren't the worst ones she'd ever seen. Maybe she'd start buying her underwear in Dunne's if she ever made it out of all this. Then she laughed at the absurdity of it.

There was a pink top and a black skirt that revealed a lot more of her legs than was strictly necessary. Maybe he wasn't so innocent after all. But it was the last item that really shocked her: a box of tampons. Was he a New Age sensitive guy after all? A thug with a heart? She had to admire him. It was more touching than any of the extravagant gifts Nick Dunne-Davis, or anyone else, had ever given her. This time, there was actually thought involved.

She finished dressing and went back downstairs.

—Ready.

Johnno got up and turned off the TV.

—What do you think? she said. She was going to give him a twirl, but resisted. She was still his prisoner, after all.

He glanced at her quickly and turned away. —Grand. Let's get you back before himself notices.

Was he actually blushing? She couldn't believe it.

The train had been struggling slowly through the immense jungle of high-rise apartments for the past hour. It reminded Barry of Gotham City.

—Dublin'll be like tha' in ten years, he assured Dunne-Davis.

When the train finally ground to a halt, they picked up their meagre belongings and said their goodbyes to Jan.

—Good luck with your journey – and with the football, Jan said, smiling wryly.

They stepped onto the platform of Moskva Station. It was enormous. Black-market money-changers swooped around them, kindly offering to take euros, dollars or anything else they might have off their hands. Barry went to get the Honda from the cargo carriage. He checked the saddle; it hadn't been tampered with.

Dunne-Davis was kicking around nervously when he got back to him.

—Any sign of them yet?

—Nah, said Nick. —It's hard to say, though. It could be anyone.

Barry saw them first. Despite Dunne-Davis's prediction, they turned out to be anything but inconspicuous. One of them was small and wore a black leather jacket over a black T-shirt and black jeans. He must be boilin' in this heat, thought Barry, who could feel himself starting to perspire lightly. The other fella was taller, with a goatee, and he too was dressed in all black.

They didn't even ask for names.

—You have it?

Dunne-Davis nodded dumbly. They were completely out of their depth. These guys were the real deal. Dunne-Davis nodded to Barry to produce the rucksack; he prised it free from the cavity and held it out.

The smaller guy looked inside and nodded.

—Follow me.

They started after him, but he turned to Barry, restraining him with a finger to the chest.

—Not you.

Barry didn't know what to say. There was no point in arguing. He shrugged and handed the bag to Dunne-Davis. He watched them melt into the crowds that thronged the station and found himself hoping, for the first time, that it wouldn't be the last time he saw Nick Dunne-Davis. There had been real fear in Dunne-Davis' eyes. And Barry couldn't say he blamed him.

He decided to venture out and take a quick look at Moscow; it wasn't as if he got the chance every day of the week. Besides, there was no telling when Dunne-Davis would be back. The question was if, rather than when. He waited until he was well outside before firing up the bike. The last thing they needed was for him to be arrested while Dunne-Davis was being held by the Mafia. He didn't know which of them would be worse off. From what he'd heard, the police and the Mafia were probably the same shower anyway.

He whizzed around to the only place he'd ever heard of in Moscow – Red Square. And he had to admit it was impressive – very fuckin' impressive, with the Kremlin behind it and the dome-topped towers rising all around it. It was the sheer scale of it that was so incredible. St Basil's Cathedral was spectacular. Barry just stood outside and gaped at the sheer wonder of it. It was like fuckin' Disneyland, only it wasn't made out of plastic or whatever else it was that Disneyland used. Another thing that struck him was the amount of building going on. There were cranes everywhere; the whole city looked like a huge building site. He remembered hearing of lads back home, chippies and sparkies and that, who came out here to work on big jobs. Now he knew why.

He glanced up at the huge clock tower beyond in the Kremlin. He'd spent over an hour just exploring on his own. It was probably time to go back.

When he got back to the station, Dunne-Davis was waiting for him. He was sitting on a bench, staring at the ground. At least he was still alive. But he wasn't his usual cocky self.

Barry sat down beside him. He tried to sound as positive as possible.

—Well?

Dunne-Davis looked at him out of the corner of his eye.
—Not good.

Barry wasn't sure how to broach it delicately, so he didn't bother trying. —Yeh fucked it up, didn't yeh?

Dunne-Davis didn't answer. That wasn't a good sign.
—Wha' happened?

Finally Dunne-Davis turned to face him.
—They took the lot. I was lucky to walk out of there.
—They took it, or they bought it?
—Yah.
—Which, but?
—Well, they took all of it and paid...
—Yeah?
—Not a lot.
—How much?
—Put it this way: by the time we get home, there won't be enough change left to buy Doyle a new suit.

Barry wasn't exactly surprised; he'd been expecting as much. In one way he was glad to get rid of the stuff. And he didn't want anything out of it. It was dirty money. But still, the fact remained that they were worse off than when they'd started. In retrospect, it had been a stupid plan anyway. Cutting the stuff with flour was exactly like trying to water down whiskey and sell it to a pub: you were never going to offload it to people who knew what they were doing – not at a profit, anyway. But they had to try something, anything, that might get them off the hook with Doyle. And they had tried – tried, but failed.

So here they were, sitting in a train station in Moscow with their sole hope of redemption gone. They had no one to blame but themselves. So Barry did.

—Yeh fuckin' eejit, yeh, he said to Dunne-Davis, just in case he wasn't aware of the fact. It helped a bit, but not as much as he'd hoped.

They were stuck between the devil and the deep blue sea. At least, they would be when they reached the sea, in six and a half days' time.

—CHAPTER FOURTEEN—

Michael was listening to Marian Finucane on the radio. Normally, he only watched the news on the telly for the young ones presenting it, but not any more. Now he was far more interested in the content of the programming.

Marian had Keith Wood on, talking about what it meant to represent your country.

—Now, d'yeh hear that? He's captain of the Irish rugby team. Just as good a player in his own right as Roy Keane – probably better, even.

—I know who he is, said Declan. —Baldy bastard, he added, to illustrate the point.

It was impossible. Not matter how hard Michael tried to make him understand, Declan just couldn't see it. At first Michael had thought he was doing it to be rebellious, but it went way beyond that. Declan actually believed that Keane was in the right. He bought into all the crap about only wanting the best for his country and personality clashes with McCarthy. Michael was beginning to despair. This was an important issue. What kind of a father would he be if he didn't try and make his son understand the value of team play?

Declan always went his own way, anyway. It was probably because he was the youngest. He had never been interested in football or anything like that, so Michael hadn't pushed him. At the same time, he admired the stance Declan was taking. Not the stance itself, more the fact that he was confident enough in his own judgement to stick by it – even if it was completely misguided. Jesus, it was like the Civil War all over again. Dev and Collins had been replaced by Keane and McCarthy. The whole country was at it. You were either a Keane man or a McCarthy man.

Whatever chance Ireland had of doing well was ruined, that was for sure. Whether Keane went home or stayed didn't really matter. He'd caused so much grief that the tournament was over for Ireland before it had even started. Michael was starting to get sick of the whole thing himself.

Declan was busy lecturing him on how McCarthy was the root cause of the whole thing. He was convinced that Keane had been forced into a corner and had no choice but to leave.

—And if the rest of them were half as professional, they'd walk as well. Keane is the ultimate pro. He shouldn't have to compromise his standards for a shower like the FAI.

Then Eamon Dunphy came on the radio and started talking about what a magnificent human being Roy Keane was. Michael thought he heard him actually use the word 'perfect' before he switched the radio off. It was too much, even from a header like Dunphy. He decided to change the subject.

—And what have you planned for the day, Jill?

—Oh, just a walk down to Sandymount this afternoon.

—Getting' very fond of the oul' walks, wha'? he said, but she didn't answer. She seemed a bit distant lately.

Relations between Barry and Nick were at an all-time low. They sat opposite each other in the four-bed train compartment, furiously avoiding eye contact.

The compartment was actually quite comfortable. Dunne-Davis had sorted them out with the carriage conductor. There had been a queue a mile long back at the station, and everyone in it had been showing passports at the ticket office. They had decided to bypass it and try their luck with the train official. He'd been surprisingly obliging, except when Nick had discreetly offered him the small quantity of cocaine he had left. The man hadn't a word of English, but his whole demeanour had instantly frosted over when he saw the little bag of white dust. Things had improved a bit when Dunne-Davis produced ten thousand roubles from the rucksack, and a further two thousand for the bike. Two packs of Marlboros had sealed the deal, and they had been led to a second-class sleeping compartment, which they had to themselves. There was a 'Reserved' sign on the door, and Barry suspected that it was reserved for any 'guests' the conductor might want to accommodate. The only problem with the privacy it afforded them was just that: it was private, so there would be nobody but the two of them in it – a prospect neither man particularly relished.

They'd been travelling a good three hours or more when Dunne-Davis finally broke.

—You don't like me much, do you?

Barry continued staring out the window.

—Look, those guys were Solsnetskaya – the most powerful arm of the Russian mob. I couldn't exactly bargain with them. They made me an offer I couldn't refuse.

He lapsed back into silence. Barry was the next one to break it.

—I wouldn't be mixed up in any o' this if I hadn't gone around to the garage that night, he said bitterly.

—And do you remember why you came around, do you? demanded Nick.

It was funny. Barry had actually forgotten what he was doing there in the first place. He remembered Dunne-Davis calling him with his knickers in a twist.

—A certain piece of vandalism? Nick reminded him. —Not to mention defamation of character?

Now he remembered.

—I didn't do tha'.

—Ah, come on! How thick am I?

—As thick as bottled shite, but that's not the point. I'm tellin' yeh, I didn't do it!

—Who did, then? Tell me that!

Nick would have to be careful if he was to avoid another puck in the face.

—My brother done it! Righ'? To get back at you for firin' me.

Nick calmed down a bit and managed to soften his tone.

—That wasn't my decision. I was only the messenger. I'm...sorry it happened.

—You're sorry? Ha! I've lost everything. And now whatever hope I had of gettin' it back is gone.

Nick said nothing. It was the first time he'd really thought about how much Barry had to lose. At least if Doyle did him, Nick realised, nobody would lose too much sleep over it. He wasn't married. He didn't have kids. Even his parents didn't seem to care very much – not that he blamed them: he'd already caused them more pain than anyone should have to put up with in a lifetime. He didn't even have any brothers or sisters. It was just him. His funeral would be a stiff, formal affair. His drinking buddies would have a few light ales in his honour and slowly forget he had ever existed. He expected it would actually be a kind of relief to his parents.

But Barry was different. Nick had never really considered what it meant to have a long-term partner waiting back at home. And he had a kid – a girl, wasn't it? Barry had a life, that was what he had. He was four or five years younger than Nick in chronological terms, but in every other respect he was light years ahead of him. It was a strange experience for Nick. He'd never felt anything like it. This, he realised, must be what guilt felt like.

Jill held the umbrella over her head as she crossed the bridge into Ringsend village. The rain was only a light drizzle, but she didn't want it making her hair go all fuzzy.

It was her second time meeting him. The first time had been a bit of a letdown, but this was going to be better. She had a good feeling about it.

She thought about what Barry would say if he knew what she was up to. He wouldn't approve, she was certain of that. But she had to do something while he was away, something to take her mind off things, to keep her from screaming — just opening her mouth and letting it all out from somewhere deep inside her. She walked past the endless traffic that choked the Strand Road all the way to Merrion gates and beyond. She thought of what Joyce had said about the paralysis of living in Dublin, the feeling that everything was stagnant, going nowhere. Was it Ulysses? She couldn't remember. She would have loved to study English at university if she'd had the chance. Joyce had meant it metaphorically, of course, but what would he say if he were alive today? His twentieth-century vision had become a twenty-first-century reality. You literally couldn't move. The city streets were constipated, like giant, clogged intestines. Jill hurried past the stationary motorists, bitter, stressed and imprisoned in their single steel cells, each one a single cog in a chain that stretched for miles and held them fast in its grip.

Jill opened the gate and made her way nervously up to the front door. She swallowed hard and took a deep breath to steady her nerves. Her hand was shaking as she rang the bell. The sound of his footsteps on the old floorboards made her heart jump. He opened the door.

The train was stopping again. It did this fairly regularly, and you could get off and stretch your legs for a few minutes. Barry had retreated into silent sulking mode, but at least the atmosphere wasn't as tense as it had been.

—You coming out for a bit? said Nick.

Barry shook his head. Nick jumped down onto the tracks and soaked up a bit of comforting sunshine. He hadn't been near a sunbed since they left, but his tan was holding its own from all the natural rays. He ran his fingers through his fringe. It could definitely do with a trim.

One of the Russian chaps came over and attempted to strike up a conversation. It wasn't a particularly intellectual one, since his English was as good as Nick's Russian, but there was one word they both understood, so they stood there repeating it to each other in various tones.

—Vodka? said Nick.

—Vodka! Da! enthused his new friend.

He held up eight fingers and produced a large bottle.

Nick scratched his chin for a bit and pointed to the bottle. —Vodka, he reasserted, and held up four fingers. His Russian friend laughed and gave him an 'I have ten children to feed' look.

Eventually they settled amicably on five fingers, and Nick hopped back on board. When he got back to the compartment Barry was still staring out the window. Nick twisted the cap off the bottle and offered it to him.

—Vodka? he repeated yet again.

Barry looked at it for a long time before taking it.

—Why not?

—Are you all right? he asked awkwardly.

—I'm fine, said Jill, brushing away the tears and his offer of a tissue. She felt terrible, like she was making a show of herself.

—Er, don't you like it? he asked. He couldn't have been more than twenty-one, fresh out of college. He was still wet behind the ears.

—It's beautiful, she whispered.

And it was. It wasn't a huge house, but it was exactly what she wanted. The view over the bay was stunning in the evening sun. There was even a patio, and a good-sized garden out the back where Sarah could play. She didn't dare to ask how much it was. She felt so silly.

She had no right to be there.

—The auction is on next month in our showrooms. We're guiding seven hundred, said the auctioneer.

Seven hundred thousand euro. It was an obscene amount of money for a three-bedroom semi-detached house. Jill knew she was crazy even to be looking at it. Even if Barry doubled his salary and she was working full-time, they'd never be able to afford it. They'd have to win the Lotto. How did anyone afford to live in these places? Even five years ago, she and Barry would have been able to afford a little place of their own, but they had been young and they'd wanted to save some money. It was ironic: now that they had a bit tucked away, it wasn't even worth talking about as a deposit. They'd missed the boat.

Jill almost ran over the agent in her hurry to get outside. The tears were streaming down her face. The poor young fella didn't know what to say.

—Would you like a brochure...?

But she was gone, practically running back towards Ringsend, back to the house they had to share with Barry's family – if he ever got back to share it with them.

It was getting dark by the time they reached the Urals. The train was well on its way, and so were they. They crossed the massive Kama River and drank another toast.

—Russia! proposed Barry.

—Russia! agreed Nick, taking his turn on the bottle.

—Ireland! suggested Barry.

—Ireland! agreed Nick.

It was beginning to sound like the Eurovision Song Contest, Nick thought, until Barry jumped to his feet and roared: —Japan!

—Japan! repeated Nick.

Barry started singing 'On the One Road', and Nick changed his mind about the comparison. The singing was dreadful, but it was nowhere near as bad as the Eurovision.

They were joined at one stage by Paul, who claimed to be the carriage's Russian guide for the journey. He had a drink and sang a Russian song for them. They made it through most of the bottle before passing out on their beds fully clothed.

The motion of the train woke Barry. There was sweat all down his back; the T-shirt was stuck to him.

—Oh, Jaysus...

His head was pounding. It was like a sauna in the little cabin. The air was close and heavy with the smell of drink and farts. He reached up and opened the window to let the fresh air in. Then he closed the curtains to block out the glaring sunlight and collapsed back onto his bed. His tongue felt like a strip of sandpaper, and his stomach heaved back and forth with the train. He picked up the large bottle of water from the bedside table and knocked it back; it was warm and stale, but he forced himself to swallow a few mouthfuls before crashing back onto his pillow. He rolled onto a cooler part of the sheets and closed his eyes again. That was better. He was bursting for a piss, his bladder felt like it was going to give way when he lay on his tummy, but it could wait. He rolled onto his side and drifted off again for another hour.

The next time he woke, he was alone. Dunne-Davis wasn't in his bunk. Barry eased himself up and drank some more water. Then he noticed the rucksack at the end of Dunne-Davis's bed. He had a quick look inside it. It was stuffed with roubles, thousands of the fuckers, maybe hundreds of thousands. Probably worth fuck all, though. Not that Barry wanted any of it. He had only ever wanted the money so he could buy his way out of Doyle's debt; now that that was impossible, he couldn't care less about it. Dunne-Davis could buy whatever he wanted with it when they got home. He wouldn't have long to enjoy it.

He struggled out of the bed, pulled on his jeans and runners and made for the jacks. After a long and messy piss (most of it went onto the floor, due to the windy track), he turned on the cold tap and drenched himself under it. He wedged his head into the sink and let the water flow right down his neck and onto his back. It wasn't as cold as he would have liked, but it was still nice.

His head was beginning to clear and his tummy was rumbling. That extra bit of kip had sorted him out. At least he didn't suffer from trainsickness as well as seasickness. He made his way down to the dining car. The train was mainly full of Russians, but Barry reckoned there were a few Spaniards and French people, as well as some Scandinavians. He couldn't be sure, though; they all just sounded foreign, and he was basing his guesses on appearances more than anything. Dunne-Davis was having breakfast alone. Barry went up and got some scrambled eggs. They were revolting, but he was too hungry to care.

—How's the head? enquired Dunne-Davis.

—OK, Barry mumbled between slurps. The eggs were so runny and wet that only about half of them were reaching their intended target. The rest fell short and clung precariously to Barry's face before sliding slowly onto his T-shirt. Dunne-Davis was appalled, but he was learning when to keep his mouth shut.

—I've been thinking, he said eventually.

—I thought I could see smoke comin' out of your ears.

Dunne-Davis let it go. He was definitely learning.

—What are you going to do when you get back?

Barry continued· plastering his face with egg. He was practically wearing his breakfast by now. He was completely aware of how it must look, but he didn't give a shit. Anything that offended Dunne-Davis was OK by him.

—I've been thinkin' about tha' too, he said, pushing the plate away from him and wiping his mouth with his hand.

—And? said Nick, trying to hide his revulsion.

—And I don't know if I am goin' back.

He waited for the information to sink in.

—I was thinkin' about gettin' Jill and Sarah out altogether.

—You mean emigrating?

—Suppose you could call it tha'.

—Where to?

—Dunno. Maybe Australia. Somewhere as far away from all tha' mess as possible.

Dunne-Davis nodded. —It makes sense. I'll probably have to do the same.

He really did feel bad now, for screwing up Barry's life and dragging him down with him. It was all just a big misunderstanding, really – the switched tyre and all of that. If only, Nick thought, he had had the time to explain it to Doyle. He could have given him the merchandise there and then and had a pint and a laugh about it – well, maybe the pint and the laugh were stretching things a bit, but at least he could have sorted it out. One simple cock-up had caused all this. And once Benny Doyle had done his Woody Woodpecker impression into that tree...well, all bets were off. Doyle was almost obliged to do Nick, and most likely Barry as well. It was much too dangerous to risk hanging around to find out.

Nick knew he would never have walked away from it unless something like this had happened. He wondered if he had learned his lesson. Would he do it again, given the chance? It was a tough call. There was a lot of money involved. But, up until now, he had only been putting himself at risk. Now his actions had hurt other people, and he had to take responsibility for them.

—That money I got from the Mafia—

He was interrupted abruptly. —I don't want it, said Barry.

—But what about your plan?

—I'll work somethin' out.

—Well, I can't keep it all for myself. You've earned your half.

—I've earned nothin'! Now I told yeh: I don't want nothin' to do with it.

—You're a fool if you don't.

It had to be said.

—Think of your family. They're the innocent victims in all of this. Take it for their sake, if not for your own.

Barry continued staring out the window. Nick knew he was getting through to him.

—There's enough for both of us to get away and get set up. Just not enough for us to stay.

Barry looked at him.

—Think about it, suggested Nick.

—CHAPTER FIFTEEN—

Over the next couple of days, Nick could tell that Barry was considering it. There was feck-all else to think about as the train wound its way towards Lake Baikal, which Paul had informed them was the deepest lake in the world.

—How do they know, but? Barry had asked.

—They just...know.

The views were stunning, and even Barry's spirits lifted. The lake was magnificent; it was more like an ocean. Waves whipped across it, and they could actually see right down to the bottom at the edges, when the train passed along its shores. The frequent tunnels made it more of an adventure than passing through the seemingly endless crop-filled steppes of the previous few days. It was definitely dawning on Barry that there was a big wide world out there. He hoped that Jill and Sarah would see it that way. They didn't have much choice, if they wanted to be together.

He thought about things like that a lot, over those few days. And he thought about the final destination of their current odyssey. There was no point in being miserable. He'd never have this chance again, so he might as well make the most of it. There'd be plenty of time to worry about the other stuff. He'd have the rest of his life to think about it. Admittedly, that might not be all that long, which was all the more reason to enjoy the next part of the trip.

Johnno knocked on the office door before entering. He immediately recognised the man inside with Tony Doyle. Vinny Purcell was one of the soldiers from the Byrne gang on the north side of the city. Johnno had been wondering how long it would take Doyle to replace Benny.

—Johnno, this is Vinny Purcell, said Doyle.

Vinny offered his hand. —How's it goin'?

—All righ', said Johnno.

He was young and hungry, just the way Johnno himself had been at that age. Doyle had always had an eye for recruitment, with the exception of that clown Benny. But he was family; that was the only reason he had been in.

—Vinny's goin' to be joinin' us for a while, explained Doyle.

Johnno knew what that meant. Vinny would be given a job to do in the first couple of weeks. It was like a trial. If he fucked it up, he was out on his ear; if he took care of it, he was in. Johnno didn't know much about him, which meant he was probably competent enough.

He wondered whether Doyle had let Vinny know about the Dunne-Davis job. Probably not. The fewer people who knew about that, the better. Appearances were all-important in this game – it was all about the illusion of power; Doyle wouldn't want it getting around that he was losing his touch. Nobody knew about the yuppie who had done Tony Doyle out of a million euro. Even Benny's accident had been brushed under the carpet as a hazard of the job. The Guards hadn't a clue, either. As long as Doyle kept the dodgy ones sweet, they didn't ask too many questions. They'd already written off the Herbert Park incident as joyriding. So the only ones who were really clued in were Johnno and Doyle. And that was just the way Doyle wanted it.

Nick sprinted down the corridor. He had to sidestep an old Russian lady, which almost cost him dearly: he could feel the worst of it coming on. When he reached the toilets, he was dismayed to find them both occupied. He had a vital decision to make: did he stay and wait, or try for the ones in the next carriage? There was no guarantee they wouldn't be engaged too.

It was his third visit to the toilet in the past hour. Where was it all coming from? In fairness, it didn't take a genius to figure it out. The food was horrific. They weren't even sure what it was, most of the time. At one point they had found their pathway to the dining car blocked by a door that refused to budge; when the obstacle behind it had finally shifted, they had been amazed to find a live sheep on the other side of the door.

—At least it's fresh, Barry had said.

It had been a bit odd eating the thing for dinner that evening. At least they knew what it was, though. Most of the time they just held their noses and swallowed.

Nick waddled back to the compartment and eased himself slowly into a seated position.

—Arse like a Japanese flag, wha'? said Barry. He was enjoying this.

Nick didn't answer. Instead, he went out to find Paul, to see if he had anything that might help. Thankfully, he did. Nick wanted to kiss him when he produced the Arret packet. He broke out a couple of pills and handed them to Nick.

—From my personal stock, he told him.

Nick was expecting to be hit with a large bill, but Paul didn't want anything. Nick thrust a fistful of roubles into his hand despite his protests. He even managed a smile at Barry when he got back. The man was a wonder, Nick thought: he had a stomach of cast iron. Nick lay down and let out a contented sigh. He could feel himself tightening up like a nut already.

Johnno was shaking like a leaf. He wasn't looking forward to this one bit. The old warehouse door made its usual nerve-chilling scrape across the floor, to add to his woes. How would he tell her? She was waiting for him; her face actually lit up when she saw it was him.

—Morning, she chirped.

She was amazing. She'd been here almost two weeks, locked up like an animal, beaten and degraded, yet she still had a sparkle in her eye.

—Mornin', he managed weakly.

She sensed it in him straight away. Was it that obvious?

—What is it?

It was difficult for him to look at her. But he didn't have any choice. He had to be honest with her. He tried to compose his voice, and failed.

—I have a proposal for yeh, he said.

When Nick and Barry finally got to Vladivostok, it was a nightmare. The Russian Mafia were everywhere. They had to pay three different taxes just to get themselves and the Honda 50 out of the station.

—Bastards, mumbled Barry, waiting till they were well out of earshot.

At the rate they were going, they would be out of money by lunchtime. Not that that was necessarily a bad thing: they figured the food would get them eventually, if the Mafia didn't.

They rode down to the huge port. Floating factories littered the horizon, enormous hulks of Japanese and Russian steel that scoured the ocean for fish. Those were their best hope. Dunne-Davis tried his luck on the Russian leviathans first, but they wanted big money. And Barry didn't trust the bastards, anyway. He'd never seen such a corrupt shower in his life. They tried some of the Japanese trawlers, but they had even less luck there. The Japanese wouldn't even talk to them; they just ignored them, or got agitated and forced them to leave.

Without passports, they were screwed. It was a fact. They'd come all this way across Europe and Russia for nothing. Nobody was willing to smuggle them on board. They were stranded eight thousand miles from Moscow, and a million miles from reality. Barry felt betrayed. They were so close; to be tripped up at the final hurdle like this was more than he could bear. He lashed out with his foot, catching the Honda on its front tyre.

—Bollix it, anyway!

The bike keeled over onto its side from the force of the kick. For a minute he thought he'd broken his toe, but the pain soon subsided. He stood looking at the bike that had helped to take them so close to the promised land.

He wasn't the only one.

—Nice motorcycle.

Barry whipped around. A little Japanese fisherman was standing behind him.

—Er, thanks.

—You want sell?

Barry looked at Dunne-Davis. He knew exactly what the bastard was thinking. He was thinking the same thing himself.

Michael settled into his armchair. He still had the dressing-gown on, but he had made sure he got up early enough to make himself a cup of tea. He wanted to be in full command of his faculties for this one. Today was the big day, or at least the big morning – seven o'clock in the morning, to be exact. Ireland versus Cameroon. The Keane debacle could be forgotten for a couple of hours; for now, it was only the football that mattered. Jill flapped into the living room in her slippers, holding Sarah, who was wearing her Man United pyjamas and dragging her teddy by the arm. She was really only interested in watching David Beckham ponce about for England, but still. Even Declan had struggled out of the bed to watch.

—They'll be hammered without Keane, was his most constructive comment.

Michael felt for a minute that the little so-and-so

actually wanted them to lose, in a twisted kind of way. Then he could say, —I told you so. That made Michael want them to win it even more – to prove that they were more than a one-man team. Deep down, he reckoned it was beyond them; but he would rather support a team of committed lads, willing to do or die for Ireland, than a collection of prima donnas like Keane, even if that meant supporting a losing side rather than a winning one. And he really meant it.

—We want volunteers, not conscripts, he replied. He was determined not to rise to Declan. Besides, he knew damn well that if Ireland did win Declan would be cheering as loud as anyone.

But Declan kept baiting him. —No matter wha' happens, Ireland won't live up to their potential. D'you know wha' the most revealin' thing about all this is? The fact tha' they're just happy to be there. Tha' might be enough for most of them, but not for Keane. He wanted to win. And isn't tha' the whole point?

Michael ignored him.

The first half wasn't going exactly as planned. Mboma scored easily after some dodgy defending. Going into the break, Ireland was one-nil down and lucky to be nil.

—I told yeh, mumbled Declan.

—Shut up, you.

—We've no shape.

Michael doubted he even knew what that meant. He sounded like one of those pundits repeating the clichés: 'It's not over till the final whistle,' 'It only takes a second to score a goal' and all of that rubbish.

Then the second half kicked off, and so did the Irish team. Maybe it really was 'a game of two halves'. It was like they'd spent the first forty-five minutes running out all of the cobwebs from the previous week. Passes suddenly started finding teammates, and there was purpose and organisation in the defence. In short, they started playing like a team again, and when Matt Holland drove a peach of a shot into the bottom corner Michael nearly hit the roof.

—YESSS! he screamed, in unison with Declan and four million others.

Declan even hugged him for a split second. It was pure euphoria. Michael felt...alive. For the first time in years, he actually felt something, other than pain or anger. And what a thing it was.

Across town, Tony Doyle was mopping up the last of his fry-up with a slice of fresh batch. It was the business. His doctor would go spare if he saw him, but he had cause for celebration. Ireland had just secured their first point of the tournament – and, more importantly, the first part of the bet was in the bag. Another draw against Germany and the job would be as good as done. If they couldn't beat the Saudis, they shouldn't be out there.

Five points from the group: that was the bet. Johnno had suggested that Keane's absence should lengthen the odds to twenties, and Casey's Bookmakers hadn't argued – particularly since Johnno had taken Vinny Purcell along with him. Vinny had offered to extract the bookie's teeth with a pair of pliers, but that hadn't been necessary. At least the lad was showing a bit of initiative. He might make a decent soldier yet. Doyle had a little job he'd been saving that would sort out whether or not Vinny was a genuine prospect.

Doyle skewered a plump sausage with his fork and folded it into the bread. The butter melted over it in his mouth. Fuck it; the odd fry never hurt anyone. And if he had to eat muesli and yoghurt for the rest of his life, he might as well be dead anyway.

Sasha wasn't as surprised as Johnno had imagined.

—So, what d'yeh think? He could hardly contain himself.

—I don't have much of a choice, do I?

She didn't sound too pissed off.

—Yes, yeh do, he said.

She cocked her head at an angle and regarded the pigeons nesting above them in the rafters. He couldn't work out what she was thinking.

Then she looked him straight in the eye and smiled.

—OK, I'll do it.

He wanted to kiss her. He'd been dreading what she might say, but it really was the only way, despite what he had said about her having a choice.

Her disappearance had finally made the newspapers. Nick had rung work to say he was suffering from a particularly nasty viral infection, and he had also claimed that he had had a row with Barry and fired him on the spot – so that just left Sasha. Officially, she was the only one missing. And Doyle couldn't allow her to be traced to him.

So this was their chance. It was now or never. And, after a moment, Johnno did kiss her – or rather, she kissed him. She kissed him for so long that he knew it had been the right decision. Now all they had to do was get past Doyle.

Barry had reluctantly agreed to exchange the Honda 50 for their passage to Tokyo. He'd been meaning to change the plug, and the shocks had taken a bit of a hammering from all the off-roading they'd been doing, but apart from that she was in perfect nick. She was a classic. It was like losing a limb, after all the work and love he'd put into restoring her and adding the unique modifications; all those nights he'd spent out in the yard, freezing his bollix off. Sometimes his fingers had been so cold he could hardly hold a wrench, but he'd kept at it.

They'd nurtured each other for years. The bike was the only thing he could really call his own. Everything else he did was for Jill and Sarah; every penny earned, every moment spare was invested into their happiness.

And he wouldn't have had it any other way. But everyone needs an outlet. There was the football, of course, but he had been reduced to a mere spectator since the injury. It wasn't the same. It was passive. The bike was different. It had been a dead thing, and he had breathed life into it. It was his hands that had given her a new engine – a new heart. It was his brain that had worked out the parts needed to make her ride and handle like a Ducati. He had given birth to her. And now his baby was being taken away from him.

He took one last look and covered her up with the tarpaulin. At least it would keep the salt water off her. A gnarled hand rested on his shoulder.

—You no worry. I give her good home.

It was Kata. He smiled knowingly at Barry, then waved cheerfully at the young Japanese man coming on board.

—Basho!

Kata rattled off something to the young man, who listened intently and then turned to Barry.

—Irish? he said, opening his eyes wide in apparent amazement.

Barry nodded. Basho bowed slightly and grabbed his hand, pumping it hard. He had an amazingly powerful grip for such a small man. Barry guessed he was about eighteen, but it was hard to tell.

—You hear result?

Barry's jaw dropped. The fuckin' Cameroon match! It must have been played by now. —Ireland an' Cameroon?

—Yes.

—Who won?

—You no know?

—No!

This was unbearable. If he hadn't known better, he would have sworn that Basho was taking the mickey out of him.

—You want know?

—Yes, course I bleedin' do!

—Excuse, please?

—YES! Tell...me...who...won!

—Cameroon, one...

Fuck it. It was typical. Losing to that shower of...

—Ireland, one.

—Yes!

A one-all draw. Exactly what he had predicted. It was a good result.

—D'yeh know who scored?

Basho looked uncertain.

—Duff?

No response.

—Keane? Barry reeled around and displayed the name of his hero across his back. Well, his hero's namesake, at least. Not that Basho would know the difference.

Basho pointed to the stained shirt and smiled. He seemed to find something funny. —Ah, Keano!

—Yes, Keano. Great player.

—Great player, agreed Basho. He pointed to his temple. —Crazy player, yes?

—Er, yeah. Sometimes. Did he score, but?

The fucker was definitely laughing at him now. —Keano, score?

What the hell was so funny? Maybe he had been sent off or something? Whatever it was, Barry was getting sick and tired of it. —Yeah. Did he score?

Basho slapped him hard on the shoulder. Barry had to grit his teeth to stop himself bursting him. —Ah, you crazy Irish.

He shook his head and skipped off to check the nets before sailing. Barry glanced over at Dunne-Davis. He was busy preening himself in front of the tiny mirror on the bridge of the little fishing vessel. He flicked his hair back and forth and pouted like a Playboy centrefold, totally transfixed by his own reflection.

—Prick.

He'd tell him later. Not that Dunne-Davis had much interest in anything that didn't involve his hair. All the same, they were on their way now.

—CHAPTER SIXTEEN—

Barry's stomach heaved and bobbed in time with the boat, up and down, up and then down again. It was like a seesaw. The constant motion made him want to hurl – again. He'd thought it might subside after the first three or four times, but it hadn't. He hung his head over the side and watched the Sea of Japan gently rise and fall all around them. Time for another dry retch.

—Yeaarrgghh…

There was nothing left in his belly to come out. Even the bile and mucus from earlier had dried up. There was a short pause in proceedings, just enough to let him catch a breath.

—Huuuggghh!

His head was hurting from the lack of oxygen. It was all he could do to draw a shallow breath before the next bout.

—Aaarrghh, he groaned miserably.

That was it for the next few minutes.

Basho shook his head and smiled. —You no fisherman.

No shit, Barry would have said, if he'd been capable of speech.

Dunne-Davis didn't take much notice of him any more. He was used to it by now. I'll never make it to Tokyo if this keeps up, Barry thought.

Kata must have been thinking the same thing, because he came over to Barry, holding a bottle of what looked like some kind of medicine. Fuck it; it was worth a try. Barry took it in his shaking hand and smelled it gingerly.

Which turned out to be a big mistake.

—Fffuuaarrgghh!

It smelled like shite. Worse, even.

—You drink. Very good medicine.

Barry wasn't convinced, but he knocked back a quick shot of the stuff. It didn't taste as bad as it smelt. That would have been impossible. He didn't want to ask what was in it; probably tiger's bollix or something. It seemed to work, though. Twenty minutes passed without any further attempts at puking.

Thanks be to Jaysus, he thought.

Dunne-Davis was helping the two lads with the nets. They hauled in a good catch of big, plump fish. They looked like mackerel. Barry watched them squirming and jumping around. Poor fuckers. He would have helped, but he was just too weak. Dunne-Davis had been eating the noodles and whatever else it was they'd been giving him, but Barry didn't want to push his luck. The medicine was definitely working – he would have been rightly screwed without it – but he didn't trust himself with anything other than water.

The sun was beating down on them and the waters were calmer now. Most of the time Barry stayed in the little cabin where the four of them slept. There was only enough room for three at a time comfortably, but Kata and Basho never slept at the same time anyway, so it was grand. Even still, you could dehydrate very quickly in the heat, despite the cooling sea breeze. Dunne-Davis was out in it every waking moment. He was practically in his fuckin' nip most of the time. He was some tulip. Barry caught him checking out his biceps a couple of times. He'd be in the middle of pulling in the nets or something and he'd stop for a minute, when he thought no one was watching; he'd actually flex an arm or one of the large muscles on his chest, delighted with the result. There was no denying he was in good shape, but he was still a prick.

Barry wondered what was going on back home. Would they be missed yet? Obviously he knew he had been, but what about Dunne-Davis? Barry doubted he had any close friends. As far as he was aware, he didn't have a girlfriend – not a steady one, anyway. He was too much in love with himself to love anyone else. Barry hoped the garage had bought Dunne-Davis's story about the virus and the dismissal. He knew he'd get all the news when he called Jill in a couple of days. He could hardly wait.

By the time they reached Tokyo, Barry was feeling very weak. He hadn't eaten in over two days, and the heat had taken its effect: he reckoned he had lost nearly a stone in weight, even though he'd been drinking water by the gallon. At first he'd felt a bit guilty about that, but he had soon realised there was plenty on board, so he wasn't depriving anyone. Dunne-Davis looked like he'd been away in Spain for a fortnight. The fucker was black. He'd been eating properly, too, for the first time since they left. Barry thought back to the fatal night. It seemed like years ago, instead of just over three weeks.

Kata gave them directions to the underground and they said their goodbyes. Barry took longest over the Honda. He patted the saddle gently and swallowed hard.

—Good luck, Ireland! said Basho, interrupting the farewell. —You no miss Keane now!

—Fuckin' sure, said Barry.

He had made it. All the way from Ringsend to Tokyo. He could feel the buzz as soon as they hit dry land. His stomach slowly began to return to normality, even though he still swayed a bit; it'd probably take an hour or two to get that feckin' boat out of his system. Basho was right, though: they were going to get tickets to see Ireland against Germany if they had to spend every last penny on them. There was no way he was going to miss the lads taking on the might of the Germans. Ballack could score as many as he liked against the Saudis, but Barry couldn't wait to see him try and get past Keano.

The first thing they needed was money. Barry let Dunne-Davis go into a bank and exchange some of the roubles for yen. It wasn't that he trusted him with the money – he just wanted as little to do with it as possible. Dunne-Davis came out eventually.

—Right, we're sorted.

—How much?

—Enough.

—Enough to buy match tickets?

—Yah, yah. Now where do you want to go first?

—Anywhere with grub. I'm starvin'.

It was just docklands and industry around here, so they decided to head into the centre of the city to eat. They made their way to the underground the way Kata had shown them. They bought weekly rail passes and Dunne-Davis got a map of the stations in different colours. There were dozens of them; the underground lines crisscrossed like a massive game of snakes and ladders.

—It must be bleedin' huge, said Barry.

They got out at a stop on the orange line. Barry spotted the Hard Rock Café from fifty metres away. The station was enormous, and there were all sorts of places to eat, but Barry wanted something familiar, just to get his system back in gear. The place was like a giant ant colony. People rushed back and forth; trains arrived every few seconds, disgorging new masses into the relentless melee. Barry had only ever seen this many people together at Lansdowne Road.

They stepped into the café and pure Americana. There were electric guitars hanging on the walls and gold discs everywhere. The video jukebox was playing 'Run to You' by Bryan Adams. It wasn't one of Barry's favourites, but at least it wasn't Westlife. Barry ordered the chicken burger and Dunne-Davis went for the steak. They had a Miller each while they were waiting.

—Cheers, said Dunne-Davis.

—To Ireland, said Barry.

His head was spinning already and he'd only drunk half of it. The ice-cold amber was mother's milk gliding down his throat.

—Ireland, agreed Dunne-Davis.

Barry's burger was suitably massive. He reckoned there was at least half a chicken in it. He shovelled it down and polished off the fries and salad that came with it.

—Lovely.

Dunne-Davis was only halfway through his, so Barry ordered a slice of mud pie and another cool Miller. He could feel his strength coming back, but it seemed to disappear again as soon as they stepped outside the cool blanket of the air-conditioned café into the street.

—Fuck's sake!

It wouldn't have passed as weather reporting on RTÉ, but Dunne-Davis knew what he meant. The weather display read thirty-three degrees, but he reckoned it was even hotter. The searing sunshine wasn't that bad – they were used to that by now; it was the humidity. It grabbed you by the throat and didn't let go. It was like hitting a wall of pressure when you stepped outside. Salty lines of sweat began streaking down Barry's cheeks as soon as they started moving.

A couple of Irish lads passed them on their way into the station and cheered.

—Come on, ye boys in green!

It was magic. Tokyo was just like Barry had imagined it. Huge buildings covered in advertising, traffic and people everywhere. Your heart started racing just at the sight of all that life. They strolled around for a half-hour or so, gradually acclimatising to the heat. There were Westerners everywhere, probably mostly football fans. They found a bit of shade and sat down on a bench to watch the world go by.

—So, Dunne-Davis eventually said, ——where are we going to stay?

Barry thought about it for a minute.

—I seen some place on that programme with Shay Healy

and Ray Treacy.

—What was it called?

—Dunno. Wayno, or something?

Dunne-Davis scanned the underground map.

—Do you know how to spell it?

—Haven't a clue, conceded Barry.

Nick ran a finger back and forth a few times.

—Ueno? U-E-N-O?

—Could be it. May as well have a look, anyway.

When they passed the shop in the train station, Barry went into raptures.

—Lookit!

He held up an Irish jersey from the rack. But it wasn't any old Irish jersey. It had 'Keane' and a number 6 on the back.

—The real Keano! he beamed.

—But you've already got a Keane jersey.

—A Keane jersey. Not the Keane jersey. Give us some money.

Dunne-Davis did as he was told. Barry insisted on pulling the thing on as soon as he'd paid for it. He threw the old one at Dunne-Davis.

—You can wear that one at the match.

—Thanks a bunch, mumbled Nick, holding the damp jersey at arm's length.

They hopped on the escalator and descended into the labyrinth below. There were Irish all over the place; Barry couldn't believe the amount that had travelled. Of course, most of them had probably chosen an easier route than Barry and Dunne-Davis, but they were here and that was all that mattered. It was a great buzz, seeing so many lads from home, even though Barry didn't know any of them. It didn't matter. It was the camaraderie and adventure that held them all together in this strange and wonderful part of the world. Fellas who wouldn't have looked at each other on the street in Dublin or Cork, or wherever they were from, were suddenly like long-lost brothers. To prove the point, a small group of them started singing when they saw the back of Barry's shirt.

—Kean-o! Kean-o! Kean-o!

This was great gas. They were actually here. In Japan. At the fuckin' World Cup! It was almost too much.

Then a rough-looking bastard spoiled the mood.

—Wanker, was all he said as he passed them.

Barry couldn't get over it. What was his problem? He was definitely Irish. He sounded Dublin, too. And he'd been talking to Barry, there was no doubt about it. He'd stared him in the eyes, like he was going to headbutt him. Maybe he recognised him from somewhere? Or had mistaken him for someone else? That must have been it. It still shocked him, though, the viciousness of it. Had Dunne-Davis not heard it? If he had, he said nothing. It had been directed at Barry, solely for his benefit, so maybe he hadn't. Barry stayed silent until they got off at Ueno.

Ueno was even more packed with Irish. They were swarming all over the place, running in and out of the bemused local commuters and office workers. It was like a school tour for adults. They definitely had the bodies of adults, anyway. Large guts hung over shorts that could never stretch enough to accommodate their load, no matter how much Lycra was in them. Milk-bottle thighs shone bright in the afternoon sun and builder's tans adorned the pavements. Scorched necks and arms looked like they'd been tattooed onto the painfully pale torsos. The Irish were definitely here. And, just in case there was any doubt, most of them seemed to have a couple of yards of green, in the shape of scarves, jerseys, hats and anything else on which it was possible to display loyalties. As ever with the Green Army, there wasn't the slightest hint of trouble. They were lads out for a good time. Nothing more.

Barry and Nick tried their luck in a couple of hotels, but everywhere was full. Barry was beginning to feel like giving up when they finally found one overlooking the park. It was called the Parkside.

—Very imaginative, said Dunne-Davis as they trudged through the revolving door. He soon changed his tune, however, when they told him that they had vacancies. The guy at reception spoke reasonable English, too.

—How much for a single room?

—Nine thousand two hundred yen.

Dunne-Davis did some quick mental arithmetic. —Can we have two?

He held aloft two fingers to illustrate.

Barry cut in. —Why don't we just get a twin?

Dunne-Davis looked at him for a second. —Would you not prefer some privacy for a change?

—Much are the rooms?

—About seventy-five euro each.

Barry scratched at the stubble on his chin.

—Can we afford it?

—No problem.

—Fuck it, so.

Dunne-Davis reached into the rucksack and dug out the cash while Barry signed in.

—You have passport? enquired the receptionist.

Barry looked at Dunne-Davis. He wanted a room, not a fuckin' international plane ticket.

—We lost them at the airport. The embassy is issuing us with new ones shortly, said Dunne-Davis, as confident as a politician.

This didn't appear to be standard procedure. The receptionist seemed unsure of what to do next.

—We should have them in a day or two. I can call the Irish ambassador if you like.

There was a short pause.

—Not necessary, sir. You sign, please.

He offered the book to Dunne-Davis, who signed obligingly.

—You need bags brought up? said the receptionist, handing over the keys.

—No, thank you.

Dunne-Davis carried the bag to the lift. Barry waited till they stepped in before he said what he was thinking.

—You've a neck like a jockey's bollix.

The rooms were grand – nothing special, just a single bed in each and a small en-suite bathroom. Barry jumped under the shower. It was fantastic. There was a layer of grime and salt covering him that scrubbed away in the hot water. Just what he needed. Dunne-Davis had taken a swim in the ocean, but even that was a couple of days ago now, and Barry knew he must have smelled much worse. He couldn't really tell any more. It was nice having the bit of privacy at last, being able to walk around in the nip without anyone looking at you. Not that Dunne-Davis would have been looking at him. He was always far too busy looking at himself.

In the adjacent room, Nick Dunne-Davis was busy looking at the soft-porn channel on the TV. He had also liberated a cool beer from the mini-bar and was generally making himself at home. He was disappointed with the quality of viewing on offer, however. The good bits were all scrambled, so you never got a really clear shot of anything pink or hairy.

—Fuck.

It was strange looking at naked bodies with pixilated private parts. He watched for another twenty minutes, in the vain hope that it might get better – or worse, depending on your perspective – but it didn't. Still, it was interesting to see the Japanese girls in action. He took a few mental notes and tried to memorise some words that would hopefully come in handy at some stage. He looked about the room. It definitely lacked something, but what? He couldn't quite put his finger on it. Then he realised. It needed to be christened.

Ten minutes later, he was still sitting on the pot. Nothing was happening. It was a first for Nick. He hadn't passed anything solid since the Trans-Siberian railway; he was beginning to wonder exactly what it was that Paul had given him. After a few short trumpet-bursts, he decided to leave it alone for a while and take a bath. Maybe that would get things moving. On closer inspection, he decided to opt for the shower instead, since he would have had to be an Olympic gymnast just to fit into the tub. After a quick twenty-minute scrub, he took full advantage of the complimentary moisturiser and settled onto the bed for a well-earned nap.

He was woken up an hour later by a loud knock on the door.

—Yeh in there? asked Barry.

There was another rap on the door.

—Wake up, yeh bollix.

Charming, thought Nick. Why did Barry never call him by his name? It was always 'yeh dozy cunt' or something equally articulate. He was feeling more refreshed after the sleep, and he slowly peeled himself off the mattress.

The door almost came off its hinges again.

—Come on, yeh…

Nick yanked it open as Barry was in mid-knock. For a split second Barry looked like he was going to follow through and jab him on the nose, but he stopped at the last second. It was like he realised, just in time, that he wouldn't get away with pretending it was accidental. Nick wondered why Barry hated him so much. He couldn't ever imagine being so bitter himself. Fair enough, he'd got the guy into a spot of bother; but he'd apologised, hadn't he? What more could he do?

He knew it was more than that, though. Guys like Barry never liked guys like him. And Nick couldn't really blame him. Barry had no education to speak of, but he certainly wasn't thick. He was what was referred to as 'streetwise', but Nick reckoned that was just a euphemism for being hard – almost to the point of being mean.

He certainly wouldn't have liked to get into a fight with Barry. He had that vicious streak that fellas from that background always did. No amount of trying to placate him or attempting to be friendly ever worked. He just had no interest. Nick and his kind were the enemy, plain and simple: us and them, management and workers, and all the rest of it. Sometimes Nick wondered why he bothered. Why should he keep pissing against the wind for someone who didn't even try to conceal his contempt? And it was all because Nick had been born with something Barry would never have: class.

He was going to forget about being anything other than civil from now on. And Barry Kelly could take a running jump if he thought Nick was going to force him into accepting half of the money. Besides, he'd never even asked how much the Russians had paid for the merchandise. And what he didn't know couldn't hurt him.

The Church bar was full of Irish and English. Barry ordered two pints of Carlsberg and handed over two thousand yen. He didn't get any of it back.

—Much is two thousand yen?

—About sixteen euro, said Dunne-Davis after a minute.

—Jaysus.

Barry took a sip. It tasted exactly like the stuff at home. He'd been expecting it to taste somehow different – better, maybe, on account of the inflated price. He took another, larger gulp, just to make sure: exactly the same.

After another three, they got talking to a lad from Galway who seemed like a good bloke.

—Any chance of a ticket for tomorrow night? said Barry.

—Nah. I'd say there's no chance, replied the Galway lad.

—Fuck it!

It was exactly what Barry had been afraid of. He spent

the next two hours asking the exact same question, and every time he got the exact same response. No amount of cajoling, persuading, threatening or bribing made the slightest bit of difference. Their whole odyssey had been for nothing. Even a tout laughed when Barry offered him a thousand euro for two tickets. They were like gold dust. People who were lucky enough to have them were never going to part with them. A couple of lads told Barry to show up at the ground and chance his arm – maybe somebody would sell him their ticket... Fuck that. He wanted it in his hand. He hadn't come all this way to watch the match on television. Dunne-Davis didn't seem unduly bothered by the whole thing, but that was hardly surprising.

It was when Barry was ordering the next round that it struck him. It was screaming down at him from the wall. How had he missed it? Had it been there all along?

He felt a tingle run down his spine. This was it. The Holy Grail. His chance to get two tickets for the match. It was a sign, like the previous ones that had guided them on their journey. This was the fucking star that would lead them to the Messiah. Only this time the saviour would be surrounded by ten disciples and wrapped in green.

Barry slipped out of the bar unnoticed, leaving the two pints and Nick Dunne-Davis alone. He was a man on a mission, and he wasn't about to fail.

Nick never even saw the sign that had shocked Barry into action. Even if he had, he would probably simply have noticed the bad grammar, or decided that only a madman would enter the Tokyo radio station's competition – even if it promised 'Two Tickets to the Match of Your Choose!'

—CHAPTER SEVENTEEN—

Barry moved with stealthy certainty. It was instinctive. The name of the radio station was indelibly etched onto his brain. He was like a tiger stalking its prey. There would be no escape. He had them in his sights. It was only a matter of time before the tickets were his.

Johnno sat looking at the bank statement. He'd been saving everything that came his way for the last couple of years. Doyle didn't pay him a set wage; he gave him a percentage of the takings each week – a very small percentage, no doubt. But Johnno was cuter than most foot soldiers. He had a couple of minor schemes going himself, schemes about which Doyle knew nothing. They hadn't made him a fortune, but he had enough to get them out of Dublin.

The plan was to head to a little village in Spain. It sounded like paradise to Sasha. It wasn't on the Costa del Sol or anywhere else where Doyle might have contacts. This place was up in the hills of Andalusia. Johnno had been to the little village once and had dreamed about retiring there ever since. They'd use the money to set up a bar or a guesthouse, and they'd watch the sun setting over the hills every evening.

It meant saying goodbye to her life in Dublin, Sasha knew, but that wasn't necessarily such a bad thing. Living alone in an apartment that could have masqueraded as a shoebox, working a dead-end job as hostess of a largely ignored restaurant, wasn't exactly what she'd dreamed about as a girl. She'd been embarrassed when Johnno had asked her how much money she could get her hands on in twenty-four hours.

—Oh, my entire life savings, she'd replied.

—Much is tha'?

—To the nearest euro?

He nodded.

—Thirty-seven, and twenty-three cents.

—Maybe yeh should wait for a bit more interest, wha'?

He hadn't been upset. She'd never been very good at saving. There were always so many things she had to buy. It was true that she only ever wore about a quarter of those things, but still, it was a compulsion she'd have to curb in her new life. She couldn't wait. España, here we come!

It took Nick a while to realise that Barry was missing. He had his mind on other things – two other things, in particular, and he couldn't take his eyes off them. He'd wait until Karen, or Clare – he couldn't remember her name – was taking a sip from her drink; as soon as she lowered the glass he'd return his eyes to hers, all the time trying not to let on that he'd been staring at her ample cleavage. And the more drinks he had, the harder it was to concentrate on anything else. If she noticed, she didn't say anything. Anyway, what did she expect, wearing a top like that? If it had been cut any lower he could have seen her belly button. When he looked hard enough, he could even see a hint of the dark bit around one of her nipples, protruding over the tightly stretched cotton that held them in place. It looked like she was hiding a couple of Tic-Tacs under her top, as well.

Kate seemed to read his mind. She leaned over and kissed him on the lips. It was a full, wet one that tasted of cranberry juice. Funny, can't taste the vodka, he thought. He wasn't sure of her name, but he was sure of what she was drinking. He must have bought her half a dozen of the things by now.

As they staggered back to his room, it started to hammer down in buckets. Large drops of warm rain soaked them through to the skin. It washed away any doubts: she definitely wasn't wearing a bra. Nick's trousers were at full mast. A subtle wrenching of his boxers partially obscured the way he was feeling. They passed the hookers and massage parlours that lined the laneway behind the hotel; there'd be no need to avail of their services tonight, but he saw no harm in a quick glance at what the various establishments had to offer all the same. When they eventually reached the bedroom, they decided to have a nightcap from the mini bar. Then they decided to have four more.

Nick was awoken the next morning by the sound of the shower. He checked the clock: 11.23. The last time he'd checked, it had been 5.18. He must have passed out on the bed. Surely he would remember if he'd got his end away? He went over the events leading up to the part when they got to the bedroom, and wondered briefly what had happened to Barry.

—Fuck him, he muttered. Barry was old enough and bold enough to look after himself. The last time Nick had seen him, he had been pestering people for tickets. Maybe he had got some and left; or maybe he had left to get some. It was all fairly irrelevant, as far as Nick was concerned. If they got tickets, well and good, but he really couldn't get as enthusiastic about it as Barry was. The main thing was that they were thousands of miles away from Tony Doyle. The fact that they were surrounded by thousands of people from all over the world didn't hurt, either – particularly since a good portion of those people were of the female variety. And then there was the very attractive local talent. Barry didn't seem to notice the significance of these facts at all, that was his problem.

Even if he was practically married, he wasn't dead yet. He was becoming obsessive about getting those tickets, like it was the most important thing in the world.

Nick was desperately trying to recall whether he'd had a good night or an amazing night, when the shower stopped.

He lay back and relaxed as best he could. He'd still get a decent look at Carol when she came out. That was her name, wasn't it? Better not mention it, just to be safe; getting it wrong would be very embarrassing, especially if they'd done the business last night. His mind drifted back to the main events of the evening. He was clear as a bell until the point when they'd started into the mini-bar. Things got very hazy after that. There had been some kissing, for sure, and he seemed to remember getting his hands on her goods; then nothing. He was a fucking eejit. He must have fallen asleep on the job.

The bathroom door-handle squeaked. Excellent, Nick thought. She was coming out. Hopefully she'd be covered in nothing but warm water. He pulled back the duvet in anticipation.

Arse, he thought. She was fully dressed. This wasn't what he'd had in mind at all. Maybe the situation could be salvaged by some smooth talking.

—Morning! she said.

—Morning, he replied. It wasn't exactly the sort of comeback that would make a girl go weak at the knees.

—Ca... he began, and faltered. It was safer not to make an attempt at her name.

—Can we meet again...? He left a blank where her name should have been.

She came over and kissed him goodbye. —Of course. We're meeting tonight, after the match, remember?

He must have looked even more confused than he felt.

—The reception at the embassy?

—Er...yah, yah, of course I do.

He hoped he sounded convincing.

—See ya then, Nick.

Damn! She knew his name. He'd have to take a stab at hers.

—See ya...then, he said. It was no use – he hadn't a clue.

—Just remember to ask for me if there's any problem getting in, OK?

And she was gone. Great, Nick thought. 'Can I see the girl with the great baps?' was sure to get him in.

Later, in the shower, he managed to piece together a few details. Her name was still a mystery. That might make things difficult at the embassy. But it was good that she worked there; it would make getting temporary passports a lot easier. That, Nick remembered suddenly, was why he had spent so long chatting her up last night – that and her other, more obvious attributes. She'd taken his details last night and promised to sort it out. He'd also given her Barry's name and date of birth, which he hoped was correct. He had it on file back at the showrooms, and he knew Barry had been born on 16 April; he just wasn't certain of the year. He had guessed (correctly, as it happened) that Barry was twenty-five – still only a young fellow, yet in so many ways he was more mature than Nick. He was definitely more responsible.

Nick tried ringing Barry's room as he dried his hair, but there was no answer. Barry must have gone out. Or else he'd never made it back last night. Maybe he wasn't so responsible after all.

Nick spent the obligatory fifteen minutes on his hair. The humidity was playing havoc with it, but there was nothing that could be done about it; he'd just have to grin and bear it. After a light brunch in the hotel restaurant, he went out for a stroll around the park. The water lilies were like umbrellas; they covered the lake completely.

After an hour or so, he got bored and went back to the hotel.

—Has Barry Kelly been back yet?

—He not here, sir.

Interesting. Where could he have gone? As far as Nick was aware, he didn't know anyone in Tokyo. He walked around to the Church Bar and checked it out: no sign of Barry there, either. He had a quick pint and got up to go.

That was when he saw the poster.

—The fucking plonker.

Only a madman would attempt that – a madman or a stubborn bastard. And Barry had legitimate claims to both, as far as Nick was concerned.

There were plenty of cute Japanese girls on the subway. Nick knew they were all checking him out. He stared down at his newspaper, pretending to be engrossed in the Financial Times; every few minutes he casually darted a glance about the carriage, his eyes camouflaged by the designer shades, which weren't strictly necessary in the subterranean darkness. He never actually caught one of the girls in the act, but he knew they were secretly marvelling at how much he resembled Hugh Grant or Jude Law. A few people had remarked to him before that he was a ringer for Hugh Grant. —Yes, but I've got a much better body, he always replied. He thrust his jaw out and nonchalantly flicked the hair from his forehead. Let them have their fantasies.

He was getting off at the next stop. Maybe he should ask the petite, olive-skinned temptress beside him for her phone number? She'd been playing footsie with him for the past three stops. It was true that she had moved her leg away every time he casually rubbed his against it, but that was just playing hard to get. In the end he decided against it – just on the minute chance that he might have misread the situation. The train disgorged him and a few dozen others onto the platform, and he made his way out onto the street.

The address wasn't exactly hard to find, and there

was a small crowd of Japanese people gathered outside the window, making it even easier to spot. They were pointing and laughing at the pale-blue figures shivering in their underwear inside. This was the place, all right.

Nick waved, but Barry didn't seem to recognise him. He had that thousand-yard stare they talked about in Vietnam. Nick checked his watch and did a few rough calculations. He estimated that Barry had left the Church yesterday around dinnertime. It was now after three in the afternoon, which meant he'd been there for at least twenty hours.

Inside the off-licence, Barry couldn't see anything beyond the window. Even that didn't really register in his brain. The competition involved sitting in nothing but your underwear in the freezer section of the off-licence, and his body had shut down all functions that weren't essential in generating the temperature necessary to keep him from freezing to death. All the blood in his body was busy keeping his internal organs working. His eyes were fixed dead ahead, staring at nothing. All he could feel was cold – extreme cold. The temperature, combined with the sleep deprivation, was causing his mind to play tricks on him. He kept getting rushes down his spine, like when he had unwittingly taken that acid back in Amsterdam – flashbacks, he thought they were called. It was like a bad nightmare. He couldn't tell what was real and what wasn't.

He was vaguely aware of the other guy in the freezer with him, though. He was definitely a reality. There had been six of them to begin with. During the long night and morning, four of the other lads had dropped out. It was just Barry and this other fella now. All Barry had to do was outlast the gobshite sitting next to him, and he'd win two tickets for the match of his choice – which would naturally be the Ireland versus Germany match. The only problem was that the gobshite beside him was waiting for Barry to capitulate so he could get the tickets for himself.

It had all started off friendly enough, but as the day wore on things had started to turn nasty. Earlier that afternoon the organisers had tried to coax the two of them out, offering to split the prize and give them one ticket each; but the fucker beside him was having none of it. So Barry was fucked if he was going to give up and let your man walk away with the precious match tickets. He'd rather let his knob turn to ice and drop off.

This was actually a stronger possibility than he realised. The organisers had come in around midnight with gloves and socks, and insisted that they put them on; they said something about not having included a waiver for frostbite in the contract. Barry had pretended he didn't need them, weakly protesting through clattering teeth when they were put on for him; he didn't want the enemy to think he was wilting. But secretly he had never been more grateful for a pair of socks in his life. He'd lost the sensation in his toes hours before. The radio station had never counted on anyone lasting this long. What had started out as a bit of a joke to get some publicity was becoming a serious worry for the public relations officer of 99FM. She was fairly certain that all publicity was good publicity, but freezing two tourists to death was surely entering a bit of a grey area. Barry hoped it wouldn't make the news back home, or they'd be on the run again.

Then Mick McCarthy came in and told him he was in the team for the German game. He had been impressed by Barry's grit and determination to succeed. It was the least he could do. Barry felt a tear of pride roll down his cheek. Outside, Nick wondered just whom it was that Barry thought he was shaking hands with. Inside, Barry took renewed strength from McCarthy's recognition. He knew he wasn't alone now. He had to do it for his teammates. He couldn't let the lads down. He'd stay in here till hell itself had frozen over – and, from where he was sitting, it might well have done just that.

Nick had been watching Barry for well over an hour. He had no idea what he was up to. The other guy was the same. Every now and again they'd start acting as if they were having conversations with somebody, but there was nobody else there. At one point Barry stood up and placed his hand over his heart. There was no way of telling from outside, but Nick was convinced he was singing the national anthem, especially when the other fella got up and joined in. It was like watching two people who were hypnotised. Barry was a fucking eejit – but a fucking eejit whom Nick had to admire. And he would admire him even more if he won those tickets for the match tonight. His nipples looked as if they would break off and come away from his body if they were rubbed hard enough. His lips were almost purple. It was getting ridiculous, but there was no doubting the infectious nature of the atmosphere. Nick was really rooting for Barry now.

He wondered what Barry's attitude to Roy Keane was now. Had he been there when that guy in the Church told Nick what had happened? He couldn't remember exactly, but...no, he was nearly sure Barry hadn't been there.

Hope he doesn't take it too badly, he thought, as Barry shaped up to take another imaginary corner inside.

Two hours later, they were on the train to Ibaraki. The competition had eventually ended when the other lad refused to use the screened-off toilet and began pissing in full view of the crowd outside. Somehow the station had managed to lay its hands on another two tickets – it was either that or cause a diplomatic incident – so both of them were winners in the end. Barry had recovered slightly faster than his opponent. The hot chocolate and the thermal duvets they'd wrapped around him had brought his temperature back to somewhere approaching normal surprisingly quickly.

Nick was delighted with the result. Now he couldn't wait for the match; he was almost as excited as Barry.

It was a two-hour trip out to the stadium, and there would be no danger of hypothermia this time: the train was crammed full of Irish supporters, with hardly a German in sight, and the heat was stifling. Every few minutes the train would stop at another station and more fellas would try to get on. The accompanying breeze every time the doors opened made it just about bearable, but in between stations it was like trying to hold your breath. Nick wasn't crazy about being in such close proximity to all these sweating, hairy blokes, but he wasn't going to let it get to him. They had two of the best seats in the house at Ireland's biggest game in years. He couldn't believe they were actually going to it, after all they'd been through. They were only a matter of hours away. It would be his first soccer international. He'd been to loads of rugby ones, but this was going to be a new experience. He even joined in some of the songs with Barry and the rest of them.

—Come on, ye boys in green,
Come on, ye boys in green,
Come on ye boys, come on ye boys in green…

It was magic. If the craic was half as good at the stadium, they were in for a treat. There were only a couple of stops to go. Nick felt proud of his green T-shirt, even though strictly speaking it wasn't his own. He'd earned the right to wear it. They were all part of one enormous green army, fighting for nothing more than the right to claim their place alongside the best. Nick had never experienced anything like it. The adrenaline was coursing through his veins, a natural high far beyond anything chemically induced. He felt like he was part of something great.

CHAPTER EIGHTEEN

There was only one word to describe the stadium: awesome. Barry was beginning to return to his old self again. He'd been quiet enough on the train, which was only to be expected; he must be absolutely exhausted. Nick had caught him dozing off, standing up, at one point. A couple of nips from the naggin of vodka Nick had smuggled in soon perked him up.

It was a beautiful balmy evening, neither humid nor chilly. 'The Fields of Athenry' began rising like a wave around the stadium. It started as a whisper and slowly built into a rousing hymn. Nick didn't want to look, but he was sure Barry's eyes were welling up. He stared straight ahead, afraid to let anyone see his own.

There was a serious lack of German support. The only Germans Nick could see were gathered behind the goal to their right, and there couldn't have been more than a couple of thousand of them. So Ireland definitely had the numbers. But who had the firepower?

The question was answered – in Barry's mind, at least – two minutes later, with the announcement of the teams. Every player from Given to Kilbane was cheered, with one notable exception. And that was because his name wasn't called out.

—Where's Keane? demanded Barry, after the midfield had been named.

This was followed by Robbie Keane's name on the PA, and a full-blooded chant:

—One Keano!

There's only one Keano!

There's only one Keano...

Barry frantically scanned the match programme for answers.

—Is he injured?

—Not exactly... Nick didn't know how to tell him.

Another chant from a couple of dozen lads behind them assisted his explanation. Nick believed the tune was lifted from that 'Daylight come' song. They gave quite a competent rendition, albeit with a slight change to the lyrics.

—Kean-o! Kea-n-o!
Keano went ga-ga and he had to go home.
Not Quinn!
Not Stan!
Not Mick McCarthy!
Keano went ga-ga and he had to go home...

Barry said nothing as Nick tried to explain the mess as best he could. There was a brief pause for the national anthems; then he continued.

—So, basically, what I heard was that Keane and McCarthy had a big bust-up and...er...Keane fucked off home...or was sent home, I'm not sure which.

Barry shook his head in disbelief. He wasn't taking it as well as Nick had hoped. Every time he tried to expand on the events as he understood them, it only seemed to make Barry worse.

—Then Bertie even got involved, and there was talk of a reconciliation if Keane apologised for calling McCarthy an English cunt...but he wouldn't.

Barry had his head in his hands and was staring at his feet with the look of a defeated man.

—Keane said he only wanted what was best for the team, from the beginning. He actually said he was quitting international football three times before the bust-up...

—Just like fuckin' Judas, said the fella eavesdropping in front of them, and he wasn't smiling.

—Something to do with the FAI being a Mickey-Mouse set-up, continued Nick.

Barry glared at him briefly but said nothing. He was in deep shock. Without a word, he got up and walked slowly towards the exit.

Nick found him locked in a cubicle in one of the dozens of men's toilets that peppered the ground. He knew there were dozens because he'd checked every one of them, pausing only when he heard a small roar to indicate Germany's first goal. He was about to give up and start checking the ladies' when he finally came to yet another locked door. He knew it had to be Barry inside, because when he knocked he didn't receive the usual response, which was a little crude for Nick's liking. But there was no response at all from behind this door. That was a good sign. Unless Barry had taken drastic measures... Panic entered Nick's head for a moment, but then logic regained a foothold.

—Barry? Are you in there? he repeated. Still no reply.

—Just knock if you're all right.

There was a pause, followed by a gentle knock. Good. At least he was conscious.

—Are you coming out? Nick waited patiently. —Knock once for yes and twice for no.

There was a knock, followed by a more hesitant one. Nick decided this must be the first ever séance between living people.

—Look, Barry. There's nothing we can do about it. Everyone's been let down by this, not just you. But we're here now. And the Irish team is here too...

There was a defiant double knock, to suggest that somehow they weren't.

—OK, so maybe our best player isn't here, but these things happen. It isn't a matter of life and death, said Nick. This probably wasn't the wisest thing to say to a Liverpool fan who believed passionately in Bill Shankly's claim that it was much more important than that. —He's just one footballer.

The door nearly came off its hinges from the force of two knocks that begged to differ.

Nick's patience was starting to wear thin. —Fine. Fuck you, then. You can stay in there for the rest of the match. You can stay in there for the rest of your life, for all I care. I'm going back to watch the Irish team play in the World Cup.

He left that in the air, to give Barry something to think about. When he got back to his seat, it was half-time and Ireland was one-nil down, but he didn't care. He took another nip of vodka and settled in for the second half. He was determined to enjoy it.

Barry joined him a couple of minutes later. There were no words exchanged, but at least he was there, and he seemed to have temporarily put the Keane affair to the back of his mind. The Irish team still looked a bit shaky at the back, but going forward they definitely had the Germans in trouble. Ireland was creating chance after chance; but no matter how many were made, no matter how good they were, that bastard Kahn stopped everything that came his way. Nick thought he was going to have heart failure on a number of occasions.

The second half was rapidly coming to an end. Another glorious failure. Half of the pundits would claim this was proof that Keane's tantrum-throwing and trouble-stirring had upset the team so badly that they'd never had a chance of playing their best; the other half would claim this was proof that Keane had been right, that true professionals would have played their best no matter what anyone else did, and that the team would never be the same without him.

'You'll Never Walk Alone' began to ring out around the ground. Nick didn't care what anybody said: the lads had been magnificent in defeat. What they'd been through in the past few weeks must have been easily as traumatic as what he and Barry had experienced. He looked at

Barry and saw the determination etched on his features. Fair play to him; he wasn't giving up, even though hope was all but lost and the whistle was about to blow any second. Nick wondered where people got that kind of faith.

He got his answer emphatically two seconds later. It came from heaven; or, at least, it was still close to the clouds when Quinn nodded the most delicate of touches into the path of the other Keane – Robbie. He took one touch to control it and then slammed it off Kahn or the post or something, and...it couldn't be! It was! It was rattling the back of the fucking net!

—Sweet fucking Jesus! screamed a voice behind them, articulating what everyone was feeling.

Ireland had scored.

The entire stadium erupted. Nick knew he hadn't done enough to deserve this; no one had. This was heaven, pure and simple. It was a feeling that only God himself could bestow on mere mortals; a little taster to say, —Here's what you can expect. He'd heard people say moments like these were better than sex; he'd reserve judgement on that one until he'd had sex with forty thousand people simultaneously, which surely was stretching it a bit, even for a man of his talents – but, in a way, that was exactly what he was doing. Even Barry was bounding up and down and screaming, just screaming his head off. The oul' lad in front was actually crying. And he wasn't alone.

The Germans were stunned by the late equaliser. It was probably just as well Ireland had scored so late, Barry thought; it meant that the Germans hadn't enough time to get another one. —Kean-o! Kean-o! rang around the perfect night air. Then the ref blew for full time and it was over. One all, against one of the superpowers of world football. It was almost unbelievable. Even Mick McCarthy joined in the lap of honour.

The atmosphere on the way back to Ueno was pure carnival. The Japanese police danced and sang with Irish supporters, suddenly friends with the same lads they had viewed with nervous apprehension two hours before. Luminous batons were lent to lunatics in green, with full confidence that they would be returned to their rightful owners. It was one giant, crazy birthday party for grown-ups in fancy dress. Nick didn't want to spoil the mood by mentioning anything about Roy Keane. Barry seemed to be flying with the rest of them – and why wouldn't he be? Qualification for the next round was virtually assured. Only Saudi Arabia stood in the way.

CHAPTER NINETEEN

Michael roared up the stairs.

—Jill! We drew!

There was no answer. He climbed halfway up and tried again.

—Did yeh hear me?

The bedroom door opened. Jill trudged out in her dressing-gown and smiled weakly on her way to the bathroom.

—That's nice.

She looked like the effort of this small concession had drained her.

—Are yeh all right, love?

Michael felt like an eejit. He knew damn well she wasn't all right. She had been getting progressively worse for the past week. She couldn't take much more of it. He wasn't sure he could take much more, either. When was Barry going to call? Even a sign to let them know he was OK would do. It was the not knowing that was the worst part.

Doyle was still looking for him and that yuppie lad, the one who had got him into this mess in the first place. The fact that Doyle hadn't come after Jill or any of the family – even now that the Guards seemed to have lost interest – proved that he wasn't really interested in Barry, as far as Michael could make out. Doyle had as much as said so, the last time he was around. All he wanted was his 'merchandise' and the other lad. He'd even said he was prepared to forget about the incident with his nephew if Barry gave up your man and the drugs. Michael wasn't so sure, though; he could never trust Doyle. But what options were there? He'd try and talk Barry into giving up the other fella, the next time he called. He was proud of Barry's loyalty, but there was no point in two of them going down if it was the other fella's deal. Michael hoped, for everybody's sake, that he'd call soon.

In the large hall of the embassy, Barry hung up the receiver for the third time. Every time he got a ringing tone, he hung up. He desperately wanted to talk to Jill, to hear her voice again and to find out how Sarah and the rest of them were; but he couldn't do it. He couldn't work out how to tell her.

He'd been over it a million times in his head. No matter how he sliced it, it still boiled down to the fact that he'd blown it – with considerable assistance from Dunne-Davis, it had to be said, but the fact remained that Barry had been too passive in all the proceedings. He realised this now. It was all very well distancing himself from the drugs and the money; but, in hindsight, he shouldn't have left it all to Dunne-Davis. Just because he had a degree and a posh accent, that didn't change what he was – which was, essentially, a bullshitter. Admittedly, a very good one, but at the end of the day a bullshitter nonetheless.

Which is why Barry was having problems phoning Jill. What was he going to say? —Howya, I'm in Japan, havin' a great time at the World Cup. We sold Doyle's drugs for feck-all and we can't come home...

It was hopeless. He didn't know what to do. They'd have to get out, somewhere far away, where Doyle couldn't reach them. He'd think of something.

For now, Barry knew he'd better get back to the party. It was his first time ever in an embassy. He and Nick had 'borrowed' a couple of white shirts from the hotel in Ueno for the occasion, since football jerseys were a bit of a no-no at these type of things – so Dunne-Davis had said, anyway. So there they were, in a pair of staff shirts they'd acquired from the laundry of the Parkside. Luckily they hadn't any logos or crap like that on them.

Dunne-Davis had freaked when he saw Barry's shirt buttoned up to his neck.

—You look like a knacker! he'd hissed, undoing the top three buttons.

—I am a knacker, Barry had said, doing one of them back up. He still felt like a young Tom Jones with half of his chest on display, but he had decided to trust Dunne-Davis in the social-airs-and-graces department. He made his way out to the large terrace at the back of the house.

It was all terribly civilised. Officially they were guests of the Irish Ambassador. Barry wasn't sure which one he was. He thought they had been introduced, but it was hard to tell; they all looked the same to him. He'd decided to keep his mouth shut after one of the oul' ones had asked him what he did.

—I'm a mechanic, he'd replied.

—A mechanical engineer? she had enquired, like she had never heard of it.

—Er, no. Just...a car mechanic.

—Really? Then she had made an excuse and left him alone.

Barry wasn't ashamed of who he was or what he did, but he just felt out of place here. Like a spare prick at a lesbian orgy. Dunne-Davis was loving it, of course. He was hobnobbing with the best of them. Some of them knew his old man, who was a judge or a barrister or something. Barry knew well Dunne-Davis hadn't spoken to his father in years, but he carried on as if they were the best of pals. He was used to moving in these kinds of circles, talking about golf and the economy and that type of shite.

Kate, the girl who'd actually invited them here, was running around like a blue-arsed fly. They hardly saw her all night. Every now and again she'd come over and apologise, but they didn't mind; Barry didn't, anyway, and Dunne-Davis was too busy chatting up Japanese oul' ones to notice. Kate seemed like a nice girl. She'd sorted them out with temporary passports, which would be handy if they ever got to leave the place. Still, it kept the options open. She had even promised to get them tickets for the Saudi game, so Barry wouldn't have to risk losing any of his extremities this time. It was her job to make sure that all the guests were having a good time, particularly the foreign dignitaries, of whom there were many. One of them was wearing a large medallion on a chain around his neck, and Barry guessed he must be the mayor – or its equivalent – of Tokyo.

He looked around at the gathering and wondered again what in the name of Jaysus he was doing there. He went over to the bar and ordered another pint of Guinness; it was like a reunion between two lovers after an eternity apart. The pint wasn't as good as the ones at Smith's on Haddington Road, but it wasn't bad either. It was very good, in fact, considering.

He strolled over to Dunne-Davis, who was temporarily between flirtations.

—How's it going? asked Dunne-Davis, slobbering down another oyster.

—Not bad.

—Want one? Dunne-Davis offered him the plate.

—Nah.

The Guinness was all Barry needed. It was like the old blanket Sarah had had when she was younger – a comforter. He felt almost normal with the big pint glass in his hand, like it was shielding him from the madness of the past few weeks, and whatever madness lay in store in the weeks and months ahead.

Better enjoy it while you can, he thought. It might be a long time before you have another one.

Dunne-Davis wasn't shy when it came to the black stuff, either. He'd thrown a fair few back already, along with copious amounts of the champagne on offer. May as well make the most of it, thought Barry, nibbling on another smoked-salmon-and-cream-cheese cracker. These people certainly had the life, wining and dining for Ireland.

Tony Doyle raised his glass.
—Here's to five points.
—Cheers, agreed Johnno.
The champagne tasted even better after a result like that. Just one more good result against the Saudis, and he'd be home and dry. He didn't exactly need the money badly, but it would be nice to clear a cool million, especially after the fiasco with the last deal. That reminded him.
—Johnno.
—Yes, boss?
—Things might have to get a little bit nasty for those two...
Johnno knew what he meant. Doyle refused to refer to the lads who had made a fool of him by name. And he was definitely losing patience. Johnno knew he'd never see his money again, but Doyle hadn't risen to the depths of the Dublin underworld by letting things go that easily – especially things that were related to such a large sum of money. And there was also the small matter of his considerable ego. These lads would have to be made examples of, just in case the word got around town that Doyle was losing his grip. The mere mention of something like that could spell the end, even for someone as powerful and feared as Doyle. Johnno was convinced that nobody knew about this little caper yet; but these things had a habit of surfacing, unless all the loose ends were dealt with.
—Yes, boss.
—We'll give them till next week, no more.
—Next week, repeated Johnno.
—That young one in the warehouse.
Johnno nodded dumbly. Doyle didn't need to elaborate.

Sasha would be first on the list, whether she knew anything or not. All the more reason to make their move sooner rather than later.

—If that doesn't work, the other young fella has a family.

Johnno said nothing for a moment. He'd been dreading this for a while now. Doyle loved to be seen as an honourable Robin Hood character, but when it came down to it he used whatever means necessary to get what he wanted – including seeking retribution from those nearest and dearest to his enemies. Johnno had only been compelled to resort to these tactics once before. Once had been enough. Afterwards, he had sworn he'd never do it again; and, up until now, he hadn't had to. It had proven to be an extremely effective technique.

—Do we really want to do that?

—We? Doyle glared. —I make the decisions around here, lad.

—Yes, boss.

—Don't ever forget it.

Johnno broke eye contact. Doyle settled back into his chair, happy that he had made his point.

—Yes, Doyle said. —I believe that young fella has a daughter.

Johnno got up and left him alone. He felt like he was going to be sick.

Barry and Nick were introduced to yet another Japanese guest of the ambassador's. Barry bowed – gently this time; he was beginning to get the hang of it now. The first time he tried it, he had narrowly missed headbutting the chairman of Sony, or was it Toshiba? The Japanese were polite in the extreme, and he didn't want to do anything to offend them. Dunne-Davis had explained the importance of not being 'seen to lose face', whatever that meant. Basically, as far as Barry could tell, you just needed to show a bit of respect, which was fine by him.

The latest guy turned out to be a football nut, so talking to him wasn't such an ordeal.

—You watch Premiership in Ireland?

—Oh, yes, said Barry.

—Arsenal very good team, yes?

—Very good, concurred Barry.

—You like Manchester?

—They're a good side. I like Liverpool the best, but.

—Ah, yes! Michael Owen!

—Great player.

—David Beckham?

—Er, yes.

—What about Roy Keane? You like him?

Barry didn't know what to say. As far as he was concerned, there had never been an Irish player quite like Keane – not in his memory, anyway. Paul McGrath was a legend, really brilliant, and he vaguely remembered Liam Brady from when he was a kid; Brady was something special, a real class act. His da always went on about Giles being world-class in any era, but Barry was too young to remember him. But Keane...he was different. He'd put Keane above and beyond any of them.

Keane had driven the team on to qualification almost single-handedly. And that was his greatest attribute. His box-to-box play, tenacious tackling and brilliantly perceptive reading of the game alone would put him up there with the best; but what set him apart from the rest was his absolute refusal ever to say die, ever to settle for anything less than one hundred per cent. And his warrior spirit was infectious; it rubbed off on, and lifted, everyone around him, whether he was playing for United or for Ireland. He was the first name on Alex Ferguson's team sheet, and he should have been the first name on Mick McCarthy's. It was all very well harping on about it being a team sport, but Keane was the team. Maybe he had gone over the top and insulted McCarthy, and even his teammates; but if McCarthy had been worth his salt as a manager, he would have found a way to overcome the problem. Sure, Keane could be an obnoxious so-and-so when he wanted, but that was what made him the player he was. And if McCarthy couldn't see that, then maybe he shouldn't have been managing the Irish team.

—I love Roy Keane, he replied eventually.

—Me too! said his new friend.

—Er, I'm just going to go … upstairs, said Nick.

Nick had been holding his breath, waiting for Barry to explode into a tirade of abuse à la Keano. He had been mightily relieved when he didn't. And another form of relief was weighing heavily on Nick's mind right now. He'd been constipated since the unfortunate incident on the Trans-Siberian Railway, but all the Guinness and oysters must have loosened up something inside him, and he thought it prudent to make his way to the nearest gentlemen's room.

It took him a couple of minutes to find it. The old ambassador's residence certainly was plush, he'd say that for it. All they were missing were the Ferrero Rochers. Opulence greeted Nick from every corner; no expense had been spared to give the impression that no expense had been spared. The bathroom itself was the size of a bedroom, with a quaint sign outside identifying it as the guests' restroom. There didn't seem to be any distinction between the ladies' and the gents', so Nick resolved to be as gentle as he could. He lowered himself into position over the target and prepared to launch at will.

Downstairs, Barry and the guests were feigning interest in the first of the speeches. Kate had managed to work herself free of her hostess duties for a few minutes and had forced another pint on Barry. He hadn't put up much of a fight.

—Cheers.

The speeches prattled on for another fifteen minutes,

in ping-pong fashion: first a Japanese dignitary would thank the ambassador for his gracious hospitality, then an Irish host would thank their Japanese guests for coming, then a Japanese representative would compliment their Irish hosts on the delicious food...and on it went. Finally, the dignified chap with the large medallion got up and proposed a toast.

—He the last one? enquired Barry.

—Jesus, I hope so, said Kate.

They were disappointed: the latest orator started telling yet another funny story.

—Ah, well, I suppose it can only get better...

Upstairs, Nick was having problems of his own. The act itself had been relatively painless – one long push had taken care of it; but, no matter how hard he flushed, the damn thing just wouldn't go down. And outside the door, someone who sounded like a Japanese lady was becoming increasingly impatient.

—Just a minute, called Nick.

He'd spent the last ten minutes trying to drown it. It was huge, like a great, brown, beached whale sticking its head out of the surf. It stared defiantly up at him, mocking his feeble efforts at weighing it down with yards of toilet paper. There was another, louder knock on the door.

—Nearly finished!

He waited until the cistern had filled completely, then bore down on the handle with all his might. Water gushed and paper swirled in a miniature whirlpool. Round and round it went, down and...pop...back up again for air.

—Fuck!

It was invincible. What was he going to do?

—Fuck, fuck, fuck!

It was the faecal equivalent of the Terminator. Every time he thought it was down for good, it would rear its ugly head again to torment him. Prodding it with the toilet brush only seemed to anger it. It might have had something to do with the booze, but Nick was convinced the thing had taken on a life of its own and was trying to glide its way up the bowl like a boa constrictor. He could hear the sound of conversation outside.

—Damn!

It was in Japanese. There must be two of them out there. There was only one thing for it. He looked over at the little brush and pan he'd discovered in the cabinet. The he looked at the open window and sighed stoically to himself.

—Desperate times...

Barry suppressed a slight yawn. He was sure this guy was the last. There couldn't possibly be any more expressions of mutual admiration between the people of Ireland and the people of Japan – not unless they wanted him to speak as well. As far as he could tell, he was the only there who hadn't.

And then it literally fell from the sky. It landed directly on the mayor of Tokyo's head, just as he was toasting the wonderful relations between the two countries. Barry was certain he was imagining it. It had to be another of the episodes brought on by the spiked drink or the hypothermia. In his confused state, he was seeing what appeared to be an abnormally large turd perched on the distinguished guest's head. And it definitely hadn't been produced by any bird – not unless they still had pterodactyls roaming the skies of Tokyo.

Needless to say, Barry and Nick weren't invited back for the next function at the embassy. Nick's party piece had put a bit of a damper on the evening, and his efforts to apologise only served to further inflame the situation – especially when he tried to blame the incident on the Japanese lady who had used the bathroom after him. That seemed to cause even more offence than the flying turd had. He and Barry were politely escorted to the front door by security; once out of sight of the guests, they were dumped rather roughly on their arses in the street.

Naturally, Dunne-Davis didn't want to leave without a fight.

—Do you know who I am? he enquired indignantly.

—I'm William Dunne-Davis's son!

—Really?

The large security officer released his grip on Nick's throat. Nick nodded, happy to be finally receiving the respect he deserved.

—I'm Alan Byrne's son, the security guard told him.

Dunne-Davis looked confused. —Who the fuck is Alan Byrne?

—Who the fuck is William Dunne-Davis? retorted Alan Byrne Jr, simultaneously launching Nick onto the pavement with a swift thrust of his considerable arm.

—You're finished! screamed Nick, clambering to his feet. —Do you hear me, you fucking knacker? My father is a personal friend of Charlie Haughey's!

Judging by the force with which the door slammed in Nick's face, this didn't have the desired effect. Nick· hammered away on the door, issuing promises and predictions as to what Alan Byrne Jr might expect to find in the way of employment after he'd lost his current job.

Finally Barry shut him up. —What's your fuckin' problem?

Dunne-Davis was taken aback by the anger in his voice.

—Did you see the way I was manhandled out of there?

—No. But I presume it was the same way as I was. I couldn't see much through the headlock.

—But it's...it's completely unacceptable, stammered Nick.

—Unacceptable? What about throwin' your own shite out the window of the Irish Embassy? Does that not count as unacceptable? Yeh'll have to excuse my ignorance on this one; I'm not used to these type of high society dos. Maybe that's considered to be appropriate behaviour?

—That was a misunderstanding.

—Oh, a misunderstanding. I see what yeh mean. I don't think Kim Whatever-his-face-is understood why a giant shite should land on him in the middle of a public speech. They're funny like tha' over here, aren't they?

Dunne-Davis had no reply.

—Yous are all the bleedin' same: it's never your fault. Like those gobshites that come into the garage threatening to have me fired because their brand new BMWs are overheatin'. When I ask them did they put oil in it, they look at me as if I should have told them that. Like it's my fault they're so fuckin' stupid.

—I always put oil in my car, muttered Nick.

—No, I always put oil in your car for yeh, 'cause yeh wouldn't lower yourself to get your hands dirty. That's for grease monkeys like me, isn't it? You just drive the fuckin' thing. Spoilt brats, the lot of yous. Yeh think the whole world is there to wait on you hand and foot, don't yeh?

Nick stared at his toes.

—Don't yeh?

—I know what I want – and I get what I want, said Nick in a low voice. —If that's a crime, you can hang me. I make no apologies. I may be a bit…arrogant at times, but it's got me where I am, which is exactly where I want to be. And if you applied half of that bitter-little-man energy you have, you could do the same. So spare me the working-class-hero bullshit, will you?

Barry turned around in silence and took off towards the subway, leaving Nick alone. And the thought occurred to Nick that maybe, just maybe, Barry might have a point.

—CHAPTER TWENTY—

The next day, nothing was said about the previous evening. Barry and Nick sat in the Church bar sipping pints of Carlsberg. England was about to play Argentina on the box, and the place was crammed to the rafters – mainly with English fans, but there were quite a few Irish lads as well. Still, Nick felt a bit uneasy. There was something about the English lads – something dangerous; he always felt that they were liable to glass him on the slightest excuse. Barry didn't seem to notice, so Nick said nothing.

They kept showing the 'Hand of God' goal from the '86 World Cup, when Maradona had duped the referee with his infamous hand-ball and cheated England out of a glorious victory. Nick was no football buff, but he was fairly sure that Maradona had also scored a rather impressive goal in that match, starting from the halfway line, as well. Naturally, they weren't showing that one. Every time they showed the little genius punch the ball past Peter Shilton, the English crowd booed.

—It's pathetic, Nick complained, quietly enough not to be heard by anybody but Barry.

Barry continued staring at the big screen. They had managed to get a decent seat in front of it, early in the afternoon, and had decided to hold on to it. It had meant sitting there drinking all day, but they had soldiered through it bravely.

—I saw that fellow Coles do the exact same thing in the last World Cup, claimed Nick.

—Who?

—Coles? You know, the ginger prick?

—Scholes, corrected Barry.

—Yeah, Scholes. Well, he did the very same thing, and they didn't even mention it – not a word!

Barry didn't seem terribly interested.

—It's the fucking British media, whispered Nick.

He had to shut up then, because 'God Save the Queen' came on and all the English supporters were singing like they meant it. Nick didn't want to ask, but he was beginning to think that Barry was actually up for England – particularly when he groaned after a near miss from Owen. If he had asked, Barry might have explained that he didn't particularly care who won. Admittedly, this was an unusual attitude for any red-blooded Irishman to adopt when it came to 'the oul' enemy', but it made perfect sense to Barry. Irish people supported English club sides – in fact, he even knew gobshites who supported the likes of Liverpool and United when they played against Irish teams – yet when it came to internationals you were expected to despise them with a passion normally reserved for paedophiles and war criminals. Barry would never have admitted this to any of his mates, but as far as he was concerned Ireland should concentrate on its own team and stop constantly obsessing over the fate of its historical oppressors. Like those sad bastards who wore Celtic tops and booed anyone who had ever played for Rangers; the night Ireland had played Denmark in Lansdowne, a few weeks ago, the fuckin' eejits had booed this Danish lad every time he touched the ball. It turned out he hadn't even played for Rangers; there had been a misprint in the programme. Barry was embarrassed that idiots like that were representing his country. He was different. He was a football man, plain and simple. All he desired was that the best team win. He didn't give a fiddler's where they came from.

Then Michael Owen got into the penalty area and did a passable imitation of a Hollywood actor being shot by an invisible bullet. He went down faster than an Amsterdam hooker, and the referee pointed directly to the spot.

—Yeh fuckin' English cunt! screamed Barry.

The replay was shown again and again from half a dozen different angles, confirming Barry's analysis: not one of them indicated the slightest hint of contact between Owen and the Argentine defender.

—Cheatin' Sassanach bastards! Barry added, after Beckham had converted form the spot. Luckily, his comments were only heard by a handful of Irish lads around them; the English section of the bar had erupted into raptures at Owen's dying-swan impression.

—En-ger-land, En-ger-land, En-ger-land! rang out around the bar. Even the handful of Japanese lads in England tops joined in.

Nick tried to stop Barry from climbing onto their table, but he was a man on a mission. He countered the English chant with one of his own.

——AR-GEN-TINA! AR-GEN-TINA!

The rest of the Irish lads joined in. Eventually Nick managed to drag Barry away from what was shaping up to be a fairly decent effort at a full-scale riot.

The next few days were spent in similar fashion, with a similar number of high-profile upsets. Argentina and France, both of whom had been high on Barry's list of potential tournament winners, were as good as gone. The Senegal upset of the world champions in their opening game had been a sign of things to come. The world order was changing; or, at least, this tournament was evidence that some of the smaller nations could compete with and even beat their more illustrious opponents. Barry was beginning to fancy Ireland's chances of causing an upset or two themselves. Even without the services of a certain Corkman.

Barry was incredulous. Somehow Dunne-Davis had succeeded in securing tickets for the Saudi game from

Kate. She had been lucky to hold on to her job, after the incident at the embassy; it was only Dunne-Davis's extraordinary arrogance that had saved her. He had actually had the nerve to suggest that he would be more than willing to furnish the Irish and local newspapers with all the relevant details of the gory proceedings. Naturally, the last thing the Irish Embassy wanted was to fan the flames and cause further embarrassment to all concerned. That would have undone all efforts at reconciliation in one fell swoop – particularly if the tabloid hacks in the British media got their hands on it.

The deal was simple: complimentary tickets and travel to all of Ireland's remaining games (including the knock-out stages in Korea), the official stamping of their temporary passports, and two first-class flights back to Dublin. All Nick and Barry had to do in return was sign a sworn statement agreeing never to mention the sordid episode again.

Dunne-Davis had wanted to push for an official apology, but Barry had persuaded him not to.

—Yeh will in your fuckin' hole!

All in all, Barry was ecstatically happy with the way things had worked out. And, naturally, he was fucked if he was going to let Dunne-Davis know it. This meant they still had a few days left to work out a plan before they had to face the inevitable. Barry even bought the first round of the day, before they got on the bus for the game. After that it was free booze all the way to the ground. Things were really beginning to look up. He would never have admitted it, but he couldn't help admiring Dunne-Davis for scoring the tickets, passports and so on. Maybe there was something more to him after all...even if he was a prick.

Back in Ringsend, Michael had the champagne on ice. Actually, it was a sparkling white from Germany that he had picked up in Tesco's, but he wasn't going to let that bother him. He popped the cork and let the overflow dribble down his hand.

—Here, he said, handing a glass to Declan.

—But, Da, I don't...

—Shut up, you. Do yeh take me for a complete eejit?

Declan didn't answer.

—Can I've some too? asked Sarah.

—You're definitely too young, chicken. Finish your Coke instead.

—Ah, Granda!

He couldn't resist the big brown eyes staring up at him.

—All right, just this once.

He took the glass of Coke from her and pretended to pour a drop of champagne into it. He shook the glass a bit to get the frothy effect.

—Now.

Ireland was through to the last sixteen in the World Cup. If you couldn't celebrate that, sure, what could you celebrate? Michael poured a glass for himself. He continued pouring until it flowed up and over the rim and onto his hand.

—Get your mammy, Sarah, he shouted, staring at the screen as the golden liquid dribbled all over the carpet.
—Quick! She won't believe this!

Tony Doyle was also sipping champagne, although his was definitely genuine: a nice little Bollinger he'd been saving for a special occasion. He had just witnessed Ireland hammering Saudi Arabia, three-nil – one from Gary Breen, of all people, another sweet strike from Robbie Keane and a bit of a waxy one from Damien Duff. They all count, though, as the man said. And now he could finally relax. It was crazy: even though it would have been a serious upset of the form book, which he firmly believed in, he still couldn't enjoy it until the final whistle blew. There had been too many scares with Irish teams in the past. Egypt in Italia '90 was one. Away to Yugoslavia was another. And he would never forget that night in Belgium in the early 80s when Ireland had been robbed of qualification. He'd lost a lot of money on that one. No matter how sure you were of winning, this was still football, and anything could happen. You only had to ask the French about that. Doyle had been more nervous in the last ninety minutes than he had been in years. It was the final hurdle, the tricky last lap where Murphy's Law might buckle your best plans.

But that was it now. He'd be collecting his money for sure. Johnno had been around yesterday to remind Casey to have it ready for him. A million in cash – no messing about with cheques or bank drafts; that wasn't the way Tony Doyle did business. The bookie had put up the usual token gestures of defiance before relenting. It was in the bag.

And then the strangest thing happened. As the camera panned across the celebrating Irish fans, it stopped for a few seconds on a group of lads singing and dancing. It couldn't be, Doyle thought. The champagne and the euphoria must be playing tricks with his mind.

—Johnno?

The look on Johnno's face suggested that he was thinking the same thing.

—That's that little prick...

Johnno nodded. —Nick Dunne-Davis. He was as surprised as Doyle.

—And that must be that Kelly young fella with him, said Doyle.

Johnno saw the glass drop from Doyle's hand and smash to pieces on the wooden floor. There was no denying it. It was definitely them.

—Ughh... A low moan emanated from Doyle. Johnno watched as he clutched at his chest. His face was white, a sickly, ashen white; his swollen eyes seemed about to pop out of his head and roll down the front of his jacket. He fumbled inside his pocket for his box of pills, but he was like a man fishing for a wet bar of soap: the little box slipped from his weakened grip and followed the champagne onto the floor, smashing open and spewing its contents all over the beechwood laminate slats. The champagne quickly went to work on them, and Doyle watched helplessly as his lifesavers fizzed and frothed away, in tandem with his own mortality. He reached and clutched at one remaining intact one, but Johnno beat him to it. He held it out to his boss. Doyle strained with all of his remaining strength to reach it.

At the last minute, Johnno slowly pulled the tiny white torpedo out of his reach. It was something he would have done years before, if he had only had the courage. Finally, he had the chance to disassociate himself from Doyle forever. The thought of Sasha gave him the strength he needed. Not even Tony Doyle could stand in their way now.

—Please... Doyle croaked, grasping at the empty air.

Johnno watched him drop to his knees like a heavyweight crumbling to the canvas. Only he wouldn't be getting up again. Doyle shot him one last furious look, fully aware of what was happening. Johnno took no pleasure in it. He merely reflected on the irony of it: a thug who had brought so many to their knees, dying the same way. Death doesn't discriminate, he thought. We may not be born equal, but we sure as hell die equal.

He waited until the last embers of consciousness faded from Doyle's eyes before reaching into his dead mentor's pocket. He had a couple of little jobs to attend to.

Jill thought they were spoofing at first, but she could tell by them that they weren't.

—You're sure it was him, now?

—Absolutely, said Michael.

—It was definitely him, concurred Declan.

She sat down on the old armchair. Her head was spinning.

—You wouldn't have mixed him up with someone else, would yeh?

—Definitely not. I'm telling yeh, it was him. That other young lad was with him...

—Lick My Anus, added Declan helpfully.

—That's righ', said Michael. He looked at Jill, willing her to say something.

—Well, I suppose it's good news.

—Exactly! At least we know he's all right now, wha'?

—He looked more than all right to me, offered Declan.
—Probably blowin' all that drug money in Japan.

Michael glared at him but said nothing. He was hoping that somehow Jill hadn't heard.

—So do you think he'll phone soon? she asked.

—Ah, yeah, I'm sure he'll be on any day now, Michael assured her.

Outside the house, Sarah stopped kicking her World Cup football against the gate to watch the large silver car pulling up. It was huge. It was shiny and much nicer-looking than her granda's. She went over to the passenger door when the man opened it for her.

—Sarah?

—Yes.

—Come here for a minute, love.

Barry was polishing off the end of his can on the bus.

—Olé, olé, olé, olé...

He joined in with the rest of them.

—Olé, olé!

Most of the lads in the group were corporate heads, but they certainly knew how to enjoy themselves. Even Dunne-Davis seemed OK to Barry now. He had that warm alcoholic glow, mixed in with the elation of Ireland's qualification from the group. It was magic, but there was still something nagging at Barry. He knew what it was, but he didn't want to spoil the party by admitting it. He just couldn't help himself, though: every so often he'd slip into quiet introspection and wonder what might have been.

What if Roy had been here? How far could Ireland go with him on board, directing the battle? It was true that they'd already gone further than Barry could have imagined they would without him; but if Keane was playing...well, anything would be possible. No matter how hard he tried, Barry couldn't help feeling a little cheated – cheated and betrayed, in a way. He wasn't sure by whom, but the fact was that Ireland was in the last sixteen of the World Cup and their best player was at home watching it on TV. Was Roy to blame? Was it McCarthy's fault? He wasn't a hundred per cent sure any more.

—CHAPTER TWENTY-ONE—

By the time they got to Tokyo, Barry was flying.

—Next stop Korea! he slurred.

Dunne-Davis didn't pay any attention. He was trying to focus on the two girls dressed as leprechauns at the back of the bus. At least, he assumed they were girls. It was difficult to tell, with the fake beards and oversized hats. The clown-sized trousers didn't give anything away either. He was definitely beginning to feel something stirring in his trousers, all the same, but he decided it was safer not to investigate in his present inebriated state.

—D'you know what we need, Barry?

—What's tha'? enquired Barry.

—A good old-fashioned massage.

Barry blinked very slowly. His head bobbed and rolled like it was resting on a rubber neck.

—You're righ'. That's exactly what we need.

Inside the massage parlour, Barry giddily accepted another drink from the young Japanese girl.

—What your name? she asked.

—Roy, he said. —Roy Keane. He had a bit of a laugh at his own joke.

—You nice boy, Roy.

—Cheers, he said, spilling half of his drink down her top without noticing.

Dunne-Davis seemed to be getting very friendly with the other young one. If Barry wasn't mistaken, and there was every possibility that he was, he was presently inspecting her dental work with his tongue. It was very dark for a massage parlour; but, then again, Barry had never been to one before, so he didn't know what to expect. The girls were wearing white fluffy robes and towering stilettos that still only raised them up to chin-level on Barry; and Dunne-Davis was quite a few inches taller than him. Barry hoped they'd have the strength for a decent back-rub. He was vaguely aware of Dunne-Davis and his companion slipping away through one of the many doors that lined the circular foyer.

—You want go now? said his hostess.

—Can I have another drink first?

—No. We go now, or you no able.

—Er... all righ', then.

She led him through one of the doors and gestured for him to begin undressing. Barry removed his Keano shirt and jeans. He left his boxers on until he was asked to remove them too.

—You wear this, said the tiny masseuse, handing him a towel.

He wrapped it round his waist, and half-climbed and was half-lifted onto the leather couch in the centre of the room. The lights dimmed even further, and he could smell scented candles burning at strategic intervals around the room. He felt her hands rubbing oil onto his back, and his whole body relaxed as a pleasure broke over it like a wave breaking on a beach.

—Jaysus, he moaned, as she eased the tension out of him.

It was even better when she got to his legs. She worked her way down from his shoulders and right back down to his feet. His brain was sure his body had died and gone to heaven.

Then she manipulated him onto his back and started on his chest. She seemed to be rubbing her whole body against his, although it was hard to tell with his eyes closed.

—You very nice boy, she whispered in his ear.

—Mmm, he replied.

—You want play mousie?

—Mmm, he repeated.

He wasn't sure if she was removing his towel, so he attempted to open his eyes to see. After the spinning room slowed to an acceptable speed, he noticed that she had disappeared. He closed his eyes, but two seconds later he opened them again: something felt even better than what she had been doing before, if that was at all possible. What the hell was she doing now? Barry couldn't quite put his finger on it, but it was warm and wet and he didn't want it to stop.

He managed to raise himself up on his elbows.

—Oh, shite...

All he could see was her dark hair easing back and forth between his legs. He couldn't believe it.

—No, stop... he protested weakly.

Then he felt the onset of an unmistakable rush that started from his toes and roared through his entire body.

—Oh, God...

And then it was over. She stopped and stood up. It was then that he realised what had felt so good against his skin: she was completely naked, except for the briefest of G-strings.

He felt something else washing over him – something different from what he had felt earlier, not as sudden or as intense, but just as powerful in its own way. It slowly enveloped him like a dark fog, and he felt his whole body sag. He knew what it was, and it would last a lot longer than those other fleeting sensations. It was guilt.

The next morning was worse. Barry woke up and felt the throbbing. It was like somebody playing the bass drum in his head. For a moment he was unsure of where or even who he was, but then it all came slowly and sickeningly back to him. He was Barry Kelly, on the run from gangsters; Barry Kelly, thousands of miles from his family; Barry Kelly, spending his ill-gotten gains on hookers and booze. He was Barry Kelly, and he was a prick. How could he do that to Jill?

He fell back into an uneasy sleep and woke a couple of hours later to the sound of Dunne-Davis banging on the door.

—Fuck off!

Barry was in no humour for him. In fact, if he could have spent the rest of his life in this room, it would have suited him fine, just as long as he didn't have to talk to anyone else. But he knew he was kidding himself. There was only one person who would judge him for the remainder of his days, and who would never forgive him for what he had done: himself. He'd realised that the moment he'd shot his load last night. Those two or three minutes of pleasure would haunt him for the rest of his life. He was no better than all those other wankers like Dunne-Davis who couldn't stay faithful. Loyalty was a quality on which Barry had always prided himself, and now he realised he didn't possess it.

Suddenly Roy Keane and the Irish team didn't seem to matter so much. It was just a game, nothing more. In the greater scheme of things, it didn't amount to much. There was only one thing that mattered to Barry now, and he was going to make sure he spoke to her this time.

Sasha directed the cab driver to her flat in Dalkey. Home. For the first time in weeks. She could barely contain herself. She seemed to be floating on air. There was only one explanation for it: she was in love. He was everything she had always wanted.

Actually, he was everything she'd always hated. He was working-class, with no money and no pretensions. But maybe that was what she needed. Her mother had always told her that she'd meet someone when she least expected it, and it looked like she'd been right. Sasha wasn't sure her mother would approve; in fact, she was almost positive she would hate him. Maybe that was why Sasha found him so attractive. Mummy would be expecting a lawyer or an accountant, a nice boy from a decent background, with a steady career and the kind of earning power that would keep her daughter in the correct manner; she would be appalled at Johnno if Sasha brought him home for dinner. Sasha half-regretted that they would never meet. She would have loved to seen the look on Mummy's face, particularly when she heard his accent.

It must have been the strangest courtship in history. The closest they had come to physical intimacy – apart from that one wonderful kiss – had been when Johnno had slapped her around in the warehouse. She knew he had only done it to buy her some more time with Doyle – cruel to be kind, and all that; he had to make it look like he was trying. She also knew it would never happen again. Violence was part of his professional life, not his personal one. And now, according to him, his professional life was over.

Johnno had instructed her to pack everything she needed into a single suitcase. Only the bare essentials – they could get the rest when they got there; all she needed was her passport and a few items of clothing. She was to wait in the flat until he called her, then take another cab straight to the airport. Under no circumstances were they to be seen together. He'd made it look like she'd escaped on her own, just in case. Now that Doyle was no longer around, Sasha didn't see what the fuss was about; but that was the initial plan they'd hatched a couple of days earlier, and they were sticking to it.

Johnno would book their flight in the next day or two. There was one more job he needed to do before they could go – something to do with collecting on a bet for Doyle, if everything went according to plan.

The phone was still ringing downstairs.
—Declan! Answer the fff...phone, will yeh? Michael

was exasperated. He knew Declan was down there. The stereo was blaring away.

—Did yeh hear me?

But Declan couldn't hear anything other than Eminem blasting from the speakers: —Guess who's back?...

Michael reefed the bedroom door open and went to the top of the stairs. He'd kill Declan if he went down there. The little so-and-so had been taking advantage of his good mood over the last few days. He was halfway down when Jill came in the front door. She dropped the shopping and covered the short distance to the phone in a couple of bounds.

—Hello!

She said nothing for a minute. Michael watched her eyes close and saw what looked like a smile lifting her features. Was it Barry? He hadn't seen her smile like that since...well, since Barry disappeared. Then the door of the living room opened and Declan came out, along with the pumping rhythm that made the light in the hall shake.

—Turn tha' rubbish off! roared Michael.

Declan looked a little surprised by the glare he was getting from Jill, but he went in and turned the music down. Michael raised an eyebrow to her. Her smile told him what he needed to know, and he retired respectfully back to his bedroom to give her some privacy.

Jill returned the phone to her ear and took a minute to gather her emotions. Eventually she found the words.

—How are yeh, love?

There was an uneasy pause at the other end.

—I'm in Japan, Jill.

—I know.

—Wha'?

—We saw you on the telly.

—Fuck off! I mean...again?

—No, honestly.

Another lengthy pause, followed by Barry's quavering voice.

—I've got somethin' to tell yeh...

—No, I've something to tell you. Sarah—

—Ah, Jaysus, no!

—It's all right, Barry. She was out playing yesterday and one of Doyle's lads had a word with her.

—What did he say? asked Barry, failing to hide the panic in his voice.

—Calm down. Everything's OK. He told her that it was safe for her daddy to come home now.

—You're jokin'.

—They saw you at the match as well.

—How, but?

—It doesn't matter. It was on the news today: Doyle was found dead this morning. They say it was his heart...

She let this hang in the air while it sank in.

—That's...brilliant! Just brilliant!

—You can come home now. Your man said that was the end of it. When are you coming, love?

—...Look, somethin' happened over here that I have to tell you abou'...

Jill didn't like the tone of his voice, but she was damned if she was going to let anything spoil the moment.

—Just get yourself home. You can tell me then.

—It's just that...

—Come home, Barry. Sarah misses her daddy. And I miss him too.

She hung up the phone and wiped the tears from her cheeks.

—CHAPTER TWENTY-TWO—

Barry didn't take long to pack his gear. Dunne-Davis took a bit of convincing at first. He thought Barry was winding him up about Doyle.

—Fuck off!

—It's true. I rang home. I even checked the newspapers on the internet. He's dead as a bleedin' doornail. Heart attack.

—Even if that's true, what about O'Neill?

—Dunno. He just said it was OK to come home.

—Well, of course he'd say that, wouldn't he? It's a set-up.

Barry visibly deflated.

—Think about it. He'll try and take over Doyle's turf, and he'll start by making an example of us. He's hardly going to let a million euro go just like that. It'd be madness.

—Wha' about Sarah, then?

—What?

—My daughter. Why didn't he just nab her as insurance?

—I don't know. These people are thugs. They think differently from...us.

—Well, I'm goin'. With or without you.

Nick looked at the absolute resolve in his eyes and knew he meant it.

—Right. Well, I suppose I got you into this...

For the briefest of moments, Barry wanted to hug Dunne-Davis. He hadn't expected him to come. He'd even told himself that he didn't give a fiddler's whether he did or not. But he knew now that he did want Dunne-Davis to come. He didn't know why; it just seemed right that they face whatever lay ahead together, the same way they had faced everything so far.

For his part, Nick had always felt that travel was a bit like sex: it was quite good on your own, but it was definitely better with company.

Getting a flight was ridiculously easy. It seemed that most of the Irish supporters hadn't expected to be going on to Korea. When the lads had qualified, the inevitable happened: they all cancelled their flights home and decided to follow the dream. Which is exactly what Barry would have done himself, under normal circumstances. But these circumstances were anything but normal. It had been weeks since Barry's life had been anything approaching normal.

And that was what he missed. It had been a hell of an adventure, and if everything worked out he would probably think back on it fondly in years to come. But he had learned something invaluable on his travels. As he settled into the big first-class seat, he smiled. It was something he'd almost forgotten how to do. They'd had a few laughs on the way, but now he was happy – genuinely happy. It had taken weeks on the run, a couple of near-death experiences and a lecture from Nick Dunne-Davis – he smiled at the irony of that one – to make him realise just how highly he valued his life. His wonderful, little life. It wasn't much by most people's standards, but it was his.

—Why not? he said, as the air hostess offered him a glass of champagne. It was his first time on a plane and he was determined to enjoy it.

—And what can I do for you, sir?

Nick displayed his famous smile for the hostess. —I'm sure I'll think of something.

She blushed slightly, but Barry could tell she was enjoying it.

Johnno had lodged the money from Casey's into the off-shore account he'd set up. It had all gone like clockwork. Nobody had suspected a thing – and why would they? He'd collected the bet long before Doyle was even discovered. Casey was used to him collecting for Doyle, so there hadn't been any argument.

He jumped into the cab and tried Sasha's mobile again. Still no answer. She must be in the shower. He was like a kid going off on his holidays.

—Are you goin' to give us a clue? enquired the taxi driver.

—Airport, please, boss.

—Airport, repeated the driver sarcastically.

Johnno sat back and smiled. The rain was pelting down outside. It was a good day to be leaving Ireland. The weather in Spain would be scorching. He couldn't wait to see Sasha in a summer dress.

—Wha' have I done to deserve this? he beamed.

—Wha'?

—Nothin'. Nothin' at all.

Barry couldn't believe the service on the flight. You got to order your food from a menu and drink as much champagne as you wanted. They made you feel like you were royalty. He went for the duck for a starter and the salmon for his main course. The food was as good as he'd ever tasted – not that he was a regular in the likes of Roly's Bistro. He could get used to this type of pampering. It was certainly a far cry from the rest of their travels. Dunne-Davis was taking it all in his stride, of course. He didn't bother with luxuries like manners; he just held out his glass, without so much as a please or thank you, until someone came and filled it.

After dinner Barry watched a movie on his personalised screen – you could even play computer games if you wanted. He was feeling a bit drowsy towards the end of it, what with all the bubbly and everything. He was deliriously happy. In a few short hours he'd be home again, with Jill and Sarah. He was even looking forward to seeing his da and Declan. Everything had worked out in the end. He could still hardly believe it.

He stretched the huge seat out to its full extension. It was as big as most of the beds they'd slept in. Then he closed his eyes and dreamed of home.

When he woke, it was still dark outside. The blinds were down and people were sleeping all around him. The sound of the engines droned into the night, but apart from that there was a wonderful stillness that gave Barry a warm feeling inside. At least he knew he didn't suffer from airsickness as well as seasickness.

He lay there trying to imagine Jill's face when he arrived home. He had told her he'd be back on Thursday, when in actual fact he would be back twenty-four hours earlier. She deserved a pleasant surprise, after everything she'd been through. He wondered how he'd tell her about the massage-parlour incident, but even that couldn't upset his mood. He felt sure she'd forgive him. He had realised, after talking to her, that she was a hell of a lot more understanding about things like that than most people were. It was just another one of the reasons he was so mad about her. Any other woman would kick him out on his arse, and he wouldn't blame them. But she was different. She was no pushover; just different.

He was still moulding happy thoughts in his head when Dunne-Davis brushed past him and sat down.

—Where were you?

Dunne-Davis seemed startled that Barry was awake.

—Er, just doing a bit of exercise.

—Wha'?

—Y'know, avoiding the old DVT.

—What's tha'?

—Deep vein thrombosis.

—Oh, yeah. I heard somethin' about tha', all righ'.

Barry was interrupted by that air hostess, who had been hovering around them all through the flight. She smiled and passed Dunne-Davis a folded-up piece of paper, made a 'call me' sign with her hand and continued down the aisle without a word.

—Well? asked Barry, staring after her perfectly symmetrical figure sashaying down the aisle.

—Well what?

—What was tha' about?

Nick pulled up the blind and looked out the window.

—Just my membership.

—Membership?

—The Mile High Club, explained Nick.

They had a couple of hours to wait in Heathrow. Barry decided to check the duty-free shop.

—I can't very well go home with me hands hangin', now can I?

Nick settled down with his coffee and newspaper, since he didn't have anybody to buy anything for. Looking at the excitement on Barry's face almost made him wish he had, but that soon wore off. Maybe he'd settle down one day, but he wasn't ready for that life yet. Not by a long way. Of course, he had his regular squeezes, like Tanya and Sonya, not forgetting Vicky and Liz and... well, quite a few more whom he could call on if the need arose. But there was no one in particular, unless you counted Sasha. In fact, he was certain that none of them would even notice he'd been away. He often went for months without calling them, but they were always available when he did. Not for the first time, he toyed with the idea of settling down with Sasha; and, not for the first time, he sent that thought straight back where it came from. No, he was quite content with his bachelor lifestyle, at least for the time being.

He was just catching up on the latest news at home, which was still dominated by the Roy Keane saga, when Barry appeared holding a large teddy bear and a bag full of assorted gifts.

—What did you get? asked Nick.

—A few bits an' pieces.

He didn't seem inclined to elaborate, so Nick didn't push it.

—Just goin' to the jacks, said Barry.

Nick waited until he was gone before opening the big plastic bag. Plenty of room, he thought.

He opened the rucksack, which he had insisted on carrying as hand luggage, and began stuffing wads of Russian roubles into the carrier bag. He was sure Barry's family would enjoy the gifts he had selected for them, and he guessed that the bones of two hundred and forty grand in cash wouldn't go unappreciated either. Maybe they could get that house in Sandymount that Barry had told him about. Or maybe he'd consider Nick's offer to go into partnership in his new garage, the one he'd been planning for the past couple of years. That was another day's work, though. For now, he'd let Barry concentrate on the big reunion and getting back to normality.

Johnno sat in the airport with his head in his hands.

He tried calling her again.

—Hi, this is Sasha. I can't answer the phone right now…

He hung up. He knew exactly why she couldn't come to the phone. He couldn't believe he'd been so naïve.

He had two choices. He could go ahead and take the flight to Spain alone, or he could go back to his life in the Dublin underworld. With a heavy heart, he made his way towards the gate.

A few days later, the story he read on the internet would confirm his worst fears.

A woman found dead in her Dalkey apartment yesterday has been named as Sasha Fitzpatrick. Ms Fitzpatrick had been missing for a number of weeks, although initial reports indicate that she was probably murdered in her home in the last three to four days. Gardaí are seeking information about a man seen leaving the building...

And there was Vinny Purcell, grinning up at Johnno from the police photograph. So Doyle had had the last laugh after all. Johnno would wish many times, in his years in exile, that he could swap places with his old mentor. He realised that dying of a heart attack was a lot easier and quicker than dying of a broken heart.

The flight to Dublin was a short one, but Barry could barely contain himself. He was rocking back and forth in the seat the whole way, until Dunne-Davis asked him to stop.

—Sorry, said Barry.

Jesus, he's definitely in good form, thought Nick. It was the first time he could recall hearing the word from Barry's lips.

They touched down without a hitch and made their way through the throngs to the baggage carousel. The place was as packed as only Dublin Airport during the summer can be. Flights from London, Manchester and Paris spewed bags and suitcases onto their shared conveyor belt. Barry joined the scrum and almost dragged two other bags from it in his haste to get his own.

—Sorry, I think that's my bag, said a low voice at his shoulder.

Barry checked the bag again and realised his mistake.

—Sorry, he said turning to face the man.

He dropped the bag to the floor when he saw who was staring back at him. There was no mistaking him, even with the baseball cap and shades. After everything Barry had been through, this should hardly have come as a surprise; but when he opened his mouth to speak, nothing came out. Instead, his jaw just hung open and swayed a bit in confusion.

Then the man was gone. Just as quickly as he'd appeared, he melted away into the crowd.

Barry smiled. Later, he would wonder whether Ireland would have beaten Spain, instead of losing on penalties, had the man with whom he'd just exchanged bags been playing. But at that moment he realised he had even more important matters to attend to than football.